C000126936

A Selection of Recent Titles by Sara Fraser

BITTER DAWNING

THE DREAMERS

THE IMPERIALISTS

THE SISTERHOOD

SUMMER OF THE FANCY MAN

SPECS' WAR *

* available from Severn House

THE LEEDS LIBRARY

1 6 NOV 2022

WITHDRAWN FROM
stock

18 Commercial Street

THE TARGET

THE TARGET

Sara Fraser

LEEDS
LIBRARY

A100917
12/5/98

This first world edition published in Great Britain 1998 by
SEVERN HOUSE PUBLISHERS LTD of
9–15 High Street, Sutton, Surrey SM1 1DF.
First published in the USA 1998 by
SEVERN HOUSE PUBLISHERS INC., of
595 Madison Avenue, New York, NY 10022.

Copyright © 1998 by Sara Fraser

All rights reserved.
The moral right of the author has been asserted.

British Library Cataloguing in Publication Data
Fraser, Sara, 1937–
      The Target
      1. Thrillers
      1. Title
      823.9'14 [F]

      ISBN 0-7278-5349-X

All situations in this publication are fictitious and
any resemblance to living persons is purely coincidental.

Typeset by Palimpsest Book Production Ltd,
Polmont, Stirlingshire, Scotland.
Printed and bound in Great Britain by
MPG Books Ltd, Bodmin, Cornwall.

Chapter One

Toledo, Central Spain

THE man who called himself Spencer walked up to the Poste Restante desk and was greeted with a smile by the clerk.

"*Ola, que tal*, Senor Spencer?"

"*Muy bien, y Ustedes?*"

"*Muy bien*, Senor."

The man handed over a letter with a British stamp and London postmark, and after a further exchange of pleasantries Spencer went back out into the glaring heat of the morning. Following his usual custom he made his leisurely way to a small bar close to the El Greco Museum and seated himself on the rear terrace. He sighed with contentment as he visually feasted on the mighty gorge of the River Tagus and the far vistas of tumbled red-gold hills beyond.

The proprietor brought him coffee and chuletas, and Spencer ate and drank with gusto. A second coffee was served to him, and Spencer then lit up his first cigarette of the day, relishing to the full the strong sweet aftertaste of the black Canarian tobacco. He finished his cigarette before opening the envelope.

It contained a single sheet of notepaper, on which was printed the address of a small hotel in Bayswater, London.

Spencer experienced a sense of regret. The letter was the summons for which he had been waiting. Yet he was reluctant to leave this ancient city where he had found such peace of mind. He gazed once more at the tumbled hills, drinking in their arid beauty for long minutes. Then dismissed that beauty from his mind and directed his thoughts into the focussed, disciplined channel which his deadly profession demanded.

Within the hour he was travelling by motor coach towards Madrid. And by 3 o'clock that afternoon he was seated on an Iberian Airways flight for London.

*   *   *

"Oh yes, Mr Spencer, Ai received your reservation. You're in room eighteen. That's on the second floor." The scrawny, middle-aged female receptionist flashed a mechanical smile, and handed across the key. "Ai'm afraid the porter isn't available at the moment, but if you'd care to leave your luggage here Ai can have it brought up to your room in a teeny while. Breakfast is served at . . ."

Spencer turned away as the woman was speaking, and she glared indignantly at his retreating back and hissed venomously.

"Well! That's very polite, Ai 'm sure!"

The room was small, containing only a single bed, easy chair, built-in wardrobe, TV, an en suite shower and lavatory; it smelled of air freshener and transient bodies.

Spencer unpacked only the minimum of essentials, then showered and lay stretched out on the bed waiting patiently.

Within two hours there came a knock at his door.

Spencer wrapped a towel around his naked torso and opened the door.

"This come special delivery for you, sir." The elderly porter handed him a brown-paper parcel. Then shuffled his feet and coughed meaningly.

Spencer gave him a pound coin, and the porter thanked him profusely, as the door was closed in his face.

The parcel contained two books, an Ordnance Survey map, and a single page torn from an upmarket glossy magazine. On it was a group photo of a schoolboy rowing eight from a famous English public school, with one face ringed in red ink. At the bottom of the page was printed in the same ink.

'Alexander Margrave. Aged 14. Penfold House. Queen's College of the Protestant Martyrs. Custodial sentence.'

Spencer studied the fresh young smiling face, and briefly wondered for what reason this boy was to be kidnapped and held alive, instead of simply executed, then mentally shrugged – alive or dead Alexander Margrave was nothing to him. For Spencer the boy was simply a target. An insentient object devoid of human attributes. If Spencer was paid to destroy a target, then he destroyed it. If he was paid to mutilate a target, then he mutilated it. In this case he was to be paid for kidnapping and holding a target.

Spencer would do whatever he was paid to do. He was a professional.

He laid aside the page and examined each of the books in turn.

"An Exploration of The Queen's College of the Protestant Martyrs". This was a detailed guide book, with many photographs and maps of the ancient College and its environs.

"Fixtures". A small blue covered paperback which was the virtual directory of the College for the current term, containing detailed lists of boys, masters, college officials, departments, phone numbers, addresses and a myriad other details.

The Ordnance Survey map was of the area around the College.

Spencer took a bottle of whisky from his luggage, and seating himself on the easy chair, began to read the books and to study the maps and photographs. When the room darkened he rose to switch on the lamp then returned to his reading, smoking continuously and periodically sipping straight from the bottle as the hours passed.

The dawn was well advanced and the bottle was empty when he finished his study. He would rest now, for a few short hours, and then reconnoitre his target area. He stretched himself on the bed and almost instantly fell into a dreamless sleep.

Chapter Two

FOR more than four centuries the Queen's College of the Protestant Martyrs had stood on the banks of the broad river, and in its classrooms, and on its playing fields future Statesmen, Viceroys, Archbishops, Admirals, Generals, Lord Chief Justices had been educated, their minds trained, their bodies toughened and their characters moulded. The ethos of the College was unashamedly elitist. Self-confidence shading into arrogance was the hallmark of its governors and administrators, its teachers, its pupils. In its corporate soul the College regarded itself as the finest seat of learning, the best moulder of character in the entire world.

The small railway station with its fanciful rococo-styled decorations served both the Martyrs College and the eponymous village which had developed over the centuries in conjunction with the school. Spencer travelled from London in a carriage filled with Japanese tourists, a people for whom he entertained considerable respect. He appreciated their ruthless ferocity in war, and their good manners in peace, but did not find them a physically attractive race, and so was content to gaze out of the window at the passing scenery rather than look at the girls in the carriage.

Spencer came out from the station and paused for a moment to stare down the main street of Martyrs village with its Georgian buildings stretching in a long, slightly curving line towards the College complex a quarter of a mile distant.

The pavements were thronged with camera-laden tourists, the majority of whom appeared to be small, chattering parties of Japanese adults, and crocodile files of noisy French schoolchildren.

Spencer walked slowly along the street and as he neared the College complex took the guidebook map from his pocket and aligned it with the buildings ahead of him through which the main street ran onwards to the north. The great greystone

Sixteenth-Century chapel with its battlements and pinnacles and flying buttresses, and the conjoined castellated facade of "Old School", with the College flag of quartered Tudor Roses and Lions flying over the arched entrance physically dominated the complex, and winding lanes and passageways dissecting the numerous large buildings which made up the campus.

As Spencer passed by the chapel a bell began to toll, and suddenly the main street, the lanes and passageways were thronged with Collegians dressed in formal black suits, starched white shirts, winged collars and white cravats, and carrying armfuls of textbooks. They spoke in loud, well-bred voices, and bore themselves as if they were the lords of all they surveyed, haughtily ignoring the camera-wielding tourists moving among them.

Spencer went without haste in search of Penfold House. It was a red-brick five-storied building which stood in a cul-de-sac. He was surprised to see an armed policeman standing in a neighbouring archway, and walked slowly past, meeting the policeman's gaze with a friendly nod and smile. The policeman smiled back, then switched his attention elsewhere.

The House name was ornately etched into the polished brass plate on the great front doors.

The doors opened and a small group of boys emerged together with a tall cadaverous man wearing the long billowing black gown of a master.

Spencer glanced sideways, and recalled the name of the Housemaster of Penfold which had been listed in the 'Fixtures' book.

I wonder if you're Hubert Hilary Mollinson? he asked himself, and carried on walking to enter a long narrow passageway between two other tall red-brick houses.

The passageway debouched onto a road, on both sides of which were other boarding houses and varied class blocks, and Spencer turned to his left, the direction which would take him past the rear garden of Penfold House. A low wall which contained a central gateway marked the garden's boundary; as he passed Spencer looked through the bars of the ornate ironwork gate and noted the wide expanses of the lawn and flowerbeds which stretched up to the rear of the house. He continued to stroll around the campus and in some of the less frequented areas he encountered the occasional individual adult or boy who regarded him curiously, but Spencer was not perturbed by their curiosity, knowing that in his Saville Row suit, striped shirt and 'Old Collegian' tie he fitted in entirely with his surroundings, and would not be challenged.

When he emerged back onto the main street another lesson period had elapsed and once again the bell was tolling to bring the Collegians swarming between their widely dispersed venues for different classes. Spencer wanted to see his 'Target' in the flesh but accepted the unlikelihood of meeting him face to face among these hundreds of boys. Then an idea occurred to him and he moved to intercept an oncoming group.

"Excuse me."

The fresh faces at first instance regarded him with a suspicious disdain, then noting his 'Old Collegian' tie, responded courteously.

"Can we help you, Sir?"

"Will the Wet Bobs be practising today?" He smiled. "I'd like to see how good my successors are."

"Yes sir, after lunch. The junior eights from two until three o'clock, and the seniors from three o'clock until four," a tall youth informed him, and glancing down at the man's highly polished shoes offered diffidently, "but the towpath is quite muddy in places past Thompson's Eyot. There's a waterpipe leaking apparently, and the workmen are trying to repair it."

"It might be best if you watch from High Bridge, sir," another boy suggested. "There's a new path to it now which is much shorter than the old one." He pointed eastwards. "If you cross 'Browns Acre' and follow the hedge line to the right you'll come to it."

"Thank you very much indeed."

"You're very welcome, sir."

Spencer stood leaning against the brick parapet of the bridge watching the long slender racing shell pass beneath him, its sweating crew rowing with precisioned, graceful rhythm, their blades cutting into the dark swirling river, lifting and scattering sun-flashing diamonds of water. As the shell emerged from under the arch he crossed to the opposite parapet and stared hard at the flushed faces of the oarsmen. He found the one he sought and glanced at the photograph held concealed in his hand. It was a good likeness. He lit a cigarette, and settled to wait for the shell's return upriver.

Soon it came back, the stroke rate faster now as the high-pitched voice of the diminutive cox urged the crew to greater effort. Spencer studied the rear of the target's head then noted what looked like a large watch strapped on the slender left wrist. Spencer quickly checked the other rowers, and saw that all of them were bare armed.

The target was tagged. Spencer frowned slightly. If the target was electronically tagged it meant that a sophisticated protective surveillance was operating. Why should this schoolboy whom he had never heard of be guarded like this?

On the towpath a track-suited cyclist followed the shell, pedalling hard to keep up with the pace. As he neared the bridge he slowed and stared at the man above him.

Spencer saw the hand radio dangling from the handlebars of the cycle, and the holstered pistol showing from beneath the hem of the tracksuit top.

He waved in casual greeting, smiling and calling, "They're doing very well, aren't they. The stroke co-ordination is much better today."

The cyclist nodded in surly response, and in his turn passed beneath the bridge. Then a little distance further along the towpath halted, and began to talk into his radio, staring back at the bridge as he did so.

Spencer was fully aware that the bodyguard was reporting back to a control centre, that a strange man was on the bridge, but he stayed motionless, staring along the now empty length of the swirling water, thinking how easy it would have been to have shot the target through the back of the head as the racing shell neared the bridge, and to have disposed of the cyclist bodyguard before the man had even realised what had happened. In this hunt however, the object was not to kill, but to take alive.

Spencer experienced a tingling of anticipatory relish for the task which lay ahead.

A smile hovered upon his lips, and his fingers tapped upon the brickwork in cadence with the merry tune that had begun playing in his mind . . .

Chapter Three

THE restaurant was fashionably select, the food good, the wine adequate, the service obsequious. The two men were seated at a discreetly positioned table where their conversation could not be overheard.

Spencer ate and drank with gusto.

The white-haired, aquiline-featured older man, Charles Hoffman, ate and drank sparingly, and covertly studied his companion. Their relationship was of long standing and Hoffman had employed the other man many times to carry out high risk, illegal assignments, but in actuality he knew almost nothing about Spencer's personal antecedents. And always, whenever they met, Hoffman felt vaguely uneasy. When he attempted to analyse this feeling of unease, he likened it to being in close proximity with a primed time bomb. A bomb which was perfectly stable and safe, but only until the mechanism ticking away deep inside its innards should trigger the detonator. The uneasiness lay in not knowing at what hour that timing mechanism was programmed to detonate the explosion.

During the meal the men chatted about a variety of subjects, in none of which Charles Hoffman had any deep interest, but he was content to follow his companion's conversational leads, knowing from past experience that the younger man would not come to the real business of the evening until the brandy and cigars were served.

Once his cigar was drawing well, and with the taste of the fine brandy on his tongue, Spencer leaned forwards and asked quietly, "Who is Alexander Margrave?"

Hoffman paused before replying.

"He's the son of Henry Cabot Macpherson."

Spencer did not hide his surprise.

Henry Cabot Macpherson had lately dominated the international news. An American multi-millionaire, turned crusading politician, Macpherson had suddenly and dramatically emerged as the front-running candidate for the Presidency of the United States of America.

He was a hardline Law and Order man, who was promising to initiate the toughest crackdown on crime that the United States had ever known, and to enforce draconian firearms control laws.

"Alexander Margrave is Macpherson's eldest son," Hoffman went on. "Some years before he entered the political arena Macpherson was very briefly married to an Englishwoman, a Lydia Margrave. The marriage was a disaster. They divorced very quickly, and Lydia Margrave returned to this country. Then, some four months after the divorce, she gave birth to Alexander, who took his mother's name and nationality.

Macpherson remarried of course, and has several children from this later marriage, but has continued to financially support Lydia Margrave and Alexander."

Spencer nodded in understanding, then queried, "Did Macpherson himself request the surveillance on the boy?"

"That is so." Hoffman confirmed. "Since the announcement of his candidacy he has started to receive death threats from extremist groups, and criminal elements. Now the general public doesn't even know that Alexander Margrave exists. But as Macpherson's presidential campaign gathers momentum, then inevitably the fact that he has a son from a previous marriage will become widely known, and that son could also become a target. So he is taking early precautions."

"The boy's mother, Lydia Margrave, is she under police protection also?"

Hoffman's cynical smile flickered briefly, and he joked, "I don't believe any offer was made to her. Frankly she could well be issuing some of the death threats herself. She is still very bitter about the divorce."

"Why do your clients want the boy kidnapped?" Spencer questioned.

The older man frowned, and protested sharply. "You and I have always conducted our business relationship on a strictly 'Need to know' basis. You do not need to know my clients' identities or motives."

Spencer riposted equally sharply. "This isn't some nobody's

son we're discussing here. If and when I snatch this boy, then my head is on the block."

Suddenly Hoffman's suave facade cracked. Naked fear showed in his eyes, and he hissed venomously. "Damm you, Spencer! Do you think that I'm oblivious to the dangers? I'm running a greater risk than you, because my clients will accept no excuse from me for failure. My head is in double jeopardy."

Spencer made no reply.

With a visible effort, Hoffman steadied himself and apologised.

"I'm sorry. I'm not so young any more, my nerves are not what they once were."

Spencer's thoughts were racing. His financial funds were all but gone, and he desperately needed this job. He accepted the proffered olive branch.

"We'll leave aside your clients' identities and motives, Mr Hoffman. Now, as to the project under discussion. My fee will be two million sterling. To be paid into separate accounts of which I will provide the details. The payments to be made in US dollars, Deutchmarks, Swiss Francs and Japanese Yen. Preferably in equal amounts of each currency. The first million to be paid before the operation. The remainder following its successful completion."

The demand caused Hoffman to raise his eyebrows. "That is a very large sum, Mr Spencer."

"This is a very risky operation, and it will cost me a lot of money to set it up, Mr Hoffman. My quote is only commensurate with the degree of risk, and expense."

Charles Hoffman's reaction was a pained grimace.

"I don't enjoy haggling as if I were a dealer in old clothes," he protested frostily.

Spencer grinned with real amusement, displaying strong white teeth, and for a brief instant Charles Hoffman vividly recalled a childhood memory of a tiger he had once seen.

The older man silently pondered for some moments, and then concurred with an inclination of his patrician head.

"I accept."

He glanced at his wafer-thin gold wristwatch.

"Goodness me, just look at the time. I'll have to leave you, there's a late sitting at the House which requires my presence. Do stay on and have whatever you want."

He rose to his feet and the head waiter hurried towards him.

"Was everything to your satisfaction, Mr Hoffman, sir?"

"Yes, thank you, Gino. It was excellent, as always. Please attend to my guest won't you. He's remaining here."

The man's head bobbed repeatedly as he babbled effusively.

"Certainly, sir, thank you, sir, thank you. I hope that we shall have the honour of serving you again very soon. Thank you, Mr Hoffman, sir."

Hoffman looked down at his guest and forced a smile. "I've greatly enjoyed our evening. We really should do this again sometime."

Left alone Spencer signalled the waiter for another brandy, and when it came cradled the glass globe between his hands, staring thoughtfully down into the golden liquid, swirling it gently so that it caught the beam from the lamp and reflected a myriad glints of dazzling light.

He leaned back in his chair and looked into the wall mirror. The man he saw there reflected in the subdued lighting of the room was well barbered and groomed, dressed with understated elegance, the epitome of worldly success.

Spencer's finely honed instincts warned him that he was being observed, and he casually glanced about him. The hour was close to midnight, and only a scattering of tables were still occupied. It was a strikingly attractive young woman with raven-black hair who was watching him. Her elderly male companion was concentrating on his food, paying no attention to anything else. Her eyes locked with Spencer's, and she smiled, her teeth very white against the moist red lips. He briefly returned her smile, then broke eye contact, finished his brandy and left the room.

Outside the night was chill and misty and he drew his topcoat closer around him as he walked slowly along the lamplit street.

He reflected on Charles Hoffman's momentary loss of control. He had never before seen the older man betray fear.

His new clients must be really heavy people if they frighten that wicked old bastard, he mused.

Spencer's eyes glittered as the dormant madness hidden within him suddenly seethed in his brain. He muttered a quotation, "Yea, though I walk through the Valley of the Shadow of Death, I shall fear no evil . . . Because I am the evillest bastard in the whole Valley . . ."

He threw back his head and roared with laughter, and the echoes of that insane merriment rebounded along the mist-wet walls.

Chapter Four

GORDY Clark lived in a shabby terraced house, in a shabby street in Brighton's Kemp Town, just a short walk from the seafront. An avid reader of newspaper obituary columns, and a frequenter of cemeteries, Gordy Clark earned his living by expertly forging passports, birth certificates, driving licences and personal documentations, and because of his expertise many dead men, women and children had been resurrected to lead long and fruitful lives.

His caution concerning his clientele verged on paranoia and he only accepted a new customer who could be vouched for by an already proven and trusted associate. Because of his caution Gordy Clark had avoided arrest for many years. Faces were his stock in trade, together with names and dates, and he prided himself on his encyclopedic memory for those three things.

When the knock sounded on his door in the small hours of the early morning Gordy Clark was neither surprised nor alarmed. His customers preferred to use the unsocial hours to conduct their business in. His asthmatic breath wheezed in his throat as he painfully levered his arthritic joints out of the chair and shuffled down the passageway to the front door.

He peered through the eyehole at his visitor, who turned his face up to the street lamp so that he could be recognised.

Gordy Clark opened the door.

"Well now, I haven't seen you for a long while, have I?" He grinned, disclosing blackened snags of teeth. "Come in. Come on in."

He used no name in his greeting. In his business a client's birth name was superflous to requirements, since so many of them used a wide variety of aliases.

Spencer followed the wheezily panting, bent-backed old man down the dark, ill-smelling corridor and into the even worse smelling rear room.

"Sit down." Clark waved towards a straight-backed wooden

chair set by a table spread with old yellowing newspapers which were smothered with grease, scraps of rotting food, dirty plates and cups.

Clark lowered himself groaningly into a battered-looking armchair by the side of the blazing gasfire. The filthy room was so hot that Spencer was already sweating heavily, but he displayed no sign of distaste or discomfort.

"What do you need?" Clark wanted to know.

"Three full sets. Passports, birth certificates, driving licences, degree diplomas, army discharge papers. I'll need altered facial features for them as well. The alterations need to be ones I can be comfortable with, and can do myself without taking much time over it."

"Do you want to be older?" Clark asked.

Spencer pondered for a few seconds.

"Just for one of them. The other two can be roughly about my own age."

Clark's dirty, pallid features abruptly twisted as if he were in pain, and he began to wheeze louder, strangulated breath rasping and bubbling liquidly in his throat. He snatched up an inhaler and squirted the spray into his gaping mouth. Slowly his breathing eased and he was able to gasp out, "How soon do you want it?"

"Within a week."

"Phewww!" Clark shook his head negatively. "It can't be done that quick. There's a lot of work in three full sets."

Spencer opened his topcoat and lifted a thick wad of banknotes into view.

"I'll pay well."

Avarice gleamed in Clark's bloodshot eyes.

"We'd better get upstairs." He levered himself stiffly out of the chair and led the way back into the dark corridor and up the flight of stairs to the upper floor.

Their feet made a hollow thumping on the bare boards as they mounted the stairs and walked along the landing; the stick-thin, mangy-furred cat which had been lying on the landing sprang to its feet, back arched, hissing with fright.

"Pay no mind to her," Clark chuckled, and spoke fondly to the animal. "Don't be so daft, you silly bugger, nobody's going to hurt you."

He grinned over his shoulder at Spencer, and told him, "That's my little mate, that is. I loves that little soul."

Spencer grinned sardonically. "By the look of it, that's all it gets to live on. Perhaps you should try giving it food, as well as love."

The room resembled a photographer's studio with its array of equipment and lights. Along one wall was an extended mirror and a dressing table strewn with various make-up items.

"Stand here, will you?" Clark requested, and Spencer moved to the indicated position where the beam from the dusty, fly-speckled light bulb fell full on his face.

Clark's lungs bubbled and gurgled as he peered closely at the taller man's features, and the stenches of his unwashed body and foul mouth invaded Spencer's nostrils.

"Now then, summat quick and simple," Clark muttered as if to himself. "I reckon a birthmark and a pair o' specs for one."

Spencer frowned doubtfully and the old man hastened to explain.

"Lissen, a birthmark catches people's eyes, and that's what they notices first about you. And that's what they remembers about you afterwards."

He fumbled among the clutter on the dressing table and produced a floppy strip of purplish-red rubbery material.

"Now, you only needs to lick it on this side and slap it on. It only takes a second."

He slurped his tongue along the strip of material and slapped into onto the side of Spencer's face. Turning, he bent with a groan and lifted a shoebox from the floor which he opened to disclose a tangled mass of spectacles.

"These has all got plain lenses. I should take a couple o' pairs if I were you, just in case you might lose one."

He fumbled to fit a pair of spectacles onto the other man's nose, and then invited with an air of triumph, "Just take a look at yourself now. Your own mother wouldn't know you."

Spencer stared briefly into the mirror, then closed his eyes and mentally recalled what he had seen there. A bespectacled man with a birthmark. The birthmark and spectacles were the dominant identifying features. Nothing else had really registered.

He nodded. "Very good. Very effective!"

The old man's black stubs of teeth bared in a conceited grin. "Told you, didn't I?" he crowed. "Now for changing the shape of your face, making you look fatter, you uses these. You can slip 'um in in seconds, and there's lots of different sizes to use."

He produced several pairs of small plastic lozenges and held them up before Spencer's eyes. "Look at how they're all different shapes. And you can talk, and drink, and even eat with 'um in. We can alter your teeth as well. You can have buck teeth, or bad teeth, or missing teeth. You can have false moustaches, and beards, you can have wigs because your own hair is short, or you can alter the style and colour of your hair. You can do anything to yourself that you've a mind to. Just look at these different coloured contact lenses. You can be black eyed, blue eyed, green eyed, even bloody pink eyed if you want to be."

For the next two hours they experimented with a variety of quickly assumed disguises, and after they had settled on three, Clark then spent a further two hours taking photographs of Spencer's new appearances.

When all was finished they returned downstairs, and in the stiflingly hot kitchen Clark told him, "This lot is going to cost you heavy."

"How much?" Spencer wanted to know.

Greedy speculation gleamed in the bloodshot eyes.

"Twenty-five grand. That's what it'll cost. Half before I start. The rest on delivery."

"That's a stiffer price than I expected," Spencer protested.

The other man chuckled, and coughed, and choked and wheezed, and desperately sprayed the inhaler into his gaping mouth.

When his tortured breathing eased, he panted, "It's not only my skill you're paying for, is it? It's my silence as well. It's for keeping my mouth shut."

After a moment Spencer chuckled amusedly, but his eyes were as cold as death.

"Very true, Mr Clark. And it's well known that your discretion is absolute."

The old man looked gratified. "O' course it's well known. That's why I've been in business for so long."

"Alright, Mr Clark. We'll do business." Spencer pulled out

the thick wad of banknotes. "There's three thousand pounds on account. I'll get the remainder of the first payment to you before the end of the week."

"That's fair enough," the other man accepted.

Spencer extracted a folded sheet of notepaper from his inner pocket and laid it on top of the wad of banknotes. "Here's three curriculum vitaes for the new documentation, Mr Clark. I shall leave the choice of names and birthdates to your discretion, naturally." He smiled with genuine amusement. "But please do try to ensure that the names and identities you select are befitting for an officer and a gentleman, won't you."

Chapter Five

ON the eleventh night following his initial visit to Gordy Clark, Spencer once more drove down to Brighton. He parked his car on the seafront and walked through the narrow streets of Kemp Town. It was late, only a few belated revellers were abroad and these paid no attention to the cloth-capped, donkey-jacketed workman who passed them.

He reached Gordy Clark's house, and before he knocked on the flaking, painted panels of the front door he pulled on a thin pair of leather gloves.

Clark opened the door and gestured for silence. He leaned forwards, and his stinking breath gusted around Spencer's head as he hissed, "I've got someone in the kitchen. Go straight upstairs to the workroom, and I'll come up to you later. Don't make any noise."

Spencer obeyed without question, moving silently up the narrow stairs. On the landing the mangy cat hissed and bared its fangs; Spencer halted and stood motionless.

From below a woman's loud, cracked voice echoed along the corridor, "Who was that at the door then?"

"Some bloody drunk looking for his lodgings," Clark's voice explained. "I sent him packing."

The kitchen door closed and the voices became muffled and unintelligible.

Spencer moved on past the hissing cat and entered the workroom, closing the door silently behind him and drawing the heavy curtains across the window before switching on the light. Then he sat down on a chair and composed himself to wait patiently. He would have liked to smoke, but postponed that pleasure until his business here should be successfully concluded.

Almost an hour had elapsed before there came the sounds of the kitchen door slamming open and voices moving down the corridor to the front door. There was a series of loud drunken farewells from the woman followed by the sounds of Clark's shuffling feet and loud wheezing panting coming up the stairs and along the landing.

"Sorry about that." The old man was the worse for drink himself, and he leered salaciously. "That's my bit of leg-over. She comes round once or twice a week. Depending on how me chest is. Only sometimes it's that bad I can't draw me breath, never mind get it up her."

"I do hope that I haven't ruined your plans for the rest of the night, Mr Clark. I'm so sorry if I have." Spencer apologised sarcastically.

"Not at all. Not at all." The old man waved aside the apology. "She couldn't stay in any case. Her old man is at home tonight. It's his night off from the ferries."

He took a key from his trouser pocket and unlocked the bottom drawer of the dressing table.

"It's all ready for you. I've been working non-stop on it."

He pulled a large manila envelope from the drawer and handed it to his visitor.

"There, take a look at that lot and see what you think."

Spencer opened the envelope and extracted the contents, spreading them out on the dressing table. He studied each item in turn. Passports, driving licences, discharge papers, and all the rest. The workmanship was superb, and he could find nothing to be faulted.

"I've enclosed the photo negatives as well, and the curriculums you gave me. I never leave anything to chance. There'll be no trace of you left here when you leave." He winked owlishly. "Discretion, that's my motto. Discretion."

"You've done a first-class job." Spencer smiled, and after replacing all the items in the large envelope put it aside, and reached into the big pocket of his donkey jacket. "And here's the rest of your money."

His hand sprang from the pocket and the leather-bound lead cosh it gripped smashed into the old man's temple.

Clark dropped as if pole-axed, but Spencer had moved with lightning speed to grip the toppling body and prevent any thudding impact upon the bare boards. Gently he lowered the senseless man to the floor, then himself dropped down upon the limp body, bringing his full weight onto the narrow chest to compress the labouring lungs within that fragile cage.

He covered the mouth and nose with his hands to stifle the breathing, and within a few short minutes Clark had suffocated to death.

Now Spencer began to painstakingly search throughout the house, poking into every dusty, dirty, stinking nook and cranny, but taking great care to replace everything that he moved so that no trace of his search might remain. He found two cunningly concealed hiding places which contained large amounts of money. But it wasn't money that he was searching for. However he smiled grimly and put the wads of banknotes into his pockets.

"Waste not, want not," he murmured.

He was uncomfortably aware of the swift passing of the hours, and knew that he had not much time left. He could not risk staying here until daylight, the danger of being seen leaving was too great. But there remained the greater risk that he was conscious of. He knew that a man as cunning as Gordy Clark would be certain to keep incriminating evidence against his clients as a means of self-protection. No disgruntled client would dare to harm the old man if there was evidence against that client waiting to be discovered.

Spencer completed his search of the house, and cursed sibilantly with frustration. Then the mangy cat ran in and out of the room, mewing plaintivly, and a fresh idea struck into Spencer's mind.

He went to the kitchen and there in a corner found the wooden box filled with fetid, rotting rags in which the cat slept. He carefully lifted the rags and smiled. In a clear plastic bag there was a sheaf of papers. They were receipts for the rental of a safety deposit box in a security vault in central London. The receipts were made out to the name of Samuel Parkins.

There was no key with the receipts, however, and Spencer experienced a sudden wave of weariness at the prospect of a further search.

The key has got to be here somewhere. But where? Where would a man like Clark keep it? Further inspiration dawned, and he smiled mirthlessly. It's a good job that I'm wearing gloves.

Returning to the room where Clark lay, he slipped his hand down inside the trousers and underpants and penetrated the dead man's rectum with his forefinger. He felt the edge of a hard object. It was the key he wanted.

"You crafty bastard," he whispered to the dead man. "You almost found the perfect hiding place, didn't you?"

He carefully stowed the key away, and checked the time, estimating that it would shortly be dawn. Then he stood for brief moments, staring speculatively at the corpse at his feet.

He glanced at the contents of the room, which he knew would certainly attract a great deal of interest from the police.

I'd best not leave them an obvious killing as well, he decided. I'll have to risk a noise.

He lifted and carried the limp corpse to the head of the stairs with an ease that demonstrated his great physical strength.

Then propped the limp body upright and sent it toppling down. The corpse thumped loudly upon the wooden planking and sprawled headfirst on the lower steps.

Spencer remained motionless, listening hard for any reaction to the sudden noise from the neighbouring houses. All stayed still and silent, and he smiled in bleak satisfaction, then moved quietly downstairs himself and carefully positioned the dead man's head so that the crushed temple bone was in contact with the edge of the stair treader.

He returned upstairs and checked the floor of the room where the dead man had lain. Blood had pooled from the head wound upon the old newspapers which bestrewed the floor. He thought hard, his gaze flicking rapidly around the room, noting the many inflammable contents and liquids, and most important for his purpose, the overflowing ashtrays and scattered cigarette ends.

He switched off the light and cautiously peered through the curtains. The street was dark and deserted. He let the curtain fall back into place, then switched the light on. He picked up the box of matches on the dressing table and struck one, allowing the flaming splinter of wood to fall onto the newspapers. The dry paper took fire, and the flames spread with greedy appetite.

Spencer walked quietly downstairs, stepping over the sprawled corpse, and opened the front door just wide enough to check that the street was still deserted, then stepped out onto the pavement, closed the door behind him, and walked away.

On the main roads the early-morning traffic was already

rumbling. He returned to his car and before starting the engine he lit a cigarette and drew the smoke deep into his lungs, savouring its hot fragrance. He felt very calm and very confident that the scenario he had left behind him would be interpreted by any interested parties as a tragic accident. The old man had carelessly dropped a lighted match or burning cigarette end, a fire had sprung up, and in panic he had rushed to escape and had fallen down the stairs. If the fire did not entirely consume the body, then a post-mortem would reveal that there was no carbon in his lungs, and the cause of death would be attributed to the fall.

Using the key and the code numbers on the receipts he could access the safety deposit box at his own convenience. In fact, he might even utilise it for his own use. It had obviously served Gordy Clark well, and so long as the rent was paid promptly there would be no questions asked as to the physical identity of Samuel Parkins.

Spencer now realised that he was feeling rather tired, and he smiled with a pleasant sense of anticipation for the food and rest he was shortly going to enjoy. Still contentedly smiling he started the car engine and drove sedately out to join the traffic stream on the main road.

Chapter Six

THE Old Manse was on the English Heritage list, and this fact, coupled with the recession in the housing market, meant that the estate agent, Solly Lustberg was finding it very difficult to sell. Potential buyers were frightened off by the prospect of having any alterations or refurbishments they wanted done to the house being vetted, and vetoed, by the English Heritage inspectors.

Unlike many of his profession, Solly Lustberg, was reluctant to gloss over these potential difficulties, and to his credit now explained to the potential buyer sitting on the opposite side of his desk just what the ownership of the Old Manse would entail. To sweeten the pill, however, he ended by reiterating just how low the selling price was now, in comparison to what it would rise to when the housing market picked up once more.

". . . so Mr Arnold, it really is a bargain. An excellent long-term investment, in fact, for a gentleman such as yourself, who is looking to expand his property interests in this country. You've seen for yourself that its exterior and interior condition is excellent. The grounds of course do need attention. But we've some very good jobbing gardeners hereabouts. They're cheap too."

The potential buyer leaned back in his chair and appeared to be deep in thought, his eyes closed behind the horn-rimmed spectacles, fingertips stroking his grey military moustache, mouth slightly open displaying his protruding, brown-stained front teeth.

Solly Lustberg couldn't help but think that the man should consider finding a good dentist. He gently pressed on.

"Of course the existing fittings and furnishings may not be to your taste, Mr Arnold. Frankly I was not at all happy at the present owner's insistence that they should be included in the sale. But there are some decent pieces, and the price addition is virtually negligible . . ."

The other man lifted his hand to interrupt the flow of words.

"Any decent golf clubs locally?" He asked, and Solly Lustberg blinked in surprise, not having expected such a question at this juncture. But he instantly seized this unlooked-for opportunity.

"As a matter of fact I'm a member of a rather select private club which is only a few miles from the Old Manse." He smiled confidentially. "There's a three-year waiting list, but I've got some influence with the committee, and I'm sure that you could join very quickly. After all, living at the Old Manse means that you're a local man, and we locals have top precedence for membership entrance."

Spencer chuckled warmly. "Do you know, Mr Lustberg, golf is my weakness. Membership of a decent club would certainly sway me towards taking the house."

Lustberg beamed, and offered his hand across the desk. "Welcome to Lower Marston Golf Club, Mr Arnold. We also have a full social calendar, and you'll hopefully enjoy taking advantage of that also."

"Indeed I shall, Mr Lustberg." Spencer shook hands with a firm grip. "Now, can you recommend a good solicitor for the legal details? I prefer to use local people whenever possible."

"Leave it to me, Mr Arnold. The chap we normally use is first class, and very reasonable in his charges as well."

Spencer nodded agreement. "Fine, Mr Lustberg. Oh, by the way, don't bother forwarding any documents to my hotel. I'll be moving out from there tomorrow. I have to travel on business for a while. I'll call here at your office when I return and deal with the final details and signings."

He pulled a chequebook from his pocket and wrote out a large cheque which he handed to Lustberg.

"There's the deposit."

The two men parted shortly afterwards, and as soon as he was alone in his office Solly Lustberg phoned his wife.

"Listen, Ruthie, you can go ahead and order that new carpet. I've just sold the Old Manse . . . Some guy who's just come back from South Africa . . . He's going to be joining the club as well. His name is James Arnold . . . Stinking rich if I'm any judge . . . I don't know if he's married or not, do I . . .

Seems a very pleasant sort of guy . . . What was that? . . .
Carol wants to know what he looks like? . . . She's a tart, isn't
she. Man mad! . . . Well, he's not bad looking, I suppose, but
he's got to be sixty, if he's a day, and his teeth need some
cosmetic treatment . . . I can't say I really noticed anything
else, except that he's got a moustache, and he's grey-haired,
and wears glasses."

Spencer strolled about the small Cotswolds market town,
familiarising himself with its streets and main landmarks.
Afterwards he drove his gleaming Bentley saloon along the
winding lanes to the stone-built Old Manse, and letting himself
into its musty interior wandered through its warren of rooms
filled with dust-sheeted furniture, and eccentrically twisting
passageways. He spent a considerable time in the cellars,
noting with much interest that they were deep and only native
sandstone had been used in their construction, rendering them
virtually soundproof.

Ideal cells, he thought with satisfaction.

He had already walked the grounds of the house in company
with the estate agent, but now he explored the half acre
of neglected lawns, shrubberies and coppices much more
thoroughly, and then walked the encircling fields and hillsides,
imprinting a mental picture of the house in relation to the
surrounding terrain.

When dusk came down he drove away.

Back in London he parked the Bentley in a lock-up garage
in Chelsea, walked to the nearest tube station and travelled
to Piccadilly Circus. There, in a cubicle in the public lavatories, he removed his facial disguise and returned to his
current hotel.

In his room he stripped and showered, then for a brief while
stood staring at the reflection of his naked body in the long
mirror fixed on the inside of the wardrobe door. His torso was
lean and hard, still bronzed by the Spanish sun. A jagged scar
ran across the ridged stomach muscles, and as Spencer studied
it, his mind filled with the visual image of the man who had
inflicted that wound. The image was of a piece of butchered
human wreckage vomiting its own blood as it begged Spencer
for mercy, begged for death to release it from its agonies.

Spencer had taken great pleasure in that particular act

of vengeance, and had ensured that death had come very very slowly.

He shook his head sharply, driving the image from his mind, clearing his thoughts so that he could consider his next move in this murderous game of which he was a proven master.

Spencer had already decided that the only viable option was to snatch the target from the Martyrs campus itself. He knew that the boys were allowed out of the College for a limited period at weekends. But there was no way of knowing in advance if the target would leave the campus, or where he might go.

The same objections disqualified the school holidays. Would the target spend time with his mother? Or his father? At home or abroad? Might he go to one of his schoolfriends' houses? It was too uncertain.

Spencer's all-imperative need now was for knowledge of the inner workings of Penfold House. Its daily and weekly routines. Its inhabitants. Its security measures. The layout of its rooms and passages. The locations of its power supplies. Above all else, Spencer must uncover its vulnerabilities.

Spencer lit a cigarette and drew deeply upon it, then exhaled slowly, letting the smoke drift from his mouth to wreath its tentacles around his head.

He knew exactly where to search for the vulnerabilities of Penfold House. He would find those among its human elements. The human element was always the weakest point in any system of defence.

Chapter Seven

TOMMY Phillpots was a small, plump, nondescript man with no striking physical attributes. In any grouping he would be unremarked, an overlooked nonentity. But his bland, bovine features concealed a sharp and shrewd mind, and he possessed the talent for being able to assemble a montage of accurate knowledge from tiny, and sometimes inaccurate scraps of information. A talent which served him well in his work as a private enquiry agent.

Phillpots had once been a highly successful practioner of his trade, numbering many famous names among his satisfied clients. But his working methods had always hovered dangerously close to the thin boundary which separated legality from illegality. Eventually his frequent forays across that boundary had brought him into conflict with the police and had cost him his operating licence, plus a lengthy prison sentence. Now, unable to openly advertise his services, he had fallen upon hard times and was dependent upon the occasional commission that came his way through word of mouth. He had long since been forced to give up his business premises, and now his office was the saloon bar of his local public house in Notting Hill Gate, where he spent most of his waking hours sitting brooding, and nursing a half pint of bitter through the long arid periods of idleness that increasingly lengthened between commissions. The only high spots in his bleak existence were the occasional drunken binges on the rare occasions when he had sufficient money.

It was Thursday afternoon and Tommy Phillpot was in his usual seat next to the pay telephone in the saloon bar. He always insisted on being next to the telephone, and each time it rang he jumped to answer it in the desperate hope that it might be a potential client seeking to engage his services.

The telephone had rung several times that day, but none of the callers had asked for Tommy Phillpots, so he was morosely

27

contemplating the emptiness of his glass, and the unlikely possibility of the landlord allowing him to have a drink on credit. The landlord was leaning over the spread newspaper on the counter studying racing form, and there was no one else in the room. Phillpots cleared his throat and the landlord's head lifted. Phillpots smiled tentatively and lifted the empty glass.

"Any chance?"

The landlord silently shook his head, and returned to his newspaper.

Phillpots gusted a depairing sigh.

Then the phone rang. Wearily he clambered to his feet and lifted the receiver.

"Hullo?"

"I'd like to speak to Mr Phillpots."

The voice was muffled, and at first Phillpots feared that he was mishearing.

"Who d'you want?"

"Phillpots. I want Thomas Phillpots."

Sudden hope swelled. "This is Tommy Phillpots speaking," he informed eagerly.

"Are you available at present, Mr Phillpots?"

For a brief, insane instant Phillpots hesitated, wondering if he should perhaps give the impression that he was a very busy man. Then he castigated himself furiously: Don't be such a silly cunt!

"Yes, I'm available," he told the caller.

"Do you know the Home and Garden Store in Welland Road?" the voice asked.

"Yes."

"Go there now, and browse in the bathroom section, until I come to speak to you," the voice instructed.

"What?" Phillpots demanded, and became angry, thinking that this was some sort of practical joke being played on him. "Are you having a fuckin' game with me, mate?"

"No. This is not a game, Mr Phillpots. I'm offering you the chance to make some money. You have half an hour. If you're not there at the end of half an hour, the chance will be lost."

The phone went dead, and Tommy Phillpots stood with the receiver clamped to his ear, unable to decide whether or not he was being made a fool of.

Well, anyway, what have I got to lose by going there. I've

been made a fool of enough times before. Once more won't hurt me, he decided.

Twenty-five minutes later he was standing gazing at the shining bathroom suites in the big warehouse, his eyes constantly flicking from side to side as he looked for his mysterious caller.

Spencer had watched Phillpots crossing the big forecourt parking area and entering the warehouse. Business was brisk at the tills, and customers and browsers constantly came and went. He studied Phillpots for some few minutes, evaluating the drink-mottled face, the shabby clothing, the aura of defeat that emanated from him.

You'll do, Spencer decided.

"Mr Phillpots?"

Tommy Phillpots turned eagerly at the sound of his name.

"That's me? And you are . . . ?"

"I'm the man who spoke to you on the phone, Mr Phillpots. That's all you require to know about me."

He handed Phillpots an envelope. "You'll find everything you need in here. Don't open it until you are somewhere more private. I'll be in touch."

With that he was gone, quickly lost to view among the bustle of customers, leaving Phillpots with the memory of a flat cap, a donkey jacket, an unsightly purple-red birthmark and a pair of horn-rimmed spectacles.

Phillpots stared down at the long white envelope, and pressed his fingers hard against what felt like a wad of banknotes. Excitement burgeoned in him, tightening his chest, drying his throat and mouth.

I reckon my luck's changed, he told himself, yet still did not dare to believe it.

He hurried to find the men's lavatories, and to lock himself into one of the cubicles. Then, with shaking hands and fumbling fingers he tore the envelope open. He moaned aloud with delight.

It's real money. It's real. This isn't a joke. I'm not being made a fool of. This is real! Real!

He stayed seated on the lavatory pan until his thudding heart slowed and his reeling senses had steadied. Then he tucked the envelope into his inside pocket and hurried back to his poky council flat.

Once there he emptied the contents of the envelope on top the table. There were two thousand pounds in twenty-pound banknotes, and a foolscap sheet of typed paragraphs. He began to read, and wild excitement burgeoned once again. More money was promised to him, and more important than that, a permanent retainer, should he complete this present assignment to his new employer's satisfaction. Reiterated constantly was the warning that complete secrecy was required. If by any deliberate or unguarded word he let slip to anyone else what he was doing, then the consequences for himself would be extremely serious.

Below these opening paragraphs there was printed an address, 'Penfold House, Martyrs College', and a further brief paragraph.

'All adults living here must be identified, and checked out. Report as fully as possible on their personal characters, sexual preferences, social habits, etc. etc. Photograph them also.'

Tommy Phillpots laughed gleefully.

It would be a piece of cake! First thing tomorrow straight to the nearest public library to look up Martyrs village and go through the Electoral Roll for the names he needed. Once he had those, the rest would be easy for an operator of his vast experience.

Celebrate! That's what I'll do now, he decided. Celebrate my change of luck. A few gins, a slap-up meal with wine, and then a visit to young Jenny to shift the dirty water off my chest.

He had actually opened his door to go out when second thoughts struck him.

Hold on, Tommy. Hold on. You've been given another bite at the cherry here. A chance to come good again. The drink messed you up before. Don't be a silly cunt and mess up again. Stay off the sauce and away from the whores until you've got the job done. Then celebrate.

He slammed the door shut.

Sitting in an old rusting van within eyeview of the front of the block of flats, Spencer saw the door of Tommy Phillpots's flat open and moments later close. Spencer never left anything to chance if he could avoid doing so. He had judged that Phillpots's professional instincts would reassert themselves if the opportunity were offered. That judgement had been vindicated.

He smiled mirthlessly as he drove away. If Phillpots had left his flat to go on a drunken spree then the man would not have lived to greet another day.

Chapter Eight

THE chain of keys jingled against the lock and the outer door was thrust open and left to crash shut against its jamb. Dermot Murphy, the stockily built handyman walked through the ground floor of Penfold House, whistling tunelessly and switching on the lights where the early daylight failed to penetrate dark recesses and passageways. His left eye flicked from side to side in wary examination as he entered each shadowed space, searching for booby traps rigged by mischievious boys. His right eye remained motionless because it was made of glass.

On the main entrance doorstep crates of milk had been deposited, together with cartons of fruit juice and yoghurt, and a bundle of newspapers and magazines.

Murphy stepped out into the chill dawn air and stood looking down at the crates and bundle. He scratched his testicles through his blue boiler suit and grumbled beneath his breath.

Across the road a uniformed police constable, holstered pistol prominent on his broad hip, paced slowly backwards and forwards upon the pavement, face set in an expression of stoic resignation.

From the entrance hall behind Murphy footsteps sounded on the stone slabs and another man came out to join him. Despite the early hour this newcomer was dressed in a smart lounge suit, collar and tie, and was freshly shaved and smelling of cologne.

"Good morning, Mr Murphy!" the newcomer wished politely.

"The fuck it is!" Murphy growled, his accent the nasal whine of the Liverpool slums.

Detective Constable Tony Kilbeck frowned at the surly response, as he crouched and carefully examined the crates and the bundle of newspapers, then nodded.

"It's okay. Take them in."

"O' course it's fuckin' okay!" Murphy snarled, and brushed his sleeve against his badly watering glass eye. "Having to wait for youse every morning don't half hold me up. I've got a job to do."

Stung into irritation the policeman snapped curtly. "And so have I."

From the Old School Yard some fifty yards away the Great Bell tolled out from Latimer's Tower, as it had done for more than four centuries to announce the start of the Martyrs College day, and within Penfold House the Rising Bell shrilled loudly on every floor to rouse the sleeping boys.

Maggie Stevens stirred into reluctant wakefulness as the shrilling bells penetrated her consciousness. She turned over in bed and swore in shock.

"Oh shit!"

She sat up and shook the sleeping youth at her side.

"Marcus! Marcus, get up! The Rising Bell's gone!"

He groaned in protest, and she grabbed his thick curly black hair and yanked hard.

"Owwch!" He came awake with a start. Then heard the repeat bell shrilling. Alarm crossed his handsome features and he ejaculated, "Oh shit! Why didn't you wake me?"

"Because I was asleep myself." She rolled from the bed and began to dress hurriedly. In her late twenties she was a handsome, full-bodied woman and despite his own haste to dress the youth felt a surge of lust as he saw her large, shapely breasts.

"Be careful when you go out," she told him, and pausing only to quickly tidy her short brown hair before the mirror, she hurried out of the flat into the end of the long corridor.

Sleepy-eyed boys were emerging from their rooms, some already wearing their uniforms, others in dressing gowns carrying towels and toilet bags.

The woman went along the corridor chivvying the boys.

"Come on now, be quick. Henry, why aren't you dressed, you're duty prefect today, aren't you? Timothy, pull your gown together, I don't wish to see your private parts. All dirty sports togs in the laundry basket please, before you go to breakfast. Sports togs before breakfast!"

"Matron? Matron?" A small, carroty-haired, bespectacled boy ran to catch her up. "Matron?"

33

She sighed impatiently and turned to face him.

"What is it, Phillip?"

"It's Marcus St Clair, Matron. He told me to wake him early because he's on 'Late Book', and when I went to his room, he wasn't there."

She eyed the small boy warily. He was one of the ones she disliked, knowing him to be sneaky and underhand.

"Well, if he isn't in his room, then he must have already gone to sign 'Late Book', you stupid boy."

Behind the smeared lenses of his spectacles his eyes were craftily knowing. "If you please, Matron, his bed hasn't been slept in."

To her relief she saw the Housemaster appear from the passageway which connected to his private quarters.

"I have to speak with Mr Mollinson, Phillip. I'll bring this to his attention. Get off to breakfast now."

He made no move, only glanced slyly at the Housemaster and asked with wide-eyed innocence, "But won't you need me to tell Mr Mollinson myself, Matron. I'll have to confirm that Marcus is missing, won't I."

She controlled the urge to slap him hard, and snapped sharply. "Go to breakfast."

Then swung on her heel and walked on towards the oncoming man.

Tall and skinny to the point of emaciation Hubert Mollinson was known to the boys as 'The Famine'. His given nickname, of which he was all too well aware, did nothing to endear his charges to him, and he walked through his days with his skull-like features set in a permanent frown.

When the handsome woman joined him he challenged querulously.

"I knocked on your door last night, and received no reply. Where were you, Mrs Stevens?"

She assumed a puzzled expression.

"At what time was this, sir?"

"At half past ten."

At half past ten she had been squeezing Marcus St Clair's lithe young body between her plump thighs, and crying out in the throes of orgasm.

"Oh, I must have been sound asleep by that time, sir. I had a bad headache, so I took a sleeping pill and went to bed early."

His thin lips pursed in distaste. "Headaches are no excuse for neglecting your duties, Mrs Stevens. You are paid to be on call twenty-four hours a day. What if an emergency had occurred?"

"I couldn't help having a headache," she protested.

"I do not allow my headaches to distract me from my responsibilities," he told her acidly. "And I expect my staff to follow my example. I hope that you will not give me cause to speak with you again about this." He dismissed her with a curt nod. "I won't detain you further. We have a busy day ahead of us."

He stalked on, leaving her seething inwardly.

Dear God, let me win the lottery, and get out of here, she begged silently.

"Good morning, Matron." A tall, good looking, fair-haired youth greeted her with a smile.

"Good morning, Fergus," she smiled back at him as she walked on thinking how attractive he was physically, and how charming in his manner. Perhaps next year when Marcus had left the school, she might well take Fergus Cochrane into her bed.

She entered the stairwell and began to climb up the stairs to the upper floors, scouring the rooms for reluctant risers. The top floor contained only six rooms, one of which was occupied by the policeman. He came to look out of his open door as she passed.

"Good morning, Mrs Stevens."

Tony Kilbeck stared at her appreciativly. He liked women with big breasts and curvaceous buttocks.

"Good morning, Constable. Did Alexander sleep well?"

"I believe he did, Mrs Stevens. Did you?"

He was an attractive man, and Maggie Stevens was not averse to exchanging some flirtatious banter with him. Although at thirty-five years of age he was too old for her sexual taste.

She smiled and ran her pink tongue over her full lips. "I slept as well as a lonely woman can sleep, Constable."

He played up to her lead. "There's no need for a beautiful woman like you to be lonely, Mrs Stevens. Not while I'm here."

"Oh, Constable, I wouldn't dare deprive Alexander of your protection." She giggled.

Before he could answer they were interrupted by the named boy coming from his room. He was already dressed in full uniform.

"Good morning, Matron," he greeted politely.

"Good morning, Alexander. How did rowing practice go yesterday?" Maggie liked the boy. He was pleasant, well-mannered, and unassuming, despite his father's power and influence.

"It went very well, thank you, Matron."

"Good!" She nodded, and went on briskly. "Be sure to take your dirty sports togs down to the laundry basket before you go to breakfast."

She went past him and began rousting the other boys out of their rooms.

"Come on, you lot, it's breakfast time. Don't forget that you've a busy day ahead of you. Take your dirty sports togs down to the laundry basket before you go to breakfast."

The boys exited the floor, but Tony Kilbeck lingered momentarily.

"Are you coming to breakfast with me, Mrs Stevens?"

She shook her head. "Not today, Constable. I've too much to do."

He shrugged as if disappointed, and left her.

Maggie thought of the Housemaster. At least I won't be seeing much of that miserable bastard today, he's got parent interviews. Thank Christ!

And decided to have a coffee and cigarette in her flat before beginning her work.

The vast, recently-built communal dining hall could seat a maximum of two thousand at its extended rows of refectory tables. It was a single-storied ranch house-style building, its outer walls vast sheets of tinted plate glass sectioned by brick pillars. The building bordered one of the minor roads that ran through the campus, and Tony Kilbeck considered it to be a security man's worst nightmare come true. There was absolutely nothing to prevent a carload of terrorists driving past and blasting the interior with bullets.

He entered the dining hall amid a stream of boys and automatically checked to see where Alexander Margrave was positioned. When on duty he tried to maintain a discreet distance from his charge, knowing that his immediate presence imposed an unwelcome constraint upon the boy and his friends. When he was in their company the boys became surly and guarded in speech. He knew that the boys of Penfold House bitterly resented him living among them, and most of them actively disliked him, wrongly believing that he had been instrumental in causing one of their number's expulsion earlier that term.

The possession of soft/hard drugs was absolutely forbidden, and there was no appeal against instant expulsion for any boy caught with them. Yet despite this rigid stricture the use of soft drugs was widespread among the pupils. The expelled Penfold House boy had had a tiny cache of cannabis resin hidden in his room, and his friends believed that it was Tony Kilbeck who had discovered the cache and reported it to the Housemaster. In fact it had been one of the maids, Mary Jeffers, who had dicovered the cannabis and secretly reported the boy for possessing it.

Alcohol and tobacco were also strictly forbidden, but the more sympathetic masters turned a blind eye to the illicit indulgence in these, realising that youths of seventeen and eighteen years of age could not reasonably be expected to live entirely like monks. They considered that the sexual deprivation and restricted freedom of term-time were burdens enough for their lively young charges to bear.

Kilbeck joined the end of the long queue of boys at the serving counter. Masters did not queue. They had their own table with a waitress to serve them. Kilbeck could not help but feel that by making him queue with the boys the College administrators were ensuring that he was aware of his lowly position in the social pecking order of the College. He slowly moved along the serving counter with his tray, receiving the carefully measured breakfast portions of scrambled eggs, toast and shrivelled mushrooms, and moved away from the seated mass of boys to the far end of the room nearest to the roadway, where he ate in solitary splendour. As he chewed the rubbery eggs and nibbled the hard, burned toast he tried to cheer his gloomy mood by thinking of Maggie Stevens's inviting curves, but with his visual memories of her full breasts and richly moulded buttocks, there came the recollection of her repeated rejections of his romantic overtures, and his gloom deepened.

In this mood it was all too easy for him to become depressed over his lack of advancement in his chosen career. He had been a policeman for sixteen years, the last five of them in SO16, the Diplomatic Protection Group, and was still only a constable. Men who had joined the force in the same recruit intake as himself, he now encountered wearing the stripes and stars of rank.

His short-lived marriage had been another failure. Fed up with the unsocial hours that his job demanded, his wife had issued him with an ultimatum.

"If you don't leave the police force and take the job that Daddy's offering you, then I'm leaving you. It's either the police force, or me. The choice is yours."

Disliking her loud-mouthed, greedy father, and despising the wheeling and dealing by which the man made his living, Kilbeck had chosen the police force, envisaging a glittering career as a thief-taker. Not believing that his wife, whom he dearly loved, would carry out her threat to leave him.

More bloody fool me, he thought bitterly.

His ex-wife had married again, as soon as their divorce degree had become absolute. Her second husband had eagerly accepted the job her father offered, and now they were million-aires owning a large estate in Berkshire, and second and third homes in Miami and Benidorm.

Kilbeck's appetite completely deserted him, he pushed the half-eaten food away and fumbled in his pocket for a packet of cigarettes. Then remembered the no-smoking rule, and cursed long and hard beneath his breath.

"Your pig is looking very miserable this morning, Alex." Jamie Grenfell drew his friend's attention to the dejected policeman.

A chorus of muted honkings and gruntings sounded from the other boys ranged along the extended table.

Alexander Margrave sighed with exasperation. He was becoming extremely tired of the constant verbal snipings and barrackings of his schoolmates, who blamed him personally for the unwelcome presence of Kilbeck.

"Tony really isn't so bad." He defended the man. "If you'd only take the trouble to get to know him, you'd find that he's an okay guy."

"I have made the effort to be friendly." Toby Levy, a tall,

slender, bespectacled, sharp-featured boy, grinned. "I wished him Good Morning, but all he did was to grunt at me."

"What else can you expect from a pig, except a grunt?" Fergus Cochrane quipped, and his sally was greeted with gales of laughter.

"Look, there's Marcus." Rupert Farquar, freckle-faced and sandy-haired sounded envious, as he pointed to the handsome, dark-haired newcomer who had joined the end of the boys' queue.

"He was with Maggie for the whole of last night, you know. His bed wasn't slept in, and he didn't sign 'Late' book."

"He's on 'Report' for not making 'Lates'," another boy informed the table. "The Famine is putting him in front of Chiefy Beaky again. I shouldn't be surprised if he doesn't get suspended, or even kicked out this time. Chiefy Beaky warned him the last time that he'd had enough of his bad behaviour."

"What will poor Maggie do then for her nooky, I wonder?" Toby Levy asked archly. "Who will be the 'Favoured One'?" he grinned provocatively at Fergus Cochrane. "Any ideas about likely candidates to become the 'Favoured One', Fergy?"

The good-looking youth the question was directed at laughed easily. "I sincerely hope that it might be me. I'm certainly training hard to fill that position."

"Oh I know you are." Toby Levy nodded vigorously. "I can hear your bed thumping against the wall every night when you wank."

Again gales of laughter erupted from the listeners, and Fergus had the grace to blush, but was laughing himself as he retorted, "Well, you know what Chiefy Beaky always tells us . . ." He mimicked the pompous manner of the Headmaster. "Gentlemen, in this life preparation is all important. Prepare, Gentlemen, prepare! Always prepare!"

Alexander Margrave laughed with the rest of his companions. Relieved that the focus of attention had been directed away from his personally unwelcome and unwanted bodyguard.

"Any more of your insolence Cochrane, and you'll be reporting to Mr Mollinson." The young, pudgy-faced, newly appointed Assistant Housemaster of Penfold House, Julian Fothergill, had sneaked up undetected to hear what the youth was saying.

Fergus winked at his friends then assumed an expression of utter bewilderment. "Insolence, sir? Me, sir?"

"Yes, Cochrane, you. Stand up when I'm speaking to you!" Fothergill barked and moved to directly confront the youth.

"But, sir, how have I been insolent?" Fergus protested as he rose to his feet, and topped the man by some inches.

"In your usual manner, Cochrane. Mocking your elders and betters."

Again utter bewilderment and further protest. "But, sir, I assure you that I would never ever even consider for one instant making mock of my elders and betters. Really, sir, I wouldn't. I've too much respect for my elders and betters to make mock of them. Ask my friends, sir. "He spread his arms wide in invitation. "They will all be able to confirm that I hold my elders and betters in the very highest respect."

The other boys were grinning and sniggering openly, and they hastened to back up their friend.

"It's true, sir, Cochrane is very respectful to his elders and betters."

"Sir, Cochrane is the humblest boy in the College towards his elders and betters."

"He's positively slavish in his attitude towards his elders and betters, sir."

"Just look at his trousers, sir, the knees are worn through because he spends so much time kneeling submissively before his elders and betters."

Fothergill was becoming uncomfortably aware that neighbouring tables were now taking notice, and that certain of the other masters were extracting malicious pleasure from seeing him being baited.

His embarrassment caused the colour of his fresh complexion to heighten, and knowing that he was flushing his embarrassment deepened.

"Quiet! Be quiet!" His voice became high-pitched, his eyes nervous, and like a hunting wolf pack the boys scented their prey's weakness, and moved in for the kill.

"I think that Cochrane needs counselling, sir, to give him confidence."

"Yes, sir, he's a nervous wreck whenever his elders and betters speak to him."

"It's true, sir. He shivers and shakes so much that the last time he went home his father thought he'd contracted St Vitus's Dance."

"Do our elders and betters ever need counselling, sir?"

"Have you ever needed counselling, sir?"

"I'm sure that you'd find counselling to be of benefit, sir!"

"But you've already had counselling, haven't you, sir? Everyone says that you have!"

Every sally was greeted with loud jeering laughter, and that laughter infected the neighbouring tables and began to spread rapidly throughout the vast room as more and more boys joined in the sport, by catcalling and whistling.

"GENTLEMEN!" The voice thundered, and shocked silence followed.

Hubert Mollinson had entered the room and had been an unnoticed spectator of what was happening.

"STOP EATING AND CLEAR THE DINING HALL IMMEDIATELY."

His long gown swirled around him as he stalked the length of the central gangway between the rows of tables. His angry glare fixed on one hungry small boy who was hastily trying to cram food into his mouth

"YOU!" Mollinson's long finger pointed, and the small boy blanched in terror.

"COME HERE." The long finger crooked, and the terrified boy gulped and reluctantly shuffled out onto the gangway.

Mollinson bent low, and putting his mouth one inch from the boy's ear snarled quietly, "I am not accustomed to being disobeyed. When I tell you to stop eating, and to leave the dining hall, that is exactly what you will do. Have you understood what I have said to you?"

"Yes, sir." The boy nodded furiously.

"THEN OBEY ME, YOU CRETIN!"

The boy physically jumped at the bellow, and his lips trembled uncontrollably as he scurried towards the door.

Mollinson straightened and glared about him, and although his voice was low, it carried clearly to every table.

"Well, Gentlemen?"

A sussuration of complaint sounded, and there were many surly looks directed at the tall, cadaverous figure, but the boys began to move from the tables and towards the doors.

Mollinson stalked against the flow, the boys parting before

him like water before the prow of a ship. The masters were still seated at their table, and Mollinson nodded as he joined them and took a vacant chair.

"Good morning, Gentlemen." He glanced at the food on the plates, and scowled. "Disgusting muck!"

Then he beckoned to the waitress. "I'll just have coffee, roll and butter, thank you."

Face still flushed with embarrassment Julian Fothergill came back to the table.

Hubert Mollinson kept his gaze fixed on the bread roll he was buttering, and ignored his assistant. Fothergill had obtained his post in the College, and his early advancement to Assistant Housemaster because of family influence with the Board of Governors, and Mollinson bitterly resented this. He himself was of lowly origin, and had had to work very hard for many years to gain his promotions.

The other masters ostensibly busied themselves with their meals, and Fothergill's resentful misery deepened as they avoided his eyes.

Mollinson's rancorous contempt was a tangible radiation, and at last Fothergill was driven to speak.

"Mr Mollinson?"

Mollinson sighed impatiently and stared at the young man, lifting one eyebrow in silent query.

"There was no need for you to intervene as you did," Fothergill stammered. "I had the situation perfectly under control."

The other men were staring in rapt anticipation.

Mollinson's thin lips twisted in contempt as then he turned away from his assistant and remarked in an amused tone to the table at large, "There was a rather interesting item in *The Times* this morning, Gentlemen. An account of pigs flying."

Broad smiles and appreciative chuckles came from his listeners.

Fothergill's face flamed, he jumped to his feet and hurried from the dining hall.

Mollinson watched his departure, then snorted disgustedly. "Incompetent clown!" And bit deeply into his buttered roll.

Chapter Nine

TOMMY Phillpots sat in the Sloughton Public Library and studied the list of names he had culled from the Electoral Rolls. Three were male, six were female. Judging from his previous experience of names favoured by the different social classes, he surmised that Hubert Hilary Mollinson and Claudia Elizabeth Mollinson were probably the Housemaster and his wife. The other couple, Dermot and Beryl Murphy, were possibly domestic servants. He couldn't picture a male domestic with a name like Julian Sinclair Fothergill. Perhaps he was another master? The other four females, Mary Jeffers, Margaret Stevens, Reena Brown and Theresa Sweeney must all be members of the domestic staff, unless the Mollinsons had a female relative living with them.

He turned to the College guide book and studied the map of the campus and a photo of Penfold House. He took note of the two doors in the front of the building, a large porticoed central entrance and a smaller, plainer door at the extreme end.

That'll be the tradesmen's entrance, he decided. Probably the one the staff and boys use as well.

Then he left the library and headed towards Martyrs village to join the wandering hordes of tourists.

The first thing that he noticed were security cameras covering the approaches to the College, and in the College complex itself. This did not surprise him unduly. Any school which included among its pupils so many sons of the ruling establishment of the country would naturally take certain precautions to safeguard itself. What did perturb him, however, was the presence of an armed policeman outside Penfold House, coupled with an even more extensive array of security cameras covering the building.

A tourist some yards in front of Phillpots approached Penfold House, camera to his eye; immediately the policeman challenged him and demanded to know his identity.

Phillpots walked on a few paces until he was in earshot of the two men, then knelt, pretending to retie his shoelaces, surreptitiously watching and listening.

The bewildered tourist produced what looked like a passport. The policeman took the passport and began to speak into his personal radio, as if he were reporting the details contained in the document. There was a brief pause and then the policeman nodded as if satisfied with the reply he had received, and handed the passport back to the tourist. The man started to ask questions, but the policeman shook his head and brusquely ordered the man not to take any pictures, and to move on.

Who's in that bloody house? Phillpots wondered. Who are they guarding?

He realised that there was more to this assignment than he had previously thought, and he wondered doubtfully, What am I getting myself involved with here? What does the guy who'se paying me want with this house?

Then he remembered the large amount of money he was being paid, and forced this uncomfortable, newly-arisen feeling of doubt to the back of his mind.

I need the cash. That's all that I've got to think about. I need the cash.

One realisation that he could not ignore however was the fact that he was faced with a much more difficult task than he had expected. Such close security meant that he could not watch the building to see who came and went, and perhaps identify some of those he sought to know. He would not be able to gain any easy access to the premises either, by pretending to be a tradesman, meter reader or deliveryman.

Then his belief that his luck had changed for the better received a fillip. A stocky man wearing a brown overall coat came out from the tradesmen's entrance carrying two empty milk crates, which he laid down at the side of the doorstep.

"Hello, Mr Murphy," the policeman greeted. "I thought you'd be in the Crown and Anchor by now."

Murphy scowled sourly. "So I should have been, if one of the little sods hadn't pulled the fuckin' knob off his door. I've been fixing that. But I'll be down there shortly."

"Have one for me while you're there." The policeman grinned ruefully. "I could murder a pint right now."

Tommy Phillpots rose to his feet and slowly walked away.

He retraced his route along the High Street until he came to the Crown and Anchor public house. It contained only one large serving room with a long bar. Phillpots felt elation rising.

My luck's running, he decided.

He ordered a pint of beer and settled himself on a bench by the window that overlooked the High Street to await the arrival of Dermot Murphy.

The man arrived shortly afterwards and greedily gulped down a pint of strong cider, not lowering the glass until it was empty, then belched loudly and wiped his wet lips with his sleeve.

"That never touched the sides, did it, Dermot?" The middle-aged barman took the empty glass and refilled it.

Murphy looked around the room, staring briefly at the small, plump man sitting by the window, then asked the barman, "Where is everybody today?"

"Been and gone. You're late coming, aren't you?"

"Too much fuckin' work to do, that's my trouble." Murphy swore disgustedly. "What between the fuckin' matron, and the fuckin Master, and the fuckin' boys, I'm run off me fuckin' feet."

The barman's eyes glazed with boredom. He had heard this complaint so many times that he could have recited it word for word.

"I got to check the cellar," he said. "Give us a shout if somebody comes in."

He disappeared and Murphy was bereft of an audience. He scowled unhappily. A compulsive talker, Murphy's constant need was for an audience for his incessant self-centred monologues. For a brief while he stood at the bar, fidgeting restlessly. Several times he looked across at the insignificant little man on the window seat. But the man remained gazing down into his beer. At last, in sheer desperation, Murphy took his drink and seated himself by the side of the stranger.

"Turned out nice again, hasn't it?"

For the first time the stranger met his eyes. He replied timidly, "Yes, it's very nice."

"Too nice for fuckin' work, that's for sure." Murphy grinned, and the little man smiled and nodded.

"I haven't seen you here before? You're not local, are you?" Murphy questioned.

Phillpots shook his head. "No, I'm just having a day out really. I thought I'd have a look at the College. I'm interested in old places, you see."

"You're interested in the College?" Murphy sounded as though he found that statement hard to believe.

"Oh yes," Phillpots timidly asserted. "I like historical places."

"Oh, the College is old, alright," Murphy stated disgustedly. "It should have been pulled down, or blown up, fuckin' years ago."

Phillpots made no answer. He knew that he had hooked his fish, and that reeling it in would present no problem.

The barman reappeared, as Murphy took a long drink and then set his empty glass down. He made no effort to order another refill.

For a little while they sat in silence, then Phillpots drained his own glass and made a show of looking at his watch.

"I think I've time for another," he said, and timidly invited, "would you care to join me?"

Murphy appeared to consider the invitation very carefully, and then accepted magnanimously.

"Well, go on then. I suppose I can keep you company for a bit longer. Work 'ull have to wait, won't it?"

"You work locally, do you?"

"I work at the College."

Phillpots feigned surprise. "Do you? Now that's interesting, I'll bet."

"Tell you what," suddenly a vista of a large number of free drinks appeared in Murphy's imagination," you get these glasses topped up, and I'll tell you a few stories about the fuckin' College that'll make your fuckin' eyes water."

For the rest of that afternoon Murphy talked virtually non-stop as Phillpots listened and frequently bought more drinks, and very occasionally ventured a timid question . . .

Penfold House was quiet in the early hours of the afternoon, when all the boys were away at classes. Mary Jeffers opened the door of her room in the staff quarters on the first floor and listened intently, mouth slightly open, breathing adenoidally.

Through the closed door of Theresa Sweeney's room next to her own there came the sounds of a television programme. Mary Jeffers crept across the landing to press her ear against the door of Reena Brown's room. All was silent within.

Jeffers's pallid features frowned. She would have preferred to hear some sounds of life coming from the room because then she would know the whereabouts of the other woman.

A key rattled in the yale lock of the door that led into the staff quarters Jeffers darted back into her own room and pulled the door almost closed, leaving a slight crack through which she could observe the landing.

It was Reena Brown who had rattled the lock. A woman of sixty years, she desperately struggled to hide her true age, colouring her thinning hair with henna, smothering pancake make-up on her withering features, spending all her scanty wages on clothes which were too young for her scrawny body.

Jeffers sneered silently as she saw the mini-skirted old woman walking unsteadily on stilletto heels. You ought to be in the knackers yard, you ugly old cow, she thought.

Brown was carrying a shopping bag, and a happy smile curved her thin, garishly lipsticked mouth as she tapped on Theresa Sweeney's door.

"Theresa, its me, Reena."

"Come on in," the warm Irish voice invited.

And Brown went into the room, saying excitedly. "You want to see the blouse I've just got, Theresa, its beautiful."

The door closed behind her and Jeffers waited a few moments, then slipped from her room and pressed her ear against Theresa Sweeney's door, listening to the women chattering happily, resenting their friendly companionship.

After a time Jeffers lost interest in the conversation and leaving the staff quarters she moved stealthily about the house, halting at every slight sound to listen hard, before moving on. On the top floor she checked that all the rooms were vacated, and then slipped into the room occupied by the policeman, Tony Kilbeck. It was furnished in the standard pattern of all the boys' rooms – a single bed, a wardrobe, a work desk, some bookshelves, a chest of drawers and bedside locker.

Behind the lenses of her spectacles the woman's eyes gleamed moistly, and her adenoidal breathing quickened with excitement. With the speed and dexterity engendered by much practise she began to open drawers and search through their contents. She found a bundle of letters secured by rubber bands, and began to quickly read them, hoping to discover secrets and intimacies in the man's private life.

An ugly, lanky-bodied young woman, devoid of any physical or mental charms, Mary Jeffers hated her fellow men. She sought always to uncover their secrets, to discover their sins, so that she could use that knowledge to cause trouble for them. Her constant pilfering was also another means to cause upset and annoyance to her selected victims, and to create trouble when those victims would suspect and blame innocent people for the thievery.

Over the years Mary Jeffers had perfected a defensive shield. She hid her native sly cunning behind a mask of dense stupidity. Everyone who met her assumed that her laziness, her greed, her miserliness, her avoidance of ever helping others, were all attributable to mental backwardness, and so these failings were excused by those who employed her. They would express their pity for her, and smile with gratification as they were praised for their understanding and benevolence towards a poor unfortunate creature. Her fellow domestic servants were less charitable in their opinions of her, since they had to do the work that she neglected.

Maggie Stevens walked quickly around the garden, frowning irritably, then returned to the house and went to the kitchen where Beryl Murphy was washing the mugs which the boys had used for their mid-morning tea break.

"Where is he, Beryl. In the pub again?" Maggie Stevens demanded.

The small woman's careworn face betrayed her anxiety as she shook her head. "No."

Maggie sighed impatiently. "Don't lie to me, Beryl. I've looked high and low for him, and he's definitely not in the house."

"He might be over in the cottage."

"I've been there as well," Maggie stated flatly.

"He must be working in the garden then," Beryl offered.

Maggie shook her head, and the small woman seemed near to tears.

"He must have gone on an errand for Mr Mollinson."

"No, he hasn't," Maggie snapped, "because Mr Mollinson is doing parent interviews, and has expressly told me that he doesn't want to be disturbed."

"Well . . . Well . . ." Beryl Murphy still struggled to think of a convincing explanation for her husband's absence.

"Oh, never mind." Maggie accepted that she was wasting her time and turned away.

As she walked through the house she grumbled to herself. There's three million unemployed in this bloody country, and I have to put up with a staff that are totally useless. The sick, the lame and the bloody lazy.

She went into the large Assembly Room at the ground floor front of the house and stared through the window.

A glossy limousine was parked outside the central door, and a uniformed chauffeur leaned against it talking to the duty policeman.

She admired the opulent lines of the car, and the familiar feeling of envy gripped her.

These people have so much, and the rest of us have so little, she reflected.

It was sometimes hard to accept her own poverty with a good grace, living as she did here in a school where wealth, power and privilege were the norm.

I wonder who you belong to. She tried to remember which parents were coming today to discuss their sons' scholastic progress with the Housemaster.

Sir Algernon Boscawen? The Honourable Mrs Travers? Lord Tolcapple? Smyth-Evans? Cochrane? Levy? Surinder Lal? Hirokoto? Walker-Simpson? The list was a rollcall of the Great and Good.

Maggie abandoned the effort of remembrance and chuckled cynically, It doesn't really matter who it is, does it? They're all arrogant, snobbish, over-privileged bastards!

She knew that she was being grossly unfair in her blanket condemnation of the boys' parents because there were many extremely nice people among them, but envy always had this unfortunate effect upon her.

* * *

In the Housemaster's study, Hubert Mollinson regarded the white-haired, aquiline-featured man sitting facing him across the desk with somewhat mixed feelings.

It was a reaction that Charles Hoffman, the Member of Parliament for West Herenford provoked in a great number of people. The man was unusually forthright for a politician. In political circles he was considered to be a dangerous maverick. Always ready to speak out against those policies of his own party with which he disagreed, and to vote against those policies if need be. A characteristic which made him an uncomfortable bedfellow for the place-seekers and yes-men who abounded in Westminster, but which gave him a popular standing among the general public, who thought him to be that rarest of creatures – a courageous, honest and principled politician.

Hubert Mollinson had never concurred with the general public's view. The Housemaster's sour outlook upon the world, and his low opinion of his fellow men, would not allow him to believe that any professional politician could be honest and principled. He regarded all politicians as greedy, self-serving hypocrites and congenital liars.

The reasons for his mixed feelings at this moment was that he was finding Charles Hoffman both personally charming, and very honestly spoken. The simple home truths the man had voiced during their conversation would be greeted with horrified abhorrence by the devotees of "Political Correctness" but Hubert Mollinson had found himself in complete agreement with the other man's sentiments, and was reluctantly having to accept that Charles Hoffman could very well be the exception to the general rule. The fabled White Crow in the midst of the black-feathered Murder.

Now Charles Hoffman, who had just finished stating his hard-line views on law and order, smiled regretfully. "I'd like nothing more than to continue our conversation for the rest of the day, Mr Mollinson. It's such a refreshing novelty for me to meet a man like yourself who is ready to say what he really thinks. I'm afraid in Westminster one meets only chameleons, who change their colours so frequently that they resemble tartans."

Mollinson also would have liked to continue talking, and he told the other man, "You must try and visit us again, Mr Hoffman, and have lunch with me."

"Oh, I certainly shall," Hoffman assured, smilingly. "Now, I suppose we really must get down to business. To speak frankly, I was not overly enthusiastic to act in loco parentis in this matter. After all I'm not a relative. But I've known Mr Macpherson for a good many years, and since he is not able to leave America at this present time, he requested that I come down to see you. I know that he's spoken with you by telephone, but he felt that you would appreciate a personal call, even if only by a substitute, to convey to you his deep appreciation for all that you are doing for his son."

"Indeed yes." The Housemaster's skull-like features smiled bleakly. "His mother was also unable to attend today, so if you had not come, Mr Hoffman, I fear that the boy might have felt he was being somewhat neglected.

Happily, you may assure Mr Macpherson that Alexander is working very hard. He's not an outstanding scholar, but progress in all subjects, with the exception of Ancient Greek, has been satisfactory. I'm confident that he will, when the time comes, achieve at least two A levels. He's also been selected for the School Junior Eight. He's an exceptionally promising oarsman."

"That will please his father. He rowed for Harvard himself." Hoffman appeared very gratified with what he had been told. Then he went on apologetically, "It's unfortunate that Mr Macpherson's presidential ambitions have created a somewhat difficult situation. He fully appreciates how unwelcome it must be for you to have a police presence in your house."

Mollinson smiled bleakly. "I rather think that the police presence is more unwelcome to the boys, than to myself."

Hoffman chuckled appreciativly. "It cramps the young rascals style, does it?"

The other man nodded. "Undoubtedly. It makes it more difficult for them to enjoy their illicit pleasures. They all believe that the police report any transgressions of school rules that they discover to me."

"And do they?" Hoffman enquired.

"They don't need to," Mollinson stated firmly. "I'm already fully cogniscent of everything that goes on in this house. I have fifty boarders here, and I know their personal characteristics, their individual strengths and weaknesses, their virtues and their faults. I know which boys smuggle in alcohol and tobacco.

I know which boys sneak out of the house at night to go to night clubs. I know which boys regularly use soft drugs."

He paused momentarily and shrugged.

"In the wider scheme these misdemeanours are of no real importance. I take no action to stop them, unless I judge that there is an actual threat to the fabric of the discipline I exercise over the house. We have over a thousand boys in this school. Their ages ranging from thirteen to eighteen. The hot blood of youth must be allowed some licence. By turning a blind eye to the minor acts of rebellion, we avert any major act of rebellion. The boys believe that they are successfully cocking a snook at authority, and this satisfies their need for self-assertion, and makes them amenable to the general disciplines of work and behaviour that we require from them.

"We are running a business here, Mr Hoffman. People pay us to educate their sons. We are like a factory, we take in human raw material, and spend five years in turning that raw material into finished products. Products which have dominated the ruling establishments of this nation for four hundred years. It is not in my own interests to begin rocking the boat, and upsetting the parents who provide me with my living, by expelling their sons for breaking what are in actuality unenforceable rules."

Hoffman listened intently, respect burgeoning in him for this schoolteacher's shrewdness.

Spencer will have to watch out for this fellow, he realised.

"Did you want to speak with the boy?" Mollinson enquired. "I can send for him if you wish."

Hoffman inclined his head.

"That's very kind of you, Mr Mollinson. Yes, I think that I would like to have a brief word with him." He smiled. "I hope he won't mind being taken out of class."

Mollinson checked a chart upon the wall. "This period will be Ancient Greek. I'm sure he'll be very happy to be taken out of that."

He lifted the phone on his desk and dialled a number.

Tony Kilbeck was pleased at the summons from Hubert Mollinson. One of the most tedious aspects of his present duty was having to wait in the vicinity of the various classrooms where Alexander was having lessons, and he welcomed this unexpected break from routine.

He and the boy walked side by side towards Penfold House chatting easily.

"Your Dad and Charles Hoffman must be close friends, Alex?"

The boy shrugged his shoulders. "I don't know if they're close friends. They've known each other for years apparently. I've never met Mr Hoffman before. I've read about him in the newspapers quite a lot though. He's quite famous, isn't he?"

"More like quite notorious." Tony Kilbeck grinned. "But fair play to him all the same. At least he's got the guts to say openly what a great many people are secretly thinking, but haven't got the guts to say out loud."

"He's a racist, isn't he?" The boy sought for confirmation.

"Well, he calls a spade a spade." The policeman grinned.

"My father says that the Blacks in America are responsible for a disproportionate amount of the total crime." Alexander's face was troubled. "Some of the boys say that a lot of Blacks will want to kill him for saying that. That's why you're here to protect me, isn't it. Because a lot of people want to kill my father, and perhaps kill me as well."

The man's pleasant features showed sympathy. "Are you scared, Alex, that someone might try and kill you?" He tried to reassure the boy. "There's no need to be scared, you know. There's nobody will try and kill you. I'm only here for show, really."

Alexander grimaced thoughtfully. "I was a bit scared at first, when you came to be with me. I thought that there must be someone who was after me. But I've realised that nobody really would gain any advantage by killing me. I'm not responsible for what my father says, am I? So there would be no point in killing me."

"Of course people know there's no point in killing you. You're as safe as houses." Kilbeck assured him, simultaneously envying and pitying his youthful innocence.

"How do you do, Alexander?" Charles Hoffman shook the boy's hand, noting that he had inherited his mother's blonde hair and blue eyes, and his father's stocky build and pleasant, homely features.

"I'm very well, thank you, sir."

They strolled upon the forecourt of Penfold House for some

minutes, chatting about the scholastic subjects Alexander was taking, and then parted.

Charles Hoffman thought that the boy was really quite likeable. Somewhat old-fashioned and grave for his years, but confident in his manner without being too assertive. To his own surprise he found himself experiencing a fleeting instant of regret about what was to happen to the boy. But that was all it was, merely a fleeting instant of regret.

Alexander and Tony Kilbeck retraced their steps towards the Ancient Greek class.

"Well, he seemed like a nice old guy," the policeman remarked.

The boy did not reply, and Kilbeck stared at him curiously.

"Didn't you like him, Alex?"

"Well, he was very pleasant to talk to," Alexander said thoughtfully. "But he has shifty eyes, hasn't he . . ."

Chapter Ten

CHARLES Hoffman remained deep in thought during the ride back to his luxurious apartment in a quiet square in Bloomsbury. Several times during the journey the image of Alexander Margrave's pleasant homely features invaded his mind, disturbing his concentration. Each time he angrily thrust the image from him.

I've no choice. It has to be done! he reflected.

On one occasion he sensed that his chauffeur was glancing curiously at him in the rear-view mirror, and for an instant he feared that he had unconsciously voiced his thoughts aloud.

In the underground car park which serviced the flats Hoffman saw the gleaming black Mercedes standing empty next to his own reserved space, and cursed beneath his breath.

"Damn them!"

"Will you be needing the car again this evening, sir?" The chauffeur wanted to know.

"No, thank you."

"Will it be the usual time tomorrow, sir?"

"Yes."

Hoffman was unusually brusque and as he left the car and hurried to the lift the chauffeur wondered, What's upset the old bastard?

The Portuguese houseman opened the door even as Hoffman was fumbling with his keys.

"The lady and gentleman are here to see you, sir. I've put them in the drawing room."

"Thank you, Tomas."

Hoffman handed the man his topcoat and gloves and breathed deeply, trying to control the apprehension which was quickening his heartbeat. After some thought he told the houseman, "You may take the night off, Tomas. I shan't need you again until breakfast."

The man grinned delightedly. "Thank you very much, sir."

And instantly scurried into his own quarters as if he feared that his employer might change his mind.

Hoffman hesitated before the door of the drawing room, his apprehension at what awaited him making him reluctant to enter. Then he summoned his resolution and entered.

The couple were sitting side by side on the antique ottoman which stretched the length of the tapestried wall. The raven-haired woman was in her late twenties, and strikingly attractive. Her companion was an elderly man who, despite his advancing years still radiated an aura of strength. Both were dressed with that subdued elegance which bore silent testimony to wealth and power.

Hoffman wasted no time in polite greeting. His apprehension forcing him to demand sharply, "Why have you come here?"

"If the mountain won't come to Mahomet, then Mahomet must come to the mountain." Stanley Schellenburg's clipped voice contained a hint of anger. "Why haven't we received any progress reports?"

"Because there is nothing to report as yet," Hoffman snapped curtly.

"Don't take that tone with me, Hoffman!" Schellenburg warned. "You can't afford it."

Hoffman leashed in his resentment. He distractedly ran his hand through his thinning white hair. "I'm sorry. I'm somewhat over-wrought."

Zora Ahksar nodded understandingly. "Of course you are, Charles." Her voice was soft and soothing, her accent charmingly foreign. "But you must appreciate that we are also under strain. We have invested a great deal in you, and given you our trust."

"As I have given you mine," Hoffman retorted.

"Exactly so," the woman agreed, and her smile was very white against the moist red lips.

The elderly man did not smile however. He frowned truculently and demanded, "This man, Spencer, that you have hired to carry out the operation? What is he up to?"

"He's making the necessary preparations," Hoffman replied.

"And how far advanced are those preparations?" Schellenburg demanded.

Hoffman became somewhat defensive. "I assume that they're well advanced."

"What do you mean, assume? Don't you know."

Hoffman grimaced unhappily. "Spencer and myself have always worked together on a strictly 'need to know' basis."

"What do you mean by that?" the other man barked.

Hoffman shrugged uncertainly, then blustered, "I tell him what I want him to do, and then leave him a free hand. It's always worked very well for us in the past. Spencer has never yet failed me."

The woman's fingers touched the elderly man's hand, as if in warning. And it was she who next spoke.

"We can't accept that, Charles. We have to know what the man's plans are. What methods he intends to employ. We have to know dates and times and locations. We have to know everything."

Hoffman automatically shook his head in negation. "That's impossible. Spencer doesn't work that way."

"But we do!" The woman stated flatly.

Still Hoffman protested. "No, he won't agree."

"Then the deal is off, Charles."

She rose to her feet, and her companion rose with her.

Fear flooded Hoffman's mind, and he pleaded. "Please! Don't go! Wait! We can sort something out surely?"

Zora Ahksar smiled sympathetically. "Poor Charles. You're very near to ruin, aren't you? Lloyds won't give you any more time, will they." She looked around the luxuriously furnished room. "I really do feel so very very sorry for you, my dear, having to lose all this." The smile metamorphosed into a cruel mockery. "Still, Charles, you must look on the bright side – you'll find lots of company in Cardboard City. There may even be some people there who you already know."

"I'll talk to Spencer," Hoffman offered desperately. "I can offer him more money. I'm sure he'll see sense."

The couple exchanged a glance and an unspoken message passed between them.

"Do that," Schellenburg snapped. "You have three days."

A groan of despair escaped Hoffman. "I don't know if I'll be able to see him in that time. I don't know his whereabouts at this moment."

Again the woman's fingers reached out to touch the elderly man's hand and he stayed silent while she asked, "When will you be able to talk with him?"

Sensing reprieve Hoffman assured, "Definitely within a week."

"Alright." She accepted and the wave of relief that washed over Hoffman was so intense that it left him feeling lightheaded.

When the couple had left Hoffman paced restlessly about the room, his forehead furrowed with anxiety. He had no way of getting in touch with Spencer. During their business contracts the man always contacted him at intervals. The same arrangement was in force now.

Hoffman glared at the phone, furiously willing it to ring.

"Damn you, where are you?" He spoke to the absent Spencer. "Where the hell are you?"

Chapter Eleven

AT seven o'clock in the morning the wicket-gate set in the huge
iron doors of Carabanchel Prison opened and several men filed
out into the sunlight. Some were met by wives and sweethearts,
others by friends, and yet others had no one to greet them and
walked away from the grim walls by themselves.

Cesar Perales was the last to emerge from the wicket-gate.
He didn't look eagerly about him for friends or loved ones. He
knew that there would be no one to greet him. He paused for
a moment and filled his lungs with the air of freedom. Then
carrying the shabby holdall that contained all his worldly
belongings he walked slowly away from the walls that had
been his horizons for four long years.

A taxi cab drew alongside, and without looking he waved
it on. He had no money to spare for such luxuries. But the
cab continued to keep pace with him, and he swung to berate
the driver, but before he could voice his anger the back door
opened and a once-familiar voice invited in fluent Castillian
accents, "Ride with me, Cesar. It's too far to walk."

Perales blinked with surprise and he bent low staring into
the shadowed interior.

"Venga . . . Come." Spencer gestured, and Perales wordlessly entered and sat down on the hot leather seat.

Spencer touched his finger to his lips in warning for Perales
to remain silent, then gave rapid instructions to the driver; the
man slammed into a higher gear and roared into the streams of
traffic heading towards the centre of Madrid.

The cab delivered them to a hotel close to the Puerta Del
Sol, and after they had alighted, Spencer spoke for the first
time since making the pick-up.

"I've reserved a room for you here. Once you've booked in
and cleaned up, we'll go shopping."

He stared disparagingly at Perales's shabby clothes. "You need smartening up, my friend."

The Spaniard had had sufficient time to recover from his initial surprise. He frowned suspiciously.

"What gives, Spencer?"

The other man smiled and rubbed his fingers and thumb together in the universal sign for money.

"That's what gives, my friend. And a lot of it. Are you interested?"

The Spaniard ejaculated a colourful, filthy oath, then asked rhetorically, "Is the Pope a Catholic?"

They booked into the hotel and went up to the room.

"I need to take a shower." Perales scowled. "I stink of prison."

Spencer examined him dispassionately.

Perales was nearing sixty years, of middle height, with the tough, hatchet features and swarthy colouring of the gitano. A fresh knife scar creased his forehead, bisecting his right eyebrow, and Spencer indicated the scar.

"What happened?"

"A Moro thought he was a macho. I shoved his blade up his fuckin' black arse. I hate those Moro bastards."

Spencer smiled with sardonic amusement. Perales was a veteran of the French Foreign Legion and in his youth had fought in the savage Algerian conflict. He hated all North Africans with an equal venom, be they Algerian, Morroccan, Tunisian, Berber, Saharan or Moor.

He stripped off his clothes, and his body was that of a young, fit man. Blocky and muscular and solid.

"You're still in good shape," Spencer complimented.

"Always." Perales scowled, and again Spencer smiled amusedly.

"And you're still a miserable sour bastard."

"Always." Perales took a towel and disappeared into the shower cubicle.

When he reappeared, drying his still thick, black hair, he demanded, "The job?"

"It's a snatch, but we might have to kill a couple of people."

Perales shrugged his thick shoulders.

"Okay. Where is it?"

"England."

"For fuck's sake, man!" Perales complained sharply." I don't like that fuckin' place. It's a miserable, cold, wet shithole of a country. And the English are all bastards. They're all fuckin' pirates like you."

"Spencer smiled equably. He found the Spaniard's blunt rudeness both amusing and refreshing. Cesar Perales always spoke his mind. His was a character devoid of hypocrisy or deviousness.

They left the hotel and visited a number of shops; Spencer bought the other man new clothes, and accessories. Then they ate and drank.

While they were eating, Spencer asked, "Do you have a passport?"

Perales scowled. "I've got two. Spanish or French. You can take your pick."

"French?" Spencer raised his eyebrows.

"Of course. I served ten years in the fuckin' Legion. That entitled me to French nationality, didn't it?"

"Okay. You use your French one. Tomorrow we go to Paris. From there we fly to London."

"Then what?" Perales scowled.

"Then you're going to be my house servant, Cesar. At my home in the beautiful English countryside."

"What?"

"I hope you haven't forgotten how to cook and clean, Cesar." Spencer teased. "It's a big house, so you'll have to work hard."

"Bollocks!" Perales scowled murderously, and Spencer threw back his head and roared with laughter.

Chapter Twelve

AFTER Spencer had installed Cesar Perales in the Cotswold house he went on with his preparations. He paid further visits to Martyrs College, where he was able to study the rear of Penfold House more thoroughly and to identify the electricity sub-station that the College power supply was channelled through. He drove along the approach roads and explored the immediate environs of the campus on foot, paying particular attention to the river banks which bordered the wide playing fields.

He spent two days at the security vault in central London going through the contents of Gordy Clark's deposit box. As he had expected he found files of incriminating details concerning the dead man's clients, including himself. The files made very interesting reading and Spencer found some names that were known to him. There was also a sizeable amount of cash and an old army Colt revolver with some rounds of ammunition. He took only his personal file away with him when he left, and destroyed it later.

One night he drove out to Epping Forest and parked his old van deep in the undergrowth bordering an isolated lane. He cautiously explored the area, checking that no other vehicles or people on foot were in the vicinity. Then he took a spade from the back of the van and moved through the trees, taking care to keep away from the moonlit glades and tracks. He reached the thicket that he sought and began to dig at the base of a tree, sweating as the hard physical effort heated his body and the heap of spoil at the side of the hole grew larger. At a depth of four feet the blade struck metal and soon three military ammunition boxes were revealed.

Spencer grunted with strain as he lifted the heavy boxes out of the hole and opened them to check their contents. In one box wrapped in oiled cloth were four Heckler & Koch MP5 sub-machine guns, two sawn-off double-barrelled shotguns and a Steyr SSG 69 bolt-action sniper's rifle, with bipod and telescopic sights. There were several hundred rounds of ammunition for the weapons and also a bulky night sight. In the second box there were more rounds of ammunition, half a dozen fragmentation grenades, some packets of Semtex plastic explosives, detonators and a selection of timers, fuses and wires. In the third box there was a Blowpipe missile.

Spencer carefully rewrapped all the items and replaced them in the boxes. He refilled the hole and scattered rotted vegetation across the disturbed earth so that no casual glance would reveal that an excavation had been made. Then he carried the boxes one at a time to his van.

He drove through the night to the Cotswold house and he and Perales spent several hours cleaning and testing the weapons.

Dawn was breaking as Spencer returned to London and the cheap, shabby bed and breakfast hotel he was currently staying in in his guise as a travelling artisan.

Despite his sleepless night he did not go to bed but sat sipping whisky and smoking.

Spencer was considering the actual mechanics of the kidnapping. The fact that the target was under constant armed guard and was electronically tabbed meant that the instant the kidnapping was attempted a central control would be alerted, and it was a certainty that pre-planned countermeasures would immediately be set in motion to prevent the escape of the kidnapper.

For long hours Spencer sat pondering different possibilities, acting as his own Devil's Advocate as he searched out the weaknesses in each formulation. Slowly a scenario began to emerge from the jumble of ideas and gradually an outline of a plan of action became distinct.

Spencer smiled grimly. If I use that plan, it will be spectacular.

The whisky bottle was empty now; it was time to sleep.

Spencer stretched out on the bed still fully clothed and within moments was peacefully sleeping.

Chapter Thirteen

THE landlord looked up from his perusal of the racing paper at the man who had just entered the empty saloon bar and exclaimed, "Hello, Stranger, where have you been hiding yourself?"

Tommy Phillpots grinned at the greeting and tapped the side of his nose with his forefinger.

"That's top secret." With a lordly air he laid a twenty-pound banknote on the counter. "Now, I reckon I'll start with a very large gin and tonic. You can make it a triple. I've been on the wagon for the last three weeks."

"Been saving up your dole money for a spree, have you?" the other man quipped.

"I've been working, my lad," Phillpots informed him.

"That makes a change, don't it." The landlord could not keep the sneer from his voice, but Tommy Phillpots was feeling too happy to take umbrage.

"It does indeed," he agreed equably. "But the bad times are over now, Charlie." He executed a soft-shoe shuffle and sang: "Happy days are here again, The show is on the road again . . ."

He lifted the glass and sniffed its contents, eyes closed and a blissful smile wreathing his plump features.

The telephone rang, and from sheer force of habit he went to answer it.

"Hello, this is Tommy Phillpots."

The voice of his mysterious employer questioned brusquely, "Have you done the job?"

"I certainly have." There was real pride in Phillpots's voice. "I've got the lot. Some of it will make your eyes water."

"Good. I'll come to your flat at eleven o'clock tonight. Have it all ready for me."

"It will be."

"If it's as good as you say it is, there'll be a bonus for you.

Don't get too drunk in the meantime. I'll need to ask you some questions."

"A bonus! It's good enough, I can swear to . . ." Phillpots became aware that he was talking to a dead line. "You're a strange bugger."

He frowned, then the thought of the extra money brought the smile back to his lips and he hurried back to the bar and poured his triple gin down his throat.

"Fill it up again," he ordered grandly. "And keep filling it up until I fall off me stool."

Then he recalled his employer's admonition.

"No, you'd better make it singles from now on. I don't want to get legless."

He cheered himself with the promise, "But tomorrow I will."

The side street was lined with parked vehicles and was little frequented at this hour of the night. In the shadowed interior of his van Spencer pulled on a pair of thin leather gloves before taking the two bottles from their brown paper bags. One bottle contained gin, the other 100 per cent proof alcohol. He opened his van door and poured half the gin into the gutter, then topped the bottle up again with the alcohol. He slipped the doctored gin into the pocket of his donkey jacket, pulled his cloth cap low over his eyes and got out of the van.

He walked steadily along the streets, sometimes crossing the roadway to avoid the occasional pedestrians and the fronts of public houses and restaurants. When he reached the road in which Tommy Phillpots lived he moved more slowly, waiting until the road was empty before going to the front door of the man's flat.

"Come on in. I was beginnning to think that you wasn't coming." Phillpots was drunk, his eyes bloodshot, his face flushed.

Spencer seated himself at the table on which there stood an opened bottle of gin and two greasy glass tumblers.

"I've got us a drink in." Phillpots grinned and wiped his saliva-wet lips with his sleeve. He blinked owlishly at his guest. "You'll take a drink with me, won't you?"

Spencer nodded. "Yes, I'll take a drink with you, Mr Phillpots. But first I'd like to see what you've got for me."

"And so you shall. "The man preened himself. "I've done a first-class job for you, even though I say it meself. I've never done a better."

He lurched to the battered dresser that stood against one wall of the poky, cluttered room and lifted a large manila envelope from one of the drawers.

"There it is." He proudly laid the envelope in front of Spencer. "Some of the stuff in that will make your eyes water."

He staggered and abruptly banged down on the chair facing Spencer across the table.

Spencer smiled and indicating the gin told him, "I'll take that drink now."

With a shaking hand Phillpots poured out two measures, splashing some of the liquid onto the table top.

"Your very good health, sir." He finished his drink in two gulps and immediately refilled his glass.

Spencer left his drink untouched while he studied the photographs and written reports, occasionally questioning Phillpots about certain points.

He encouraged the other man to drink more and more and praised the work he had done.

Phillpots needed no encouragement to drink as he poured down measure after measure, and then the bottle was empty; he sat slumped and swaying, staring at the empty bottle as if it had grievously offended him.

"Here. I brought this for you." Spencer smiled as he produced and opened his own bottle.

Phillpots gurgled happily and grabbed the bottle with both hands, his lips sucking greedily at its open mouth, the liquor overflowing to run down and drip from his chin.

Spencer replaced the reports and photographs in the envelope and for the first time sipped from his own glass.

The doctored gin bottle was now half empty and Phillpots was almost incoherent, his face purple hued, his eyes glazed and unfocussed, his body swaying uncontrollably.

Spencer sat patiently watching the other man, waiting for the collapse.

When it came it was like watching a slowmotion film. The bloodshot eyes rolled up in the man's head and he gently crumpled from his chair and onto the floor to lie snoring.

Spencer moved to roll the unconscious man onto his back.

For a moment he stared down at the purple-hued face and the slack, gaping jaw, then he lifted the bottle, and poured more of the doctored gin down Phillpots's throat. The senseless man gagged and began to choke, and then to vomit; Spencer's gloved hands rammed the gaping jaws closed and his legs straddled the heaving body.

It was over very quickly and Phillpots was dead. Choked on his own vomit.

"Didn't anyone ever warn you, Mr Phillpots, that excessive drinking can damage your health very severely?" Spencer whispered into the bulging, bloodshot eyes. "Even lead to premature death in some cases."

He stood up and checked the time. There were some hours to wait before the early morning traffic would begin to fill the streets. He preferred to journey in the safety of traffic. A lone vehicle travelling during the early hours of the morning was likely to attract the attention of bored police patrols.

He carried out a painstaking search of the corpse and of the tiny flat, but found nothing to link Tommy Phillpots with the Martyrs College.

He washed the glass tumbler he had used and replaced it with the other crockery. Then he took a cigarette from the dead man's packet on the table and lit it, drawing the smoke deep into his lungs and exhaling it slowly.

He reseated himself at the table and began once more to study the reports and photos from the manila envelope, seeking for the vulnerable chink in the defences of Penfold House, imprinting on his memory names, faces, and the personal vulnerabilities discovered by Tommy Phillpots during the past weeks.

He eventually selected two for immediate action, annotating their reports with his own remarks.

'Reena Brown. Boys' maid. Frequents local "Lonely Heart" clubs and dances. Possible means of entry for internal reconnaissance of house?

'Julian Fothergill. Assistant Housemaster. Dermot Murphy claims that a drinking crony saw Fothergill entering the "Pink Heaven" gay club in Holburn some weeks past. If Fothergill is homosexual, he could be the source for obtaining details of internal procedures of house?'

Spencer leaned back in his chair and extracted another

cigarette from the packet on the table. He let the smoke dribble from his lips and his gaze fixed upon the bulging, sightless eyes of Tommy Phillpots. Despite his intimate familiarity with death in all its forms, he still experienced a faint sense of wonderment at how completely all personality was stripped from a corpse. How death turned even the most familiar being into a stranger. Spencer held no religious beliefs, yet did not dismiss the possibility that another existence lay beyond this present life. He was contemptuous of those who feared death. When the moment of his own death should come, Spencer was prepared to meet it with the same cold-blooded courage with which he had confronted and challenged death so many times during his life, and to confront and challenge whatever might lie beyond.

He turned his attention back to Reena Brown and Julian Fothergill. He picked up both photographs, holding them side by side, contrasting the soft, pudgy features of the master with the gaunt, raddled face of the maid, and whispered to the images, "You're both going to have an exciting adventure."

Chapter Fourteen

PICCADILLY Circus and the network of sleazy streets and alleys surrounding it were a maelstrom of traffic and noise. Music blared, people swarmed in search of fun, excitement and adventure, eyes eagerly seeking for the objects of their multi-varied desires. And in the shadows of doorways and buildings other predatory eyes evaluated and voices promised, invited and enticed.

Spencer slipped through the jostling crowds of pleasure-seekers, his body evading contact, his gaze moving across faces as he sought for his target. Outside a coffee bar two youths, brightly coloured shirts worn Cuban fashion, and skin-tight jeans moulding their hips and buttocks, were eyeing the passing crowds.

Spencer sighted them and recognised the features of the taller youth. He moved to their side and the feral-featured, pimpled-skinned, smaller youth smiled archly at this tall man in the dark trenchcoat.

"Hello, Handsome, are you looking for a naughty boy?"

Spencer ignored him and spoke to the taller youth.

"Is Shafto still on the scene?"

The smaller youth tossed his long blue-dyed hair and pouted petulantly. Telling his companion huffily, "This one's looking for old meat, Tracy."

Spencer held a ten-pound note under the taller youth's nose. "Where can I find Shafto?"

Dirty-nailed fingers snatched, but the note had disappeared into Spencer's fist.

The taller youth scowled and his voice was spiteful. "Well, dearie, Shafto can't flog her mutton under the bright lights any more. She's bloody well past it. So you won't find her here. It's only the sweet young things like us around here."

"Suit yourself." Spencer shrugged dismissively and began to move on, but the smaller youth stopped him.

"Make it twenty, and I'll tell you where to find her."

Spencer waited silently.

"Shafto's had to go on the S and M." The youth seemed to take a malicious pleasure in stating this fact. "That's the only punters who'll touch her nowadays."

He held out his dirty, painted-nailed hand expectantly and after a moment Spencer held two ten-pound notes against the sweaty palm, but did not release them.

"Now is it worth more than this, I wonder?" The feral features were greedy and calculating.

"Oh, Stella, stop arsing about, will you, you silly whore." The taller youth exclaimed irritably, and told Spencer.

"You'll find Shafto down at Terry's Club, just off the square."

Spencer allowed the smaller youth to clasp the banknotes and moved on.

The doorman was black and huge, and as Spencer went to enter the doorway he stepped to block the passageway.

"Members only, Mister."

Behind the massive body the flight of dimly-lit stone steps led steeply downwards and the pounding beat of rock music came pouring upwards from the depths.

Spencer gave the huge man a conciliatory smile. "This place has been recommended to me by a friend."

"Who's the friend?" The tone was still hard and unyielding.

"Shafto."

The huge man repeated the name. "Shafto?"

Spencer nodded. "We're very old friends."

"Alright, but you'll have to pay for temporary membership, Mister. It's valid for one night."

"How much?"

"Thirty quid."

The money changed hands, and there was an almost miraculous change in attitude. Gold teeth shone in a beaming smile of welcome.

"Have a good time, sir."

"I hope to." Spencer smiled.

The cellar room was long and low-roofed, and the thudding bass overpowering. The air was hot and moist, thick with the fug of smoke and over-heated flesh. Black leather gleamed, metal chains and studs glinted beneath the flashing strobe lights, shaven heads, stubbled chins, naked muscled arms and chests mingled with sober business suits, manicured hands, expensively styled hair. Young men fluttered and preened and screamed with girlish laughter. The atmosphere was heavy with lust and feverish need, and eyes constantly flickered and met and broke or held contact.

Spencer threaded his way along the crowded bar, and his appearance attracted many lingering stares. He saw the wild mass of bright blonde hair and knew he had found the person he was looking for.

"Spencer! It's been years since I saw you last! What are you doing here?" The flat Mancunian accent was unchanged.

The heavy make-up did not completely hide the incipient bags under the man's eyes, or the lines on the forehead, but the thin face framed by the cascading masses of blonde hair was still exceptionally handsome, and there was still the slender grace of the boyish figure dressed in sweatshirt and jeans.

Spencer placed his lips close to the other man's ear and told him. "I came to find you, Shafto. I might have a job for you."

He nodded towards the far corner of the bar where the shadows were darkest, and there was a paleness of writhing, intertwined bodies.

"Let's go over there."

They moved and then stood close, Spencer deliberately putting his arm around Shafto, as if he were sexually propositioning him.

"I'm told you've been having a hard time of it lately."

"Who told you that?" Shafto tossed his head petulantly. "I'll bet it was that rotten little cow Stella. She's always having a go at me. Was it her? Was it?"

"Never mind who it was," Spencer snapped curtly. "Is it true?"

Shafto pouted and again tossed his head. Then shrugged and admitted it.

"Yeah. I've been in hospital and my usual punters all think that I've got AIDs. The silly cunts! All I had was me piles cut out." He mimicked a sepulchral voice. "Just a normal hazard of the trade, my dear, one's arse can only stand so much."

"You want to get out of the S and M scene, don't you, Shafto?"

The blonde head nodded violently. "Of course I do. I don't enjoy being whipped by bloody maniacs. I need to get away from the scene and rest up for a bit."

"Of course you do." Spencer was sympathetic. "And I'm going to give you enough money to rest for years, if you want to."

Hope shone in the mascarad eyes.

"Do you know this guy?" Spencer showed the picture of Julian Fothergill.

Shafto held it to the light, and pursed his lips. "There's something familiar about him. How long has he been on the scene?"

Spencer shook his head. "I don't know. But I'm told he uses the Pink Heaven. Especially on Saturday nights."

Shafto's orange-painted lips sneered. "He'll be a closet queen then. Butch as hell all the week, and screaming to get fucked on a weekend. All the closet queens flock to the Pink Heaven on Saturday nights."

He stared with arch enquiry at Spencer. "Don't tell me that your tastes have changed, Spencer?"

Spencer chuckled with genuine amusement. "No, Shafto."

"Haven't I always told you that you don't know what you're missing, Spencer. Remember what the Arabs say, 'Its a woman for pleasure, but a boy for paradise.'"

"I'll bear that in mind." Spencer's smile faded, and he became brusque and businesslike. "Now listen carefully. This is what I want you to do . . ."

Spencer talked and Shafto listened intently, nodding his consent at intervals. Finally Spencer surreptitiously slipped an envelope into the other man's hand.

"Here's the first instalment of your money. I'll be in touch."

Shafto began to babble words of gratitude but he was speaking to Spencer's disappearing back.

The doorman wished Spencer a smiling goodnight, Spencer returned the smile and disappeared into the night.

Chapter Fifteen

IT was Saturday evening and in Penfold House the boys and staff were entertaining themselves in a variety of ways.

Maggie Stevens lay in her bed, her hand cupping her Venus mount, her fingers stroking the hot wetness between her legs as she watched the handsome youth slowly undress, unbuttoning his shirt and slipping it from his broad shoulders, sliding his trousers down his thick muscular thighs, shucking his singlet over his curly head to reveal his firm pectorals and the arch of his ribs above the sharply defined abdominals.

Marcus St Clair was proud of his body – it was lithe and muscular and the only blemishes on the smooth skin were the abrasions and bruises from that afternoon's game of rugby. He enjoyed displaying himself like this before the woman's hungry eyes. He smiled now and his hands rested on his slim waist, his thumbs tucked beneath the waistband of his pants, but he did not pull the garment down to reveal the erect manhood which was bulging beneath the thin cloth.

Maggie's desire was almost unbearable.

She threw back the sheets and reached out her arms; when the youth saw her breasts and jutting nipples, and smooth round belly, his own excitement overcame him, and he tore off his pants and came to her. No foreplay was wanted by either and he instantly entered her, driving hard and deep, grunting with each thrust, as she ran her hands down the firm lines of his back, fondling and kneading his small, tight buttocks, lifting her hips and bucking furiously against his pounding body, moaning deep within her throat.

The bed rocked with their passion, creaking and shaking, and in the storeroom below Mary Jeffers lay on a makeshift mattress of cardboard, listening to the noises from above, visualising what was happening, her fingers ramming deep into her body, in frantic need to achieve her own sexual satiation.

*　　　*　　　*

In the huge dusty loft directly beneath the roof tiles a group of senior boys sat in a circle, around a row of lighted candles, and passed a joint from one to another, each boy in his turn dragging the acrid smoke deep into his body, and holding his breath, keeping the smoke trapped in his body, until oxygen starvation forced his straining lungs to expel it and draw in air.

In the Assembly Room on the ground floor actors were blasting thousands of bullets from inexhaustible magazines, and bodies were gouting blood and screaming and falling from great heights. Seated on rows of chairs before the huge television screen, junior boys gloried in the toughness, violence and bravery of the make-believe heroes, and wished with all their hearts for the day to come when they might emulate their exploits.

Other boys were playing pool and table tennis, listening to music, reading, visiting each others' rooms, or simply doing nothing for the few hours of free time before Evening Assembly and Roll-Call.

In the maids' quarters Reena Brown peered into her mirror and painted her collapsed, lipless mouth, spreading the garish scarlet colour wide in the vain hope that men would believe she had full, juicy, tempting lips.

Afterwards she plastered her withered skin with foundation cream and powder, adjusted her false eyelashes, and treated her denture plates with fixative so that they would not slip or fall as they had done on some terrible occasions in the past. And all the time that she was adorning her body Reena Brown was praying fervently that tonight would be the night. That tonight she would meet the man of her dreams. That tonight she would finally find her true love.

In the neighbouring room, fat and blowsy Theresa Sweeney sat in her dressing gown watching *Hearts of Gold*, and periodically shedding sentimental tears into her brimming glass of stout.

Alexander Margrave was in his own room playing chess with Fergus Cochrane, while Toby Levy looked on. The door opened and Rupert Farquar's freckled face appeared around its edge.

"If you've got some cigarettes then come in, if you haven't then fuck off!" Toby Levy told him.

Farquar grinned and entered fully, closed the door and brandished a packet of cigarettes above his head.

"Where's the pig?" he wanted to know.

It was Toby Levy who gave him the information.

"He's gone across to the Security Office in Old School, with his apprentice piglet."

Farquar grinned. "Fuckin' Ace, man."

He opened the packet, gave each of the boys a cigarette and they all lit up.

Clouds of smoke billowed from their mouths.

"Better open the window," Fergus advised. "We set the fire alarm off in Willie Goldblum's room when there were only two of us smoking."

Toby Levy got up and opened the window, then poked his head out and looked up at the clear moonlit sky.

"It's as light as day, Fergie. We'll have to be careful tonight."

He resumed his seat and rubbed his hands together, grinning with eager anticipation. "I can't wait!"

"How many of you are going tonight?" There was envy in Alexander's voice.

"We three and Andy Boscawen," Fergus told him. "My brother is going to pick us up and bring us back."

"Which club are you going to?"

"There's a new one just opened in Wandsworth that my brother says is great. We'll probably go there."

"I wish I could go with you," Alexander said wistfully.

"You can, as soon as you no longer have a pig as your nanny," Toby Levy told him.

"What time are you going?"

"Straight after Final Assembly. The Famine has gone to a dinner party somewhere, so the Precious Jewel, is doing duty beak. When he does Saturday duty he always sneaks out himself after he's done roll-call, so he won't be doing late check on our rooms."

"I don't like it when the Precious Jewel does late check." Rupert Farquar grimaced. "He always makes me get out of

75

bed and unbutton my pyjamas. He says it's to make sure that I'm not wearing my underclothes, because that's unhygienic. I think he just wants to look at my dick."

"There's no think about it," Toby Levy stated firmly. "He does want to look at your dick. He's a bloody queer, just ask Wynne-Davies. He'll tell you all about the Precious Jewel. He was a beak at Wynne-Davies's prep school before he came here."

"The next time that he wants you to unbutton your pyjamas, Rupe, you must tell him that he has to pay for the privilige of admiring your dick," Fergus advised laughingly.

"Yes, that's a good idea," Toby Levy chortled. "He can admire my dick for a pound any night he chooses to."

"He can admire mine for a cigarette." Fergus blew smoke into the air. "On second thoughts, it will have to be two cigarettes. I'm not cheap."

Alexander was laughing uproariously. These senior boys were his heroes and he thought they were wonderful.

In the Security Office the bank of screens of the closed-circuit television network were displaying various areas of the College campus, but no one was watching them.

The three dark-uniformed College security officers on duty were sitting smoking and drinking tea, chatting quietly.

Tony Kilbeck looked through the glass panel of the outer door and told the man he was with, "This lot are bloody useless. They might as well get rid of the cameras for all the attention they pay to them."

He pushed open the door and entered, and the security men stared at him sourly, one of them muttering, "Hey up, lads, here's Rambo."

"Good evening." Tony Kilbeck regarded them with an equal sourness and introduced his companion. "This is Detective Constable Willets. He's my relief for the next couple of days, so he'll be using my callsign."

The crew-cutted young relief nodded. "Evening."

"Do you mind if I explain the set-up to my relief?" Tony Kilbeck requested. Not waiting for any reply he pointed at the screens and told Willets. "This row here are the cameras covering Penfold House. If any suspicious or unidentified party hangs about near the house, then you'll be immediately alerted by the guy who's acting as control here. Control will also alert the uniformed patrol outside the house. Just follow normal Orange Readiness procedure then.

"If the party tries to gain entrance Control will notify you, and you go to Condition Red. Control will alert SO19 at Sloughton, and there'll be a couple of Armed Response teams put on standby."

"What about the uniformed patrol outside the house?" Willets asked.

"He's the tripwire. His job is to tackle the party, and to see what it's getting up to. He'll be backed up by the College Security".

"How will I know what's happening to them?"

"You stay on frequency all the time. There will always be someone keeping everybody in the picture."

"And suppose the shit hits the fan?"

"We'll have Armed Response cars here in a couple of minutes. You'll have to cover until they arrive."

"And then we'll see what you're made of, won't we!" The eldest of the security men, a grizzle-haired veteran with a row of campaign medals on his tunic, interjected sneeringly. "We'll see if you lot are any use when the shooting starts."

The crew-cutted young policeman grinned. "I'll be a hero. Mel and Bruce have trained me. I've seen all the *Lethal Weapon* and *Diehard* films eight times each. I can't wait to show how good I am."

The two younger security men laughed at the riposte, but the eldest scowled, and muttered sullenly beneath his breath.

Once the two policemen were outside the Security Office Willets asked, "What's upsetting that old bastard?"

"His name's Snagg. He was a sergeant major in the Parachute Regiment. He takes it as a personal insult that we've been brought in to cover young Alex. He reckons that his blokes could do the job . . ." Tony Kilbeck paused reflectively. "If they were allowed to be armed, they probably could. They're all old soldiers. They've probably seen more bullets flying than I ever will."

"What's the kid like?"

"Young Alex? He's a good lad." He grinned wryly. "Most of the lads here are alright. They're over-privileged little cunts, but they're okay. It's the bloody adults who get up my nose."

"Why's that?"

"Because most of them have got delusions of grandeur. Even some of the bloody matrons seem to think that they're royalty. I'm glad I'm getting a couple of days away from them, and that's the truth."

As they neared Penfold House they could hear bells ringing in its interior.

"That's Final Assembly call," Kilbeck explained. "All the boys have to gather in the Assembly Room on the ground floor there, and answer the roll-call. Then the house is locked up for the night and none of the boys are allowed out until tomorrow morning."

"Christ! It's like a bloody nick!" the younger man exclaimed.

"Oh no. It isn't so luxurious here as in the nick and the inmates have less freedom. "Kilbeck laughed.

". . . Pierce?"

"Here, sir."

"Richardson Major?"

"Sir."

"Richardson Minor?"

"Present."

Julian Fothergill ignored the undercurrent of whispering and giggling as he called the roll. He was praying inwardly that no boy would be absent, which would then entail him having to make an enquiry and search for the delinquent.

"Thornton-Penrose?"

There was no reply.

Oh, fuck it! Fothergill cursed silently, and glared at the mass of young faces, repeating in a louder voice, "Thornton-Penrose? Answer to your name."

Boys were grinning and nudging each other as the young master felt the familiar nauseating churning in his stomach which always began when he was faced with potential ragging from his charges. He was sickeningly aware that the boys had no respect for him. He wasn't athletic or physically tough enough for them to admire him as a man, and he wasn't a good enough teacher for them to respect his academic prowess. The only thing which enabled him to exert any control at all over the boys was their own awareness that the College administration would show no mercy to any boy who transgressed too blatantly the Draconian code of discipline. Any boy who was foolhardy enough to openly challenge them was very quickly shown the error of his ways. No matter how rich or powerful or influential that boy's family might be, he would still be expelled from the College without recourse to appeal. The Corporate Body of the Martyrs College bowed to no one.

"Has anyone seen Thornton-Penrose?" Fothergill demanded, trying to keep his voice firm.

"Perhaps he's resigned his position here, sir?" Fergus Cochrane offered, his handsome face a picture of innocent concern. "He was rather stressed, sir, when I saw him earlier. I remember remarking to Farquar at the time, how stressed Thornton-Penrose appeared." He turned to Rupert Farquar. "Wasn't that so, Farquar. I made that remark to you, didn't I?"

"You certainly did, Cochrane." Rupert Farquar vigorously nodded his sandy head.

Toby Levy's hand shot up and he beseeched, "May I speak, sir?"

With a sinking heart Fothergill assented.

"With all respect to Cochrane, sir, I have to say that I also saw Thornton-Penrose earlier this evening, and I was most concerned by his manner and appearance. I have a different theory regarding the reason for his present absence."

Even while inwardly castigating himself for being stupid enough to take the bait Fothergill asked, "Why were you concerned, Levy?"

"Well, sir, Thornton-Penrose gave me cause for grave concern because he was threatening to hang himself, sir."

"Don't talk rubbish, Boy!" Fothergill shouted and could have wept with chagrin as he heard the muted explosion of glee from the boys.

"I'm sorry that you think it to be rubbish, sir." Toby Levy assumed an aggrieved air of indignation. "But Thornton-Penrose kept on pestering me to advise him on the length of rope he should use, and what type of knot."

Now the muted glee became loud guffaws, and at the rear of the group Alexander Margrave was forced to thrust his handkerchief hard against his mouth to stifle his roaring laughter.

Fothergill lost control. "You're on Report, Levy," He screeched in fury.

The tall youth's face instantly became the picture of injured innocence. "But, sir, I'm merely trying to help."

Just at that moment the door opened and the lanky figure of the missing boy appeared.

"Where the hell have you been?" Fothergill bellowed. "You're on report for absence."

Thornton-Penrose was an admirer of the early Victorian poets, and he modelled his physical appearance on them, with his hair centre-parted and falling in long flowing waves, his school cravat loosely bowed, his waistcoat unbuttoned. He also cultivated an ethereal vagueness of manner which he considered to be in keeping with his poetic persona.

"What am I on report for, sir?" he fluted.

"For being absent," Fothergill snarled.

The youth stared about him with an air of puzzlement, then enquired politely, "This is the Assembly Room of Penfold House, is it not, sir?"

"You damn well know it is, you fool." Fothergill's body was shaking, his face red with fury, and the boys watched with huge delight.

"Well, sir," Thornton-Penrose smiled charmingly. "Then if that is the case, I am not absent, am I, sir? I am here, sir, therefore it is physically impossible for me to be absent."

Bellowing laughter erupted, and Fothergill, raging with an impotent fury, could only shout, "You're late. I'm putting you on report for being late."

"That isn't my fault, sir." The youth stated calmly.

A warning bell sounded in Fothergill's heated brain. This boy might have a reason for his lateness which he, Fothergill, would have to accept. He managed to control his fury sufficiently to grit out, "Why were you late?"

Thornton-Penrose's charming smile beamed out once more. "Well, sir, on hearing the assembly bell I put aside the sonnet I had been composing and I began to make my way here. I followed my customary path, sir. After leaving my room I turned left and travelled to the end of third landing and down the stairs. Much to my dismay as I reached second landing I experienced a sharp pain within my inner organs. Approximately in the area of the lower descending colon, sir.

I think that is the correct term for that area of the intestinal tract. But I would be prepared to be corrected on that, if any member of the medical profession were to disagree . . ."

"Get on with it, boy!" Fothergill snarled impatiently.

"Well, sir, it was of course a signal. And that signal was my body's method of telling me that I must defecate that instant. Or failing that, deposit a large amount of waste matter within my trousers."

A cheer shattered the air, and Fothergill knew that he had lost it.

He went on gabbling out names, not caring if he received any answer or not. Then snapped the book shut and warned the chattering, laughing boys, "Mr Mollinson is due to return within the next half-hour. Any boy who is not in his own room by that time will answer to him."

He hurried out, and feeling near to tears escaped to his own quarters.

As he bathed his burning face in cold water, his anger metamorphosed into a searing self-pity. He bitterly regretted ever having come to the College, and tears filled his eyes and spilled down his pudgy cheeks.

I try to be a good teacher. But they won't let me. The bastards just won't let me.

Envy racked him as he thought of those other masters who so effortlessly controlled the boys. Subjugating the unruly ringleaders to their own will. Enforcing discipline with merely a frown. Evoking admiration from their pupils by displaying superior physical and intellectual prowess.

I should never have come here, Fothergill told himself miserably. The boys and the other masters despise me, don't they? I'm sure that they've realised that I'm gay. That's why they torment me so badly. They think that I'm an easy target. A soft poofter!

A terrible loneliness assailed him, and he felt very vulnerable, very afraid.

His father and grandfather had been regular soldiers, his mother the daughter of a soldier, his two brothers were professional soldiers. All of them tough, hard-bitten individuals, who loathed and despised sexual deviants.

It was Julian Fothergill's greatest dread and terror that his family would discover that he was homosexual. A fact that he had realised as a young teenager, and that had initially filled him with horror and despair, but which over the years he had struggled to accept and to come to terms with.

He regarded himself as an honourable person, who would never take advantage of his position to try and seduce the boys and youths in his charge. And he prided himself on his record in this area. Naturally there had been, and were still times when some boy or youth would fire his desire, but always he had successfully resisted the temptation, even when he recognised in that boy or youth the same sexual hungers that he himself possessed.

'Closet Queen'. He knew that derisive term so well. He knew the contempt that his fellow Gays had for the Closet Queens, those Gays who kept their sexual identities hidden from the world and passed themselves off as 'straights'. He derided and despised himself for his own cowardice in remaining a Closet Queen. For not having the courage to come out into the open and declare to the world what he was. But he knew that he would never possess the courage to do what he yearned to do. He knew that he would always try to keep his sexual identity hidden from the world he moved in.

But his sexual hungers needed to be satisfied. The frustrations of his body must be relieved. And so he regularly went into London, and there in the anonymity of the gay clubs he searched for transient sexual partners and with them satiated his greed for male flesh.

Tonight, when the house was quiet, he would again journey into the city, and for brief hours he would throw aside his defensive shield and allow his true self to emerge from hiding. He would hope to find love, but would settle for sex.

It was three hours after Final Assembly and only the dim amber nightlights glowed in the darkness as the four boys moved stealthily up the stairs. They were wearing their Cadet Corps camouflage smocks and trousers, and black trainers on their feet. Each had a pack strapped to his back and the lead boy also carried a small aluminium stepladder. The house was quiet, but from some of the rooms muted voices and music could be heard.

At the top of the flights of stairs there was a small landing in front of the door to the top floor. A trapdoor was set into the ceiling above this landing.

Fergus Cochrane placed the stepladder, swiftly mounted it and pushed the trapdoor open. He disappeared into the black hole and one by one the other boys followed. The last boy drew the stepladder up after him by means of the rope tied to its top rung, and then the trapdoor was silently lowered back into position.

In single file they traversed the wide expanse of the loft, finding their way by torchlight, stepping over and ducking under the pipes and cables that snaked in all directions.

Low down on the tiles of the front-facing roof was a skylight; Fergus carefully levered it upwards and cautiously poked out his head to stare around him. Then he clambered out onto the tiles and again the boys followed one by one, the last boy closing the skylight behind him.

Fergus snaked up the steep incline and slid over the gable ridge. The other boys waited, lying back against the cold tiles until he returned.

"All clear," he whispered and in single file they moved up and over the ridge.

At the bottom of the incline there was a balustrade shielding the sheer drop of the blank wall to the roof of the old stable block some twenty feet below. Fergus felt for the coiled rope hidden at the base of the balustrade, tied one end to the coping stone and lowered the rope until it touched the stable roof. Then swarmed down the rope, to be followed by his friends.

Up to this point they had remained above and behind the arcs of the security cameras, and the infra-red censor-controlled security lights which automatically switched on to illuminate the immediate environs of the building if a body broke into the infra-red field. Over a period of many months by trial and error Fergus Cochrane and Toby Levy had established and mapped out the range perimeters of the security light censors.

They had also carefully plotted the locations of the various security cameras on the campus, calculated the overlaps of the camera arcs, and established the many blind spots that the cameras could not overlook among the warren of ancient buildings.

They had discovered that if they crawled along the roof ridge of the stable block for twelve metres, then descended directly to gutter height and travelled for a further five metres to reach a drainpipe, they would be just inches beyond the ranges of both Penfold and the neighbouring Stallard House security light censors. They would also be in the cameras' dead ground.

Directly in front of the stable block were beds of flowering shrubs. Evergreens which bore thick leaf cover on their branches. By dropping from the low guttering and snake crawling, they could remain shielded from the cameras, and were out of range of the light censors. From that point on it was a comparatively easy matter to crawl through the bushes and reach the public highway. During the evening hours there was always plenty of pedestrian and vehicular traffic on this road. The boys would hide in the bushes, take their civilian clothing out of their backpacks, change, leave their packs and camouflage outfits hidden, and slip out to mingle with the passing traffic.

The return to the house simply entailed the same procedure in the opposite direction. And was easier, because the boys knew that in the hours just before the dawn the police patrol and the security men became weary and less alert.

Now, Fergus Cochrane and his friends followed their customary route, changed their clothing and slipped from the grounds of Penfold House. They ran swiftly across the wide expanse of the playing fields, climbed through a hedge onto another main road and, laughing and hooting with excitement, hurried along to the layby where Fergus Cochrane's brother was waiting for them in his car.

Chapter Sixteen

TEETERING on high heels, scarfs held over their tight-permed hair, the two women hurried through the drizzling rain towards the building that was festooned with strings of coloured lights and surmounted by the flashing neon sign that proclaimed 'Garden Pavilion'.

Spencer sat invisibly in the dark interior of his van and watched them pass.

"Good evening, Ladies. You're looking very beautiful tonight. Who's the lucky man?" the thickset bouncer greeted gallantly.

"That's for us to know, and for you to find out." Reena Brown was delighted by his compliment.

"If I wasn't working, then I'd be after you meself. You look good enough to eat."

"We'd only give you indigestion, my bucko," Theresa Sweeney laughed.

"I'd only get indigestion because I'd make a pig of meself with you," he insisted.

"Take no notice of him, Theresa. He's just a sweet talker." Reena fluttered her false eyelashes in what she fervently hoped was provocative invitation. "If we offered, he'd run a mile."

"Will you come on, Reena," the Irishwoman snapped impatiently. "Me throat's that parched it's like a desert."

Reena directed a languishing gaze at the bouncer. But to her chagrin he had already seen other women approaching the door and was greeting them.

"Good evening, my lovelies. You're looking gorgeous tonight."

"Come on, Reena," her friend urged, and she snapped irritably.

"Alright! Alright!" Muttering angrily beneath her breath as she followed the massive, fat buttocks. "You spoil all my chances, you jealous cow."

As they passed through into the large room a hundred hostile female eyes instantly fixed upon them, and spiteful comments were exchanged in throaty whispers. There was no friendly sodality in this room. It was an arena where the air was charged with tension and rivalry.

"Girls juss wanna have fu-u-u-unnn!" Cyndie Lauper was telling the gathering, and on the dance floor sweating, panting men and women were bouncing and writhing in frantic efforts to demonstrate their continuing virility, desperately apeing the joyful abandon of their lost youth.

Reena's gaze moved down the tables that edged the dance floor, probed the shadowed spaces behind those tables, then switched to the dancers.

The familiar feeling of disappointment and depression whelmed over her. The men's faces were the same faces that she had met a hundred times before at 'Singles' gatherings, and 'Over-Thirties' nights. They were the faces that answered her advertisements in the Lonely Heart columns, the faces she talked with on the phone, arranged to meet in pubs and clubs. The faces that minutes after meeting her made excuses and left, or crueller still merely looked at her and turned away.

She took the glass of vodka and tonic that Theresa handed her, and greedily drank it down. Then she pushed to the bar and bought two more. After four or five she knew that the world would seem a happier place. She poured down drink after drink until the alcohol took over her mind. Like some miraculous elixir the vodka made her feel young again. In her mind her wrinkled skin was again smooth and sheen, her shrivelled breasts plump and firm. Her dulled eyes began to shine and her sadness become gaiety.

"Hello Reena."

She stared at him blankly.

"I see you don't remember me." He appeared to be very disappointed.

"Yes, I do," she lied, and in her heart hope suddenly flowered.

"No you don't." He shook his head, but then he smiled and jerked his head towards the dance floor." It's a slow one. Come and have a dance with me and I'll remind you."

He took her hand and led her amongst the dancers; unre-sisting she followed him, hoping against hope that she was not dreaming. That this was not some figment of her drunken imagination. He held her close against his taut body, and his breath was warm and moist upon her cheek, and she closed her eyes and prayed fervently. Dear God, let this be the one. Please let this be the one.

"Looks like Reena's found herself a chap."

The woman standing talking to Theresa Sweeney pointed to the dance floor.

The Irishwoman squinted short-sightedly but could see only blurred outlines.

"What's he like?"

"He's got glasses on, and there's a big mark down his face. I wouldn't fancy him meself."

Theresa grinned drunkenly. "Ah well now, beggars can't be choosers, can they. Poor old Reena's desperate for a man, God bless her! Cummon now, whose round is it? Me throat is as parched as a desert."

"Gurlsss juss wanna have fuu-u-unn. Gurls juss wanna have fun!" The young man wore only a leather thong, and his sweating body glistened beneath the bouncing strobe lights, as he danced alone in the centre of the floor, screeching hoarsely, "Gurlllsss juss wanna have fu-u-unn . . ."

Julian Fothergill started to become tumescent as he watched the sinuous writhings, and visualised himself locked in the embrace of those muscled arms.

"Tasty, isn't she?" the blonde-haired man whispered into Julian's ear. "But too much of a screaming queen for my liking."

Julian's stomach churned with excitement. He had noticed this blonde with his wild mane of hair as soon as he had come into the club, and found him very attractive.

Now he glanced sideways. Close up the blonde was older than he had appeared at first sight. But he was still attractive. Very attractive, in fact.

"Would you like a drink?" The blonde invited.

Julian hesitated. He didn't want to appear to be too easy a pick-up. Easy pick-ups very quickly acquired the reputation of being cheap slags.

Shafto hid a contemptuous grin. He felt that he could read this pudgy little closet queen as if she were an open book. She wants romance. The poor little chicken is looking for love.

"I'm going to have another drink myself," he said softly. "And I'm lonely."

The simple statement touched Julian's heart. He knew all too well what loneliness was.

Shafto's shrewd gaze caught the momentary softening in the pudgy features. Got you! he crowed inwardly.

He reached to gently take the half-filled glass from the other man's hand.

"It's a Thunderball, isn't it?"

Julian looked fully at the thin handsome face, and felt shy and uncertain. He nodded.

"Don't you dare to disappear on me," Shafto warned jokingly.

"I won't."

Julian's eyes followed the trim, slender figure, and his excitement quickened. This could be the love affair that he had always longed for. Not the furtive, loveless couplings of the flesh that was all he had known until now. This could be the union of bodies and hearts and souls, the end of his loneliness.

"I danced the last waltz with you
  Two lonely people together.
  I fell in love with you.
  The last waltz should last
  Foreevvvveerrrr . . ."

The dance floor was packed with scarcely moving couples, arms tight wrapped around bodies, lips greedily seeking and finding lips, hands fondling thighs and buttocks.

Reena was in a daze of drunken happiness, locked in the arms of this man who had so miraculously come to her. This man who was tenderly caressing her hips, whispering in her ear, telling her how beautiful she was. She wanted this waltz to go on and on and on, she wanted this night to never end.

Theresa Sweeney had come to her, telling her that it was time they left. That she, Theresa was tired, and wanted to go home.

Reena had sent her packing, with a flea in her ear. And serve the fat cow right, as well. She was only jealous because Reena had found herself a man, and she couldn't. The fat cow was always spoiling Reena's chances. But not tonight! She hadn't managed to spoil Reena's chances tonight. Reena had made sure of that. And now Reena had her man to herself. And she wasn't going to let him go. It was destiny. That's what it was, destiny! All the rotten bad years were behind her now. She had her own man at last, and her life from now on was going to be wonderful.

She pressed her belly hard against her man, grinding and pushing, and her mouth sucked feverishly on his lips.

"That's it, folks. It's all over, Guys and Dolls. That's the Last Waltz for tonight. Don't forget that next Saturday Night is Ladies' night. When all you lovely gals will only be charged half-price entrance for another night of music, fun, laughter and rrrooomance . . ."

The music ended, and the disc jockey's phony American accent jarred into Reena's dreams. The lights came on, bright, harsh and revealing, and suddenly Reena was afraid.

When he sees me in the light, he won't want me. He'll turn away from me, like all the others.

The long, dark birthmark showed clearly as he pulled back his head, and utter despair filled her.

That's it. He's turning away from me.

Then he was smiling down at her, the light reflecting from his glasses.

"It's time for us to go, Sweetheart. I'll take you home."

Relief flooded and her heart sang.

Outside the rain still drizzled, but Reena was uncaring of any rain, as with arms around each others' waists they hurried across the car park.

Reena wanted to bind her man to her, to give him her body, so that he should know how warm and sweet her loving could be, and want to come back to her again and again to taste that sweetness.

When they reached the van she clung to him before he could unlock its doors, kissing him passionately.

"Let's go to your place," he whispered urgently.

"We can't."

"Why not?"

"We'll be seen going in. There's lights and security cameras. The lights come on when anybody goes towards the doors."

"What do you mean?" He demanded roughly. And she

hurried to explain how the lights were triggered by someone's approach, and when the lights came on it showed on the television screens and the security men checked to see who had triggered the lights.

"Can't you go in first, and then switch the lights off so that they won't come on again?" he wanted to know.

She shook her head. "No. It's all covered by steel plating. Only the security men can get to the switches."

She thought that she detected a movement of withdrawal, and the terror of losing him made her plead desperately.

"We can do it in the back of the van, can't we? Or we can find somewhere else."

"Be quiet," he ordered her, and there was a silence which seemed to stretch for an eternity.

A fury was seething in Spencer. Fury engendered by the recognition of his own stupid mistake in thinking that this domestic servant, this menial could be of use to him. He lusted to punish this ugly old woman. To make her pay for his own error of judgement. The fury became a white heat and the madness that lay dormant in him suddenly exploded. Visual images, vivid memories crowded his mind, mingling one with another like filmic scenes coalescing and dissolving and coalescing. Brutal violations of virgin flesh, terror in dark faces, blood spurting, choking cries of agony, horror in stricken eyes. Spencer's sexual excitement mounted unbearably, his manhood engorged into throbbing erection, and insanity took control.

The last car left the park and they were alone, then the lights of the Pavilion went out, and the darkness closed around them.

Opposite the van beneath the trees there stood an old bicycle shelter built in the form of a lean-to. He pulled Reena across the muddy ground and into the shelter. His mouth clamped on hers and he pushed her back against the wall. She felt his hands tugging her short skirt high on her hips and then pulling her wispy pants down. They fell about her ankles and she lifted her foot to free them. He was panting harshly now as he spread her thighs with his own and his fingers dug with brutal force into her flaccid buttocks. She cried out as he rammed his manhood deep inside her.

"You're hurting me, darling. You're hurting me!"

He ignored her protests, silencing them with the crushing pressure of his mouth, pounding against her until orgasm shuddered through him and the madness of his lust spent itself with his spurting semen.

Then he withdrew from her body and turned and walked away without a word. He unlocked the van, got into it and drove off.

She stood motionless, skirt still rucked high up on her hips, making no attempt to cover her nakedness, watching the van until its tail lights disappeared beyond the trees. And only then did the harsh wrenching sobs of heartbreak burst from her bruised, scarlet-smeared lips.

The haunting strains of the 'Saraband for Dead Lovers' pulsed through the scented darkness of the room, and Julian knelt before his new-found lover and took the warm, silky-skinned rod of maleness into his mouth.

"No, wait." Shafto gently pushed the young man's head back, and stepped away from him. He reached out and flicked a switch and concealed lights shed a soft warm glow across the room.

"I want to see you, Honey," he told Julian huskily, and bent to kiss him. "You're beautiful and I want to see you while we're making love."

Then he raised Julian up and deftly undressed him, before casting his own clothes aside. He kissed Julian on the mouth, and then ran his hands and lips over the pale, pudgy flesh, sucking, fondling, teasing, until Julian was trembling with the force of his own wanting.

Shafto stared searchingly into the flushed features of the younger man, then smiled and nodded.

"Now. Do it now."

His hands pushed downwards on the narrow shoulders, and Julian knelt and hungrily kissed and sucked the throbbing, erect manhood.

Shafto waited for some time, judging his moment, then again withdrew from the young man's mouth, and turned him and pushed him face down upon the carpet. He spread the plump cheeks of Julian's buttocks and thrust between them, and Julian gasped and moaned and lifted his face, his mouth open, his eyes glazed, and the hidden camcorder whirred softly as it captured his raptures, and recorded these long long minutes of sexual abandonment . . .

Chapter Seventeen

THE phone burred in the luxurious apartment, and Charles Hoffman hurried to answer it.

"Charles Hoffman speaking."

"Good evening, Mr Hoffman, I'm calling on behalf of Makesafe Incorporated. You may have seen our television advertisment for security doors and shutters?"

Hoffman sighed with thankful relief, then confirmed.

"Indeed I have."

"Security measures are becoming a necessity in these days of soaring crime rates, Mr Hoffman. No home is safe without them. We have presently a representative of our company in your area. I do think that it would be to your advantage to discuss the security of your own home with him. Of course his advice would cost you nothing and would place you under no obligation to purchase our products".

"Well, if it wouldn't place me under any obligation to buy, I suppose that I could spare him a few minutes. And you are?"

"Tate, Mr Hoffman. David Tate. When would it be convenient for our representative to call on you, Mr Hoffman?"

"I'm free this morning actually. He could call in an hour from now?"

"Certainly, that will be admirable."

"What's this chap's name?"

"Turner, Graham Turner. I'm sure that you'll find his visit to be of great value to yourself, Mr Hoffman."

"I'm sure I shall, Mr Tate."

"I'll wish you a Good Morning, Mr Hoffman. Our Mr Turner will be there in exactly one hour from now."

"Very well, in an hour."

Spencer replaced the handset and left the phone booth, then strolled across the Waterloo Station concourse.

He checked his watch against the large station clock. It

was half past ten. At half past eleven he would meet Charles Hoffman in the Turner Room of the Tate Gallery on Millbank.

The lofty halls of the Gallery were swarming with the normal assortment of schoolchildren, tourists, casual visitors and art lovers.

Charles Hoffman was gazing at a seascape.

"To be perfectly truthful I've never much cared for Turner's work." Spencer's tone was dismissive. "I much prefer the Flemish School. I like clarity in pictures."

The older man turned his head, his eyes flicking around to make sure that no one was close enough to overhear what he said.

"My clients agree with your sentiments."

Spencer instantly understood the veiled import of the words. "Haven't you made it clear to them that I don't work in that way?"

"They won't accept it."

"They'll have to."

"For God's sake!" Hoffman's desperation caused a momentary loss of control. "You don't know these people. They have stated categorically that they either be kept fully informed as to methods, locations and times, or they withdraw from the contract. They are not bluffing. Believe me!"

Spencer saw the fear in the other man's eyes and realised that he was telling the truth. He broke eye contact and moved slowly away to stand and gaze at another huge canvas.

Hoffman gazed at the first picture for a brief while longer, then moved in the opposite direction.

Spencer was thinking hard. He had survived in his violent, merciless world by being always wary. Always on guard. Always prepared for treachery. And now his finely honed instinct for survival was warning him that he must tread very very carefully.

For a half hour more he moved slowly from picture to picture, mentally exploring the connotations of Hoffman's clients' insistence on knowing the details of the plans for the kidnapping of Alexander Margrave. And his survival instinct continued to sound its warning note.

"Well?" Charles Hoffman had come to stand beside him once more.

Spencer mentally shrugged. So be it!

He nodded. "Your clients will get what they want."

Hoffman's relief was palpable.

Spencer walked out of the Turner Room and towards the main entrance. His gaze moving swiftly over the bodies criss-crossing, entering, leaving the great main hall and its branching rooms.

At the entrance to the American Abstracts he noted a strikingly attractive, raven-haired woman in company with an elderly man. The couple were talking to an attendant and a sudden chord of memory struck Spencer as he saw the woman smile, her teeth gleaming white against the moist red lips.

The restaurant. They were in the restaurant.

He averted his gaze and sensed rather than saw her eyes rest briefly upon him as he passed.

Coincidence. Spencer dismissed the encounter from his mind as he ran down to the pavement and hailed a taxi.

Shafto was waiting for him in a bar off Leicester Square, his wild mane of blonde hair tied back in a long ponytail, his face powdered and painted.

Spencer frowned. If Shafto was going to continue to be included in his plans, then he needed a more subdued, less noticeable image.

Shafto grinned happily as Spencer joined him.

"I've got it, Spencer. That fuckin' Closet Queen will shit herself when she sees it."

He noticed the other man's grim expression and displayed instant concern.

"What's up, Spencer?"

"You are."

"What?"

"If you're going to continue working for me, then you've got to get your act together. You can't look like Goldilocks any longer. You've got to look like a 'straight'."

"Look like a 'straight'?" Shafto's thin face twisted in utter distaste. Then he bridled, and questioned waspishly, "And suppose I don't want to look like a fuckin' straight'?"

Spencer stared at him wordlessly and fear lanced through Shafto's mind. The dark grey eyes boring into his own were as cold as death.

"Okay Spencer," he muttered hastily. "Okay."

"Get it done as soon as I leave you," Spencer ordered brusquely, and Shafto nodded a jerky assent.

"I will."

Spencer's mood lightened abruptly and he asked pleasantly. "It went well then?"

Shafto's fear eased a little and he laughed nervously.

"I'll say it did. The Closet Queen is a star. Captured on the silver screen for ever."

Spencer held out his hand and Shafto took two video casettes from an inner pocket and gave them over.

"This is the original and this is the copy."

"Now listen carefully," Spencer instructed. "From now on you stay away from the scene. You lie low and wait for me to contact you".

"Will I have to wait for very long, Spencer?"

Spencer shook his head. "No. I've got to go away, but it will only be for a few days."

He slipped the casettes into his own pocket, and then gave the other man an envelope.

"There's some money for you to be going on with."

"Thanks, Spencer. Thanks. That's really great of you." Shafto's fulsome protestations were sincere.

Spencer nodded and left.

He walked with apparent aimlessness through the busy streets. Yet that aimlessness was in fact a highly skilled practise in detecting any possible pursuit or tail.

By the time he reached Oxford Street, Spencer was satisfied that he was not being tailed, so he hailed a cab and settled himself comfortably in its capacious leather seat.

He was unhappy about Charles Hoffman's clients' insistence on being privy to his plans. He strongly suspected that they might be plotting some sort of double-cross and he assumed that if that were the case, then Hoffman himself would undoubtedly be involved.

Spencer frowned viciously. At this stage he would continue in his pre-planned course of action, but he would also begin to prepare an alternative plan for use in case of double-cross.

"Heathrow Airport," he instructed the cab driver.

Spencer was en route to begin the recruitment of his strike force.

Chapter Eighteen

THE curtains were drawn in the windows of the first-floor flat and seeing this Terry Macrae cursed sibilantly and turned back. He made his way to the bar on the corner and went in.

The counter was lined with men and the atmosphere was loud with drink-fuelled laughter and talk.

"G'day Terry," one of the seated men greeted and shouted to the bartender, "give us a beer for me mate."

Macrae shouldered through the close-packed customers and taking the foam-topped glass drank it dry, in continuous gulps, then shouted in his turn, "Let's have two more here, Spinky."

The seated man noted Macrae's sour expression, and guessed shrewdly, "I'll bet your bloody missis is up to her old tricks again?"

Macrae scowled angrily and momentarily his sun-reddened, freckled features were threatening. Then he shook his head.

"Just mind your own bloody business."

"All right, Terry, all right," his companion placated. "Only I told you when you married her what 'ud happen, didn't I? I know what them slanty-eyed bitches are like, mate. A man can't trust 'em as far as he can throw 'em. Look what happened to me." The man paused, wary of Macrae's uncertain temper, which was as fiery as his red hair. Then he demanded, "How long have we been mates, Terry? Ever since we was in Nam together, ain't we? And if an old mate can't speak plain to you, then who can?"

Macrae nodded, and admitted grudgingly, "Yeah, you're right, Dugg. I know I should never have married her. Once a whore, always a whore."

"Exactly!" The other man emptied his schooner of beer and belched loudly with satisfaction. Then shouted for more.

The two drank more slowly now, and for a time they were silent. Then Dugg asked, "Any luck with the job?"

Macrae sighed dispiritedly. "No. They gave it to a bloody Vietnamese." Again he emitted a gusty sigh. "My luck's run out, I reckon Dugg. Nothing's going right for me these days. I wish I'd stayed in the mob. I'd be on full pension by now, wouldn't I?"

The other man's broad, fleshy features betrayed smugness. "I told you, didn't I, not to pack in the army. But all you could think about was the bloody fortune you'd be earning as a mercenary. And that game was soon played out, wasn't it?" He grinned with self-satisfaction. "I did the right thing. I stayed on, and now I'm on full pension. I ain't rich, Terry, but with my bit o' security work I manage all right."

Macrae had by now tired of his old comrade's company, and he grunted a farewell and left the bar. Reluctant to again face the drawn curtains at his flat he wandered morosely through the pullulating streets of King's Cross, breathing in the fumes of traffic, sweating in the hot sunlight, being jostled by the thickly thronging crowds. As he walked he thought about his wife, and what she was doing back at the flat.

She's gone on the game again. He knew with an absolute certainty, and fierce fury coursed through him. But that fury was overlaid by a bitter sense of resignation.

What else did you expect, you stupid sod? he castigated himself mercilessly. You pick up a tart in a Bangkok club, and you marry her and bring her back home with you, and you think she's going to change. You knew when you married her that all she was after was a ticket out of there, but you just wouldn't face facts, would you.

He caught a glimpse of himself in a show window mirror, and scowled. She never was marrying you for your good looks, that's for sure. You've always been an ugly bastard. And whore though she is, she's beautiful. She can get any man she wants to. And she's made it bloody clear that she don't want you any more. Not now she's got her citizenship.

He thought back over the last months, reliving the endless fights and bickerings that had made a misery of his marriage.

I'd leave her today, if I'd got anywhere else to go. Or any money to go with.

Reluctantly he made his way towards his home.

The curtains had been drawn back, the windows were open and he thought disgruntedly, She's getting rid of the smell of the guy.

As he climbed up the narrow flight of stairs which stank of dried urine he felt acutely depressed. His earlier anger had left him, and he felt no urge to challenge his wife, or to upbraid her for what she had been doing. All he wanted was to be free of her, free of his mockery of a marriage, free of this slum he lived in, free of his failure.

"You back too early. I got nothing ready to eat for you. You back too early."

Her heavily accented, sing-song voice accused him as he let himself into the cramped room.

She came to face him, petite and dainty in a brightly coloured blouse and skirt, her black hair worn in a long plait, looking like a schoolgirl. And he found himself yet again marvelling at how fresh and sweet she appeared. Her appearance completely belying the reality of what she was.

He did not question her when he saw the empty wine bottle and the two glasses on the table, and the ashtray filled with cigarette stubs that were a different brand to what he smoked.

He walked into the bedroom and saw that the bed had been freshly made, the sheets and pillowcases changed for clean ones. He sniffed the air and despite the open windows detected the faint scent of an expensive male perfume. When he went back into the living room she instantly demanded, "Did you get job?" Aggression glimmered in her almond-shaped, black eyes.

"No," he told her curtly and when he saw the instant contempt in her expression gave in to a sudden urge to wound. "They gave it to a bloody Vietnamese. A bloody Slant, like you."

Her eyes flashed with actual hatred and she spat a string of epithets at him in her own language. He itched to hit her, but he was a man who was reluctant to use physical violence against women, and so he turned away.

"Terry? Are you in?"

A female voice sounded from the bottom of the stairs. It was the neighbour who lived in the ground floor flat.

He went out and peered down at her. "What's up, Moira?"

The fat elderly woman waved an envelope at him. "A young kid brought this for you. He couldn't get any reply from your place so he left it with me to give you."

Her eyes were speculative and her expression prurient as he went down to her.

"I thought you was in, Terry. I reckoned I could hear somebody bouncing around in the bedroom. But I couldn't get an answer either. Was you having a bit o' nooky with your missis?"

He ignored the question knowing that she knew what had been going on, and not wishing to give her the satisfaction of admitting to his own knowledge that he was a cuckold.

"Thanks Moira." He took the envelope and examined it curiously. There was no stamp or postmark, only his name neatly printed. He opened it, scanned the brief message, and exclaimed in surprise.

The fat woman questioned eagerly. "What is it, Terry? Good news, or bad?"

He shrugged his broad shoulders. "I dunno, Moira. It's from an old mate of mine I haven't seen in years. He wants me to phone him."

She moved to peer over his arm at the brief note, and read out aloud, "Call me." It was signed simply, "Spencer", and followed by a Sidney phone code and number.

Then she said wonderingly, "That ain't much of a letter, is it?"

"No, it ain't. Anyway, thanks Moira." Macrae returned slowly upstairs, memories flooding into his mind.

The last time he had seen Spencer had been in Columbia where they had been training the private army of a drugs baron.

"I wonder what that mad Pommy bastard wants with me after all this time?"

It took several attempts spread across several hours for him to make direct contact with Spencer at the given number. When he finally did so the conversation was comparatively brief.

"Hello, is that you, Spencer? This is Terry. Terry Macrae. What are you doing here, mate?"

"Are you interested in doing a job for me, Terry?"

"What sort of job, mate?"

"A very well paid one."

"Too right, I am."

"Meet me in the Whalers, in Waterloo Square. The upstairs room."

The room was crowded with loud, brash, successful, young executives and their decorative female counterparts. It's walls were covered with the works of local artists. On the small raised stage there was a jazz combo blaring.

Terry Macrae shouldered his way through the pack clustering around the bar and tried to attract the attention of the busy barmen. Again and again he gestured, and again and again they walked past him as if he were invisible. He began to get angry, his face reddening and his big fists clenched as he thumped the bar.

"Still the same sweet tempered, placid, pussy cat, I see. Here, this will cool you down."

A schooner of cold beer was thrust under his nose and he turned to find Spencer smiling at him.

Macrae grinned delightedly. "How are you, you Pommy Bastard?"

"I'm good." Spencer told him, and jerked his head. "Let's get out of the crush."

He led the way out onto the balcony and stood with his back to one of the cast-iron pillars that supported the roof.

"Jesus, Spencer!" Macrae grunted in surprise as he examined the other man's tall, lean body, and suntanned features. "You ain't changed a bit. You don't look a day older." He cursed in mock exasperation. "Fuck you!"

Spencer looked meaningfully at his companion's beer belly, and Macrae laughed shamefacedly and slapped the bulging flesh.

"I've let meself go a bit, ain't I. But I can soon get into shape again."

"You'll have to," Spencer told him gravely, "if you're going to work for me."

"What's the job, and where?" the Australian asked eagerly.

"It's in the UK, and its heavy. Very heavy," Spencer informed him. "But the pay is very good. Can you still fly a chopper?"

"Yeah, I've kept me hand in."

"Any loose ends here?"

"Not any more there ain't." Macrae snorted.

"Okay." Spencer nodded. "You're hired."

He slipped a thick, narrow envelope into the pocket of Macrae's shorts.

"Here's an advance on your wages. Will you be staying at your present address?"

"Yeah, too bloody true I will. That slant-eyed bitch I'm married to won't be staying there with me though. I'm kicking her arse out of it the minute I get back there."

"Okay." Spencer nodded as if satisfied. "I'll be sending for you to join me in the UK shortly. Be ready."

"Jesus H. Christ!" The Australian's sandy features split in a huge grin. "I'll drink to that, mate, 'til it's coming out of me ears!"

Spencer shook his head. "No, you won't. You can have a good piss-up tonight. But from tomorrow lay off it, and get in shape. I need you to be fit."

He smiled briefly, clapped the other man's meaty shoulder, and then was gone.

The Australian shook his head admiringly. "Mad Pommy bastard. Am I glad you showed up again."

Chapter Nineteen

IT was Foundation Day, the principal festival of the Queen's College of the Protestant Martyrs, and from mid-morning the Rolls Royces, the Daimlers, the Bentleys, the Mercedes, BMWs and Jaguars had rolled down the road passing between the vast green swards of the playing fields to enter the precincts of the school.

The luxurious vehicles carried royalty, aristocrats, plutocrats, people of wealth, power and fame. They had all come to celebrate Foundation Day.

The winding streets and lanes which dissected the numerous buildings were thronged with boys and their families, the boys wearing the archaic College ceremonial dress of short purple cloaks and tasselled Tudor caps over their formal uniforms, their families, although widely disparate, yet appearing strangely alike. The women and girls were in designer clothes and broadbrimmed hats, their menfolk in pinstriped suits of grey and blue and black. They radiated confidence and regarded the world around them with an arrogant hauteur.

A group of Japanese tourists chattered excitedly, smiling and hissing with gratification and taking aim with their cameras as a procession of frock-coated masters, wearing long gowns, richly hued scholar's hoods draped on their shoulders, and mortar boards on their heads, crossed the road and entered the arched gateway of the Old School, the boys raising their floppy caps and bowing as their mentors passed.

A crocodile file of casually clothed French teenagers shepherded by their own teachers came to a halt on the opposite side of the roadway to stare at the spectacle before them, the French youths exchanging gibes and sneering resentfully at their female companions for staring admiringly at the Martyrs scholars who, secure in their privileged elitism, performed their bows with extravagant flourishes.

More tourists of differing nationalities had now gathered to stare eagerly at the colourful scene.

"They look so cute in those old-fashioned clothes," a pretty American woman exclaimed.

"They look damn silly," her male companion scoffed and she rounded on him angrily.

"They've got something that you'll never have, Buster, and that's style!"

"Oh yeah?" He scowled.

"Oh yeah!" She scowled back and then made a show of ignoring him, while he reddened and muttered and snorted impotently.

"I wouldn't mind wearing that clobber meself, if a sheila like that reckons it's cute," an Australian voice chuckled in Spencer's ear, and he turned his head and glowered at Terry Macrae.

"Where the hell have you been?"

"Jesus!" Macrae exhaled a gust of whisky breath. "There's no call for you to look at me like that, mate. The bloody train was late."

"You should allow for that, and take an earlier one," Spencer snarled, and the other man nodded sheepishly.

"All right, mate. I'm sorry."

They walked on in silence for some moments, then Macrae grinned. "How will we pick the little bastard out from all this lot. They all look the same to me in them fancy rigs and big hats."

"We'll see him later. When they have the 'Homage of the Boats'. What I want you to have a look at first is the rear of the house."

They walked slowly past the front of Penfold House which was festooned with flags and bunting in honour of Foundation Day. The armed policeman was standing to the side of the boys' entrance, through which there was a constant coming and going of boys and their families.

Spencer was momentarily tempted to try entering through that door and take a look at the interior of the house, then decided against it. These people were almost certainly all known to each other, at least by sight, and the chances of being challenged were too great.

A line of shining luxury cars were parked in the roadway at

the rear of the house, and Spencer took particular notice of a Range Rover in which a dark-suited, cropped-haired man sat in the driver's seat, while another burly dark-suited man was standing outside the vehicle, leaning casually with his arm resting on its roof.

But the searching stares he fixed on the passing pedestrians were not casual.

"They look like SO16, Diplomatic Protection Group," Spencer muttered. "I wonder if Macpherson is here to visit the boy?"

He smiled at the watching man as he neared him.

"Lovely day, isn't it?"

"It certainly is." The man smiled back, but remained tense and watchful.

They passed the Range Rover and reached the open ironwork of the garden gate and Spencer led the way through.

A large group of people were standing talking and drinking on the patio of the house, and Spencer told Macrae, "Just take a quick look, and then we'll go."

There was a rustle of movement in the shrubbery to his left and he turned to face yet another tall, dark-suited man who asked in an American accent, "Can I help you, sir?" The man smiled affably.

Macpherson has to be here, Spencer decided.

He smiled in return and shook his head, then lied fluently. "Thank you, no. I was only taking a quick peep at the old place. This was my house once."

He gestured towards the rear wing of the house which jutted at right angles to the main fabric.

"That was my room, third from the end on the second floor."

"Is it a long time since you've been back, sir?" The American seemed interested.

"Good Lord, no." Spencer laughed. "I come back most years. My boy is here now. Not in this house unfortunately. But I always try to sneak away from the family for a few moments and relive old memories. I was telling my friend as we were coming here about the occasion when myself and some school chums . . ."

The American had lost interest. He had judged Spencer and found him harmless. Now he was anxious to avoid listening to any long-winded, boring anecdote. He interrupted Spencer politely.

"That's very interesting, sir. I'm sure the old place must hold many pleasant memories for you. I only wish I could stay and hear all about it, but you'll have to excuse me. I'm wanted elsewhere."

"Of course. Goodbye." Spencer nodded pleasantly, and asked Macrae, "Okay?"

"Sure." Macrae grinned.

They retraced their path back out into the roadway and casually strolled on.

"Can you do it?" Spencer wanted to know.

The Australian nodded. "Sure. It'll be easy. I can bring it down on the lawn or hover above the flat roof."

"Okay." Spencer was satisfied. "Let's take a look at the river now . . ."

"I must say that your visit is a very unexpected pleasure, Mr Macpherson." Hubert Mollinson was uncharacteristicly smiling. "I'm sure that Alexander was delighted to see you."

"He seemed to be." Macpherson's homely features momentarily saddened. "I wish that I could spend more time with him. But unfortunately this can only be a very fleeting visit. I'm flying back to the States in a couple of hours."

"It's a great pity that you won't be able to see the 'Homage of the Boats'. It's one of our most colourful traditions. Did Alexander show you his boat hat?"

"Indeed he did," Macpherson chuckled. "We certainly didn't have anything like that at my old school."

The two men were in the centre of the crowd of parents on the patio, and there were many covert glances being directed at the American politician who was becoming almost as notorious here in England as he was in his own country for his hardline views.

On the fringe of the crowd Charles Hoffman was talking in an undertone to the tall, elderly man, Stanley Schellenburg.

"You'll be returning to the States with Macpherson?" Hoffman sought confirmation.

"That's right. I can't stay over here any longer. I've been here too long as it is."

"And Zora?"

"She'll stay to receive your reports." Schellenburg frowned. "I'd hoped that everything would be settled before I left."

A flash of anxiety crossed Hoffman's eyes. "I'm sure that it very soon will be."

"How is your man progressing?"

"Everything is progressing very well," Hoffman informed him guardedly.

"When did he last report to you?"

"Two days ago," Hoffman lied.

"Is everything set up?"

"He told me that there are still a few more details to settle," Hoffman lied again. "But they're only minor."

"They had better be only minor," Schellenburg snapped, and then warned, "on your head be it, if anything goes wrong." He gave Hoffman his empty wine glass as if the other man were a servant, ordering curtly, "Get rid of that, will you." And turned to make his way through the crowd to Macpherson's side.

Hoffman's patrician face hardened at this gesture of humiliation, and he cursed inwardly as he looked down at the empty glass in his right hand, and his own half full glass in his left hand. "Arrogant American bastard!"

"Henry, it's time we were moving." Schellenburg rudely interrupted Macpherson's conversation, totally ignoring Hubert Mollinson.

The Housemaster's skull-like features darkened ominously. He resented the elderly man's bad manners, and he reacted by telling the interrupter acidly, "I was discussing a private matter with Mr Macpherson."

Schellenburg did not even glance at him. Instead he told Macpherson, "I'll wait in the car for you, Henry." And stalked off.

Macpherson's homely features displayed some embarrassment.

"I'm afraid Stanley lacks social graces, Mr Mollinson. He's a dear friend and a most valuable colleague, but . . ." He allowed the sentence to hang in the air.

He took Mollinson's hand and shook it warmly. "Thank you for looking after the boy. I'd better say Goodbye to Charles Hoffman."

Hoffman walked through the garden with Macpherson.

"When will you be coming back to see us again, Henry?"

"That's hard to say, Charles. Why don't you come over and visit with me?"

"But surely you'll be too busy with your campaign," Hoffman demurred.

"Never too busy not to have time for old friends, Charles. Try and come over in time for the primaries. I'm sure you'll find our way of doing things very interesting to witness."

"I'm sure I shall."

"Are you staying to watch this 'Homage' ceremony? I feel guilty at having to miss Alexander's big moment."

"Yes, I shall stay," Hoffman assured him.

"Is his mother coming down to watch him?"

"I believe she is." Hoffman's smile held a hint of spite. "But I can't be sure. Lydia has a tendency to alter her plans at the final moment."

"Don't I know it," the other man agreed ruefully. "Changing her plans at the last second is Lydia's speciality."

Chapter Twenty

LYDIA Margrave was tall and slender, and still dressed with the panache and style of the top fashion model she had once been, but she was now forty-three years of age, and despite all that the plastic surgeons, the beauticians, the hairdressers, the masseurs and the personal trainers could do, the passing years had taken their inevitable toll. Men still looked at her, but now their gaze did not linger, and after brief study passed on to younger, fresher faces, perter, firmer breasts, softer, smoother skin.

Of course, she still attracted some admirers. Some men pursued her. But Lydia Margrave was all too well aware that their professed love and desire were not for herself, but for the wealth they erroneously believed she possessed. As soon as discovery was made that she lived on an allowance from her ex-husband and had no money of her own, the intimate dinners, the flowers, the phone calls came to an abrupt end, and the empty, seemingly pointless hours engulfed her once more.

Lydia Margrave was not a self-sufficient woman. She lacked the intellectual resources and strength of character to be capable of enjoying, or even merely coming to terms with a solitary existence. She needed human companionship, yet did not possess the capacity for selfless friendship which would attract and bind that companionship to her. She desperately wanted a man in her life. A warm and loving partner to care for her and to cherish her. Without such a partner, Lydia Margrave was a sad and lonely woman, dreading the coming years she seemed fated to spend alone.

Her relationship with her only child, Alexander, had always been an emotional dichotomy. Whenever she was apart from him, she wanted to be with him. Whenever she was with him, she found after a brief period that he irritated her intensely.

She had imagined motherhood to be a rosy, smiling baby, a delightful well-behaved child, a charming teenager.

The reality of the squalling, smelly red-faced scrap of humanity, who had for long months grotesquely disfigured her perfect body, caused her physical agony at birth, and to add insult to injury then demanded her constant attention, had come as a horrifying shock, and she had instantly relinquished this newly born nightmare to a succession of nannies.

Through the years of Alexander's infancy, childhood and early teens, Lydia had suffered periodic torments of guilt for not being the ideal mother she had envisiaged herself as becoming. Driven by this guilt, she would dismiss the current nanny and take on the care of her child herself.

But the tearful toddler, the secretive child, the sullen teen-ager, never ever displayed appreciation or showed gratitude for the sacrifices of her precious time and effort his mother was making for him, and she would grow resentful and angry, and give him once more into the care of nannies and boarding schools. And yet, despite this seemingly endless cycle of guilt, frustration and anger, she was convinced that she deeply and truly loved her child. The harsh fact that she loved the dream, and not the reality, continued to elude her.

Today she was being escorted to Martyrs College by Alan Cadwallader, an aging, florid-featured, pot-bellied actor, with luxuriantly curling locks of dyed black hair, whose profes-sional career had mainly consisted of resting between engage-ments. He claimed that his lack of roles was because he refused to betray his artistic integrity, and that he was wealthy enough only to work when he chose to, but in reality he was a ham and in desperate financial straits.

Lydia was under no illusions about Cadwallader. He pro-fessed his adoration, but he had not yet discovered that she had no money of her own, although he constantly tried to inveigle her into telling him how she was situated financially.

The couple had travelled to Martyrs College in her small saloon car, and Lydia had spent the journey berating her ex-husband's miserliness in not allowing her sufficient finan-cial resources to enable her to run a more expensive mod-el.

"But surely, darling, you could use some of your own money," Cadwallader fished.

Lydia evaded the hidden bait with practised ease.

"Why should I use my own money for necessities?" she

demanded angrily, "when he lavishes so much money on that American bitch and her pups."

Her resentment boiled at the thought of the luxurious lifestyle the second wife and family enjoyed.

She parked her small car alongside a huge, gleaming, custom-built, foreign limousine, and envy was a bitter taste in her mouth.

Alan Cadwallader stared superciliously at the car. "Obviously owned by a nouveau, darling. Seriously rich, but seriously nouveau." He smiled bitchily. "Could it be one of the younger Royals, do you think? One of the later accretions to our revered House of Windsor? It's just the sort of vulgar display that they go in for."

His sarcasm irritated her, and she retorted sharply, "I never realised that you were a snob, Alan."

He laughed. "Well, I'm entitled to be a snob, aren't I? After all we Cadwalladers are of a very ancient and noble lineage. We were the true Princes of Wales when the Windsors were still only German nobodies."

Although he spoke jokingly there was an underlying seriousness in his tone. He had long before begun to actually believe in his invented lineage. He had convinced himself that he was a true Cadwallader, despite his paternal name of Jones.

As they left the long ranks of luxury cars behind them, Lydia began to feel a little more cheerful. She had taken especial care with her appearance, spending many hours on her hair and make-up. Now as she secretly compared herself with the other mothers who were parading through Martyrs College she congratulated herself that the time had been well spent. She considered most of the women to be plain and ordinary looking, and thought that the pretty ones lacked her flair for glamorous clothes and looked either dowdy, or over-dressed.

But then her spurious cheerfulnes faded as she compared her escort with some of the tall, lean, elegant escorts the other women were proudly displaying. She glanced sideways at Cadwallader, and was sickeningly aware of how seedy he looked, with his pot belly bulging out of his cheap suit, and his ridiculous dyed hair which shed a continual spattering of dandruff.

At Penfold House boys in ceremonial dress were waiting in front of the main entrance to greet the guests and lead them through the house and out to the patio, where there was a hubbub of talk and laughter.

Alan Cadwallader's eyes immediately sought the drinks table.

"I'll go and get us a tipple, darling," he told Lydia, and she nodded uncaringly, her own gaze sweeping across the assembled faces, hoping to encounter a friendly, welcoming smile.

"There you are, Lydia, my dear." Charles Hoffman came to her and she was pleased. His patrician bearing and his success in his profession were in welcome contrast to her own escort's lack of either. She was more than happy to be seen with Hoffman because she believed it increased her status among her fellow guests.

"Henry was here a while ago," Hoffman told her. "He only stayed very briefly. I had a chat with him."

"Was she with him?" Lydia asked tartly, referring to Macpherson's wife.

"No, my dear. He came with Stanley Schellenburg. Do you know him?"

"No." She shook her head. "Is he anybody important?"

Hoffman's voice lowered and became confidential. "He's a very powerful man, my dear. He's regarded as a kingmaker by the American political establishment. An *eminence grise*."

"Is he? How interesting." Lydia felt boredom already invading her. She had little knowledge of, and even less interest in, American politics.

That her ex-husband was challenging for the presidential nomination was a matter of supreme indifference to her. She was only concerned with the financial support he gave her.

"Here we are, darling." Alan Cadwallader was offering her a glass of white wine.

She took it from him, irritably wishing that he would disappear.

The actor stared hard at Charles Hoffman, then asked, "Excuse me, but aren't you, Charles Hoffman? The politician?"

"Yes." Hoffman regarded the other man with actual distaste, thinking, Why can't Lydia at least find a presentable chap?

Then he instantly excused himself. "I have to leave you now. Perhaps we'll see each other later at the 'Homage', Lydia."

The woman hid her disappointment at his abrupt departure. "Perhaps, Charles."

"Not very friendly, is he?" Cadwallader complained. "Couldn't wait to get away from us." He stared about him and observed disparagingly. "Dull looking bunch."

Lydia kept the fixed smile on her face and inwardly prayed for the time to pass quickly.

Chapter Twenty-One

ALEXANDER Margrave was walking with his friend Jamie Grenfell, Jamie's parents and pretty younger sisters, across the wide, cloistered courtyard of Old School.

Jamie's father, Major General Sir Hawley Grenfell DSO, was a bluff, laughing man, and his mother a sweet-faced, dowdily dressed woman, who spoke little but smiled a lot. The two girls were very self-assured young ladies who were well aware of the admiring glances their lissom bodies and long shining hair drew from the passing boys.

Alexander was greatly enjoying their company, but could not help contrasting his friend's family group with his own, and envying him. His upbringing had made Alexander a somewhat solitary boy, who in his heart was very lonely. As a small child he had been eager to give love, but through the years as nannies came and went in quick succession, and his mother alternately cherished and rejected him, he had learned to guard his inner feelings. To protect himself against hurt by not allowing any deep emotional committments to dominate his life.

This became easier to achieve during the years of boarding at Prep School and later Public School, because then he came to realise that there were many boys such as himself whose parents displayed little love or interest in them. Who paid others not only to educate their children, but also to provide a substitute parenting.

Today's earlier brief meeting with his own father had been stiff and awkward. Despite the ties of blood, there were no bonds of shared experiences, or childhood memories which would enable father and son to talk easily and laugh together. Henry Cabot Macpherson had always been a distant figure, and a virtual stranger to his eldest son. Alexander desperately wanted to feel love for his father, but could not.

For his mother he did feel affection, but this emotion was overlaid with a shadow of contempt. He recognised her shallowness of intellect and character and he despised her continual whinings about how harshly life had treated her. Her promiscuity troubled him greatly. All through his life there had been a succession of men sharing his mother's bed, and some of his earliest memories were of the violent quarrels, the drunken maunderings, the floods of tears, the tantrums, the threats of suicide, which inevitably marked the progress of each succeeding affaire.

Now, in the next few minutes, he was going to have to leave the friendly shelter of the Grenfell family and return to Penfold House to meet and spend some time with his mother and her latest man. It was not a prospect that he relished.

"Excuse me, ma'am, I'm to tell you that Alexander is waiting in the front hallway to speak to you."

Lydia sighed with relief. She was bored out of her mind from listening to the inane smalltalk which surrounded her. And Alan Cadwallader, who had been drinking since early morning, and had made frequent visits to the drink table since their arrival here, was definitely beginning to show the effects of the alcohol that he had consumed in such large quantity.

"Why can't Alexander come and see his mother here?" he demanded aggressively. "Is he too damned lazy to walk a few yards?"

The tall young messenger's eyes flitted over the actor's cheap rumpled suit, and there was derision in their blue depths. Lydia noted that derision and was furious with the actor for provoking it.

"He isn't permitted to come onto the Master's Walk between the hours of sunrise and sunset, sir," the youth explained condecendingly, and then baited with seeming innocence. "I thought everyone knew that rule. It's been in place since the year Dot."

Cadwallader bit. "Then why are you here if there's a rule against it?"

The blue eyes sparked with malicious pleasure. "Of course, you're not an Old Collegian, are you, sir. That's why you cannot know our customs. They're esoteric, I must confess. I'm a Praetorian. Perhaps you've noticed my waistcoat?" He indicated his brocaded garment. "The Praetorians are the prefectorial body of College, and on days of festival we have free access to any part of the campus. That's another custom dating from the year Dot, sir."

He made a slight bow to Lydia. "Shall I tell Alexander that you'll join him, ma'am."

"Thank you." She forced a smile, and as the elegant youth sauntered away rounded angrily on Cadwallader. "And I'll thank you not to make a fool of yourself."

"Me? Make a fool of myself?" He blustered. "I only asked a simple question."

"Yes, and displayed how simple-minded you really are," she retorted witheringly.

"I only asked a question, that's all." Still protesting he followed her as she returned into the house.

"Where have you been? I've been waiting for hours?" She attacked as soon as she saw her son.

"I came as soon as I could, Mother," Alexander told her. "Jamie Grenfell wanted me to meet his parents and I've been talking to them."

"And keeping your own mother standing around, bored out of my mind." Her face became pinched and ugly in temper. "You show no consideration for . . ."

Alexander sighed inwardly, and in stoic silence endured the familiar diatribe.

Outside in the roadway Tony Kilbeck could clearly hear the raised tones of Lydia Margrave, and he felt a genuine pity for her son.

I don't think I'd like to be in the poor young sod's shoes, for all the money his dad's got. It would do that spoiled cow good to have to do a day's work for a change.

Chapter Twenty-Two

THE buzzing of the disconnected line sounded yet again in Julian Fothergill's ear, and with a sickening sense of disappointment he replaced the handset of the phone. Why had Shafto, his new-found dream-lover, given him a useless number to call? Why hadn't Shafto phoned as he had promised to do? Was Shafto giving him the brush-off?

"Sir?" The high-pitched call was accompanied by a knocking on the door of Julian's room. "I know that you're in there, sir."

Pre-occupied with his own distressing thoughts Julian opened the door and the huge spectacles of the carroty-haired Phillip Gamage-Walker glinted up at him.

"What do you want, boy?"

Behind the smeared lenses sly eyes noted the master's troubled expression. Something had really upset the Precious Jewel.

"If you please, sir, Mr Mollinson wants you to join him immediately in the private side for the 'Boat Farewell'."

Julian nodded absently, and reclosed the door.

I wonder what's the matter with him. The small boy was always tormented by his own insatiable curiosity concerning the lives of the adults in Penfold House.

He turned and ran down the corridor, then jumped the stairs three at a time in headlong descent.

In the Assembly Room on the ground floor the House Wet Bobs were excitedly laughing and talking, while around the door the younger boys clustered gazing at the House heroes with admiring eyes.

The Wet Bobs were mainly tall, strapping youths, fit and muscular from constant rowing practise. They wore the "Homage Rig" today. Short blue nautical jackets, striped shirts, coloured neckerchiefs and white duck trousers; on their their heads they sported straw boaters which were decorated with masses of fresh rose blossoms. The diminutive cox of the House Boat was resplendently uniformed in the full dress of a Nelsonian naval captain, while his brother, who came from another house and was the cox of the College Boat, was wearing the cocked hat and magnificent gold braided full dress of an Admiral of the Fleet.

Alexander Margrave was talking with Fergus Cochrane and Rupert Farquar. Alexander was for the first time that day truly happy. He was the youngest oarsman in the House Boat, and extremely proud of that achievement, and prouder still to be accepted as an equal by his heroes. Fergus was Stroke Oar and Rupert was Bow Oar, and they were lordly, dashing figures in their Homage Rig.

Lydia Margrave had left the house some time before, telling Alexander that she would come to say goodbye to him after the ceremony. But the boy knew that she wouldn't come. She never did stay for the full ceremony, because she found it boring. He felt a yearning for the type of parents that Rupert Farquar had, who had flown in from Singapore especially to see him take part in the "Homage". Or Fergus Cochrane's parents, who had travelled down from the far north of Scotland for this day only. Both boys would be taken out by their parents after the ceremony and wined and dined. Alexander experienced a momentary sadness. His father had spoken to him for only a few minutes and his mother had done nothing but nag and berate him during her brief time here. He wished that there could be someone to watch him take part in the "Homage" and feel pride in him.

"It's time for the 'Boat Farewell'," the diminutive cox shouted. And the Wet Bobs filed out to the roadway in front of the house where they formed two ranks under the directions of the cox, a dominant dwarf commanding giants.

Hubert Mollinson came out of the main entrance and took position facing the ranked Wet Bobs. Julian Fothergill, Claudia Mollinson and Maggie Stevens stood slightly behind and flanking the Housemaster.

The cox called the Wet Bobs to attention, and Hubert Mollinson lifted his mortarboard to them in salute, Julian Fothergill following suit.

"God speed your boat, and send you a safe return, Gentlemen!" Mollinson shouted.

"AMEN!" The Wet Bobs bellowed in unison.

"Boat Crew, left turn!" the cox screeched. "By the left, quick march."

Like a squad of soldiers the Wet Bobs marched away; in other houses throughout the College the same scene occurred, and the crews traversed their differing routes all converging onto the road that led to the riverside boathouse.

The crowds came hurrying to line the route, cheering and clapping, and Alexander Margrave swelled with pride as he marched to the sounds of that applause.

"That's Margrave." Spencer pointed out the boy to Terry Macrae as the squad swung past in slightly ragged cadence. "We'll have another look at him later."

"I've marked him," the Australian assured him. "You know me, Spencer. One look and I never forget a face."

"We'll still take another look at him later," Spencer insisted.

His dark grey eyes were searching the throngs who were making their way to the river bank. He found the face he sought.

"And that's Fothergill. The short one walking with the tall thin guy. He's got the amber coloured scholar's hood on his gown."

The two masters were walking side by side, and a couple of yards behind them followed Claudia Mollinson and Maggie Stevens.

"I've marked him." Macrae nodded, and then his gaze wandered to the two women. He whistled softly in appreciation when he saw Maggie Stevens, shapely in her smart costume, with a broad-brimmed hat shading her handsome face. "I wouldn't mind giving that one with the big tits a seeing to." He mentally pictured the photographs that Spencer had shown him. "That'll be the Matron, won't it, Margaret Stevens. Jesus! Look at the way her arse wiggles. It's making me sweat!"

Spencer scowled. "Concentrate on Fothergill, and leave the rest out."

Still his gaze raked the thronging crowds. He had not yet found Alexander Margrave's police bodyguard. He needed to know the man's location, before he made the next move he had planned.

Then he saw the bodyguard walking with a uniformed

College security man, and he waited until the pair had passed, before telling Macrae, "Come on." And followed them.

The river banks were already crowded and Spencer and Macrae sat down on the grassy slope in a position overlooking the roped enclosure where the College hierarchy clustered in a tight phalanx of tasselled mortarboards, vari-coloured scholars' hoods and long black gowns on serried ranks of wooden benches, together with minor royalty, high-ranking military and civil officers, and an Old Collegian Archbishop.

There was a sudden stirring and pointing of fingers and craning of necks throughout the onlookers as the procession of racing shells came into view, led by the ten-oared "Regius", the College Boat, with its Admiral coxswain.

The shells came downstream in slow stately procession, the long oars moving in measured unison, the blades cascading glittering sparklets of water, and as the Regius came abreast of the VIP enclosure the cox stood up and began to shout a series of commands in a shrill, high-pitched voice.

"Five and six blades up!"

The two centre oars were lifted upright.

"Five and six, stand up!"

The two strapping youths slowly stood upright and stayed motionless, holding their oars as if they were pikemen at attention.

"Four and seven blades up!"

"Four and seven, stand up!"

"Three and eight blades up!"

"Three and eight, stand up!"

Two by two in sequence the entire crew rose and stood to attention, the shell rocking in the water.

The cox, hands down at his side, holding the rudder lines, then shouted, "God send you a good deliverance Master Ridley!"

The oarsmen's left hands moved in perfect unison to lift the flowered hats from their heads, hold them out towards the College in salute, then shake rose blossoms from the hats onto the water.

They replaced their hats, and the cox shrilled, "God send you a good deliverance, Master Latimer!"

This time the oarsmen used their right hands to salute and shake the blossoms into the river.

Now the cox shrilled, "God send our Noble Founder the Queen a good deliverance."

This third and final salute was held longer than the previous, and the rose blossoms fell thick and heavy onto the water.

The crowd applauded continuously as boat after boat in its turn repeated the salutes.

As each boat completed their salutes the oarsmen reseated themselves on the orders of the coxes.

"Bow and Stroke sit down!"

"Bow and Stroke, blades down."

"Seven and two, sit down!"

"Seven and two, blades down!"

When all the oarsmen were seated the cox seated himself and the oars moved in fast cadence to propel the boat downriver leaving the masses of colourful rose blossoms to float slowly behind them.

The final salutes were made and the last boat disappeared around the bend of the river. The smiling, chattering crowd began to slowly disperse.

Spencer sat watching the VIP enclosure until he saw Julian Fothergill start to leave it. He quickly checked the locations of the uniformed College security men, and saw that Alexander Margrave's bodyguard was already walking rapidly away towards the College.

He nudged Terry Macrae.

"Okay. Do it now."

The big Australian got to his feet and sauntered slowly towards the College, allowing the faster moving Julian Fothergill to draw up and come alongside. Then he moved close to the schoolmaster and spoke to him, smiling in a friendly way.

"Good day, Julian. I've got a message for you."

The pudgy, flushed face stared in surprise.

"Do I know you?"

"No, but I know you, Julian. And I know what a naughty girl you are."

Julian's heart pounded in sudden fear, and he blustered, "I haven't the faintest idea what you are talking about. And if you don't go away I'll call for our security people."

Macrae grinned, and shook his head. "I don't reckon that 'ud do you much good, mate." He took a video tape from his pocket and showed it to the smaller man. "See this. It's a tape we made. It shows you being fucked by Shafto."

Julian's face blanched, and he came to a stumbling halt.

The big man gripped the master's soft upper arm and pulled him on. "Keep walking."

He pushed the casette into the smaller man's pocket. "We've made a few copies, so you can keep this one."

"Who are you? Why have you done this?" Julian could hardly articulate the questions his mouth was so dry.

Macrae's big yellowing teeth flashed in a friendly grin. "All you need to know is that if you're a good girl, and co-operate, then you've got nothing to worry about." He released his bruising grip on the smaller man's arm. "So long, mate. We'll be in touch. Hope you enjoy the film. You're a real star in it!"

The big man walked away at a sharp tangent.

Julian's stomach churned sickeningly, and the bitter taste of acid bile filled his mouth. Terror overwhelmed him, and he ran, his long gown flying up from his legs, unconscious of the curious stares he was attracting, driven like some terrified hunted beast to seek dark shelter where he could hide and find safety.

Chapter Twenty-Three

THE phone call came in the early hours of the morning. But Julian Fothergill was not sleeping. For seemingly endless hours he had sat watching the video casette, replaying it over and over again. Storms of anguish continually tore through him, and he sobbed until all tears were spent, and then lay moaning in utter desolation.

Images of his family rose in his mind and he foresaw their disgust and horror should they ever see this video.

I'll have to kill myself, he decided hysterically. There's no other way. I'll have to kill myself!

But even as he voiced that decision he knew that he would not have the courage to take his own life, to destroy himself.

Now, when the phone issued its strident summons he sat staring down at it, unable to find the courage to lift the handset.

The ringing continued remorselessly, and at last, fear and dread chokingly constricting his throat, the young man snatched it up.

"Hello, Sweetheart. Are you all right?" It was his lover's voice.

"How could you?" Julian accused tearfully. "How could you do this to me? You told me that you loved me!"

"Now just calm down. I've done nothing. Believe me, Honey, it's not me doing this." Then Shafto soothed, "It's not so bad as you think it is."

Perversely, even in the depths of fear and anguish, Julian suddenly became conscious of how low-class the flat Mancunian accent sounded. How like a common oik. Sudden fury pulsed through him and he screeched into the phone.

"You want to blackmail me, don't you. You filthy oik!"

"No, Sweetheart. I don't want to blackmail you. We're in this together." Shafto sounded distressed. "But it's not so bad as you think it is. If you do what I tell you, then we've nothing to worry about. Really now, we've nothing to worry about at all. We just have to tell them a few things, that's all."

"Who are you talking about?" Julian demanded hysterically. "Who are them?"

"The ones who filmed us making love."

"But who are they? Why have they done this?"

"I don't know why they did it? But we've got to co-operate with them, Sweetheart. Or they'll ruin you. They say if we don't do what they want, they'll send copies of the tape to your family, and to the College."

"I'm going to kill myself! And it'll be your fault. I'm going to kill myself." Hysteria shook Julian's voice.

"Kill yourself? Don't talk so bloody daft!" Shafto ordered sharply. "Just think what that 'ud do to your mam and dad? It 'ud break their hearts, and likely kill them as well. Stop talking daft. It's like I'm telling you, if you'd listen. All they want is a bit of information. That's all. Just a bit of simple information."

Julian was weeping now, his nerves all but shattered.

Shafto's voice became soft and caressing.

"Listen, Honey, we've got to meet. You've got to trust me. I'll save you. Listen, I do really love you, you know. But I could get killed meself if we don't do what they want."

"Good! I hope you do get killed!" Julian sobbed.

"Listen, Honey, just come and meet me later on today. I promise you I can save you."

Distraught as he was, nevertheless a germ of hope started to wriggle in Julian's brain. Yet still his terror drove him to accuse.

"You used me, you rotten bastard! You never loved me, did you? You just used me. You've ruined my life!"

"Listen, Honey," Shafto begged desperately now. "You've got to believe me. I do love you, and I'm going to save us both. I do love you, Sweetheart. But I can't save you from this unless you help me! Please meet me, Sweetheart. Please."

Julian's sobs hiccuped in his throat.

"You know I love you." Shafto's voice soothed and caressed. "You're the only one I've ever loved, Honey. I can save us both. We can put all this behind us, and make a new life for ourselves. I love you, Sweetheart, and I know that you love me. Please meet me, Honey. Please . . ."

Julian hiccuped and sniffed and hiccuped, and then, unable to protest further, agreed.

"Alright then. I'll meet you."

"Do you know the Cofton in Bleriot Street?" Shafto asked.

"Yes."

"I'll meet you there tonight, at eight o'clock. Can you make it, Sweetheart?"

"Alright." Julian hiccuped. "Eight o'clock."

"I love you, Honey. I really do! I'll make all this up to you, I swear. Eight o'clock, Sweetheart. Eight o'clock."

The line went dead.

Shafto turned and triumphantly stuck up his thumb. "The stupid bitch don't know whether she's coming or going. She'll be no trouble."

Spencer patted the other man's narrow shoulder in congratulation.

Chapter Twenty-Four

THE long bar was crowded with Gays, the air thick with tobacco smoke and the scents of perfumes, and from the garish jukebox poured the tuneless strident warblings of Margarita Pracatan, the latest rage of the Gay world.

Julian Fothergill pushed through to the counter, searching for some sight of his lover's wild mass of blonde hair.

"Hello, Sweetheart." The flat Mancunian accent sounded in his ear.

Julian turned and his eyes widened in shock.

The man at his side had short mousey-coloured hair, neatly barbered and parted, and was wearing a sombre dark suit with a white shirt and regimental tie.

"What do you think of me new image, Chuck?" Shafto smiled wryly. "Do I look straight enough?" He took Julian's hand and led him to a corner table. "I've got the drinks in. I've got you a Brandy Sour." He peered closly at Julian's pale, drawn face. "I reckon you need it, Chuck. You look like death warmed up.

Julian's fearful anxieties burst from him in a flood of angry recrimination. "Why are you doing this to me? Why are you being so cruel? You're a rotten bastard! You want to blackmail me, don't you?"

"Shurrup!" Shafto ordered fiercely. "Just shurrup and listen!" He twisted Julian's hand cruelly; the sharp pain caused the smaller man to cry out and then to subside into a fearful silence as he gazed at Shafto's face, which was suddenly the truculent face of a stranger.

"Siddown!" Shafto pulled Julian down onto the leather bench. "Now just keep quiet, and listen to me."

He glowered into the frightened, tear-filled eyes of the smaller man.

"You've nothing to worry about, so long as you do what I tell you to."

A small spark of defiance ignited within Julian. "Why should I? Why should I do what you tell me?"

The defiance was greeted with an abrupt metamorphosis in Shafto's manner. The truculent glare was replaced with a grimace of disgust and he immediately released his hard grip.

"All right, Chuck. Don't do what I tell you. Leave now. Go on. Just fuck off!"

This unexpected reaction disconcerted Julian, and he shook his head in bafflement, muttering brokenly.

"What sort of game are you playing?"

The grimace disappeared from Shafto's face, and now he looked distressed.

"It's no game, Sweetheart," he said softly. "I only wish it was."

"Why are you doing this?" Julian begged to know. "Why are you behaving so strangely?"

"Because I'm fuckin' scared to death!" Shafto spat out. "I'm fuckin' terrified! I don't know what's going on, any more than you do, Sweetheart. And that's the truth, that is. All I know is that some big ugly bastard broke into me flat and showed me that fuckin' video tape. And told me that if I didn't do what I was told, then he'd ruin you, and fuckin' well murder me! I don't know why he's doing it? I swear on me Mam's grave I don't know."

Julian was totally confused, and very very frightened. He felt that he was experiencing a nightmare, but he knew that this was a nightmare from which he could not escape by waking up.

His stomach twisted and churned sickeningly.

"I'm going to be sick," he gasped.

Shafto was instantly tender. He cuddled the pudgy body close and whispered comfortingly, "There now, Sweetheart, just try and keep calm. I won't let anything harm you. I swear I won't."

He half carried Julian into the lavatories and supported the smaller man's heaving body as he retched and vomited into a closet pan.

Another man came into the lavatories and chortled.

"What's up, Ducky? Did he swallow it?" He stared archly at Shafto's flies. "My God, you must be a big boy!"

126

Shafto grinned and winked, and the newcomer wriggled his hips seductively.

"I'll be in the bar when you've finished doing your Florence Nightingale impression. I'm dying to find out just how big you are."

He made a sucking noise and poked his tongue through his painted lips, then giggled and flounced out.

Shafto helped Julian to the washbasin and used paper towels to bathe and then dry the smaller man's pallid, cold-sweated face and neck.

"Are you better now, Honey?" he asked tenderly.

Julian felt weak and his body trembled, but the awful nausea had passed with the voiding of his stomach, and he nodded.

"Come on," Shafto encouraged. "We'll go and get a breath of fresh air; that'll make you better."

They walked the streets until colour came back to Julian's pudgy cheeks and the trembling of his body stilled.

He was the first to break the silence.

"What have I got to do?"

Shafto pulled a sheet of notepaper from his pocket. Shaking his head in apparent puzzlement he answered, "There's a lot of questions on this paper, and the big bastard says that you've got to write the answers down."

Julian scanned the typewritten sheet and his bafflement increased.

"They're questions about the routine of my house. And about the layout."

He came to a standstill and faced his companion. "Does he want to rob my house, this man who gave you this?"

Shafto grimaced and shrugged his shoulders. "I dunno, Honey. But I should think that's what he wants to do. All he kept on telling me, was that if you answered everything all right, then nobody was going to get hurt. And you and me 'ud be safe."

Julian found the motive of robbery perfectly believable. There had been several recent robberies at the College and the thieves had taken rich hauls of computers, money, valuables and other artefacts from classrooms, storerooms and boys' houses.

He studied the list of questions more closely and the feasibility of a projected robbery was strongly reinforced when he found several questions about the locations of computer equipment, house silver, the safe for valuables etc.

An inner battle was raging as he studied the questions. He was basically an honest man, who took his reponsibilities very seriously. He was in a position of trust in the College and to answer these questions would be a betrayal of that trust.

Shafto watched keenly and shrewdly surmised what was passing through the other man's mind.

"Would that man really kill you?" Julian's troubled eyes mirrored his inner turmoil. "Would he really ruin me? Suppose we went to the police, and told them what he was doing? What could he do then to harm us?"

Shafto smiled sadly. "I don't think he'd really kill me, Honey. But he'd cripple me. He'd break both me legs and kick me face in, that's for sure. And he'd make sure that your headmaster got to see that video."

"But if we went to the police, he couldn't hurt us then, could he?" Julian argued desperately. They would lock him up, wouldn't they?"

Shafto despairingly shook his head.

"If we went to the police, we'd have to tell them everything, Sweetheart. And then they'd have to tell your headmaster about you being gay, wouldn't they? They wouldn't keep quiet about it, because you're working with young boys, aren't you?"

"But I'd never harm any of the boys'" Julian protested.

"I know you wouldn't, Honey," Shafto was quick to assure him. "But you know what the 'straights' are like, don't you? We're all the same to them. They think we're all bloody paedophiles who go round shagging any little kid we can lay our hands on. No, they'd tell your headmaster, and he'd tell your parents why he was sacking you, wouldn't he? Just think what it will do to your mam and dad, Sweetheart. From what you've told me, it would more than likely kill them both to find out that you're a Gay."

Julian's overwrought emotions caused him to dissolve into tears and he sobbed heart-brokenly.

Shafto cradled him in his arms and stroked his head.

"We'll have to give this guy what he wants, Sweetheart. We've got no choice. And it's better to lose a few bits and pieces from your house rather than have me crippled and you ruined, and your mam and dad's lives destroyed. Let's just give the bastard what he wants. He'll pinch a few things from your house and then it'll be all over and done with. And we'll be safe, Sweetheart. We'll be safe."

Chapter Twenty-Five

SHAFTO was jubilant when he met Spencer the following night in the bar close to Leicester Square.

"I've got the lot, Spencer." He handed over a large manila envelope.

"Will he keep his mouth shut?" Spencer questioned.

"Oh yeah. He's too shit scared to do anything else." Shafto grinned. "What are you drinking?"

"Just a beer."

Spencer briefly examined the contents of the envelope while Shafto was ordering the drinks. At first glance it appeared that Spencer had got what he wanted. Sketch maps of the house interior and detailed explanations of the house routines.

He pushed the sheets of paper back into the envelope and laid it on the table, tapping it with his fingers while his cold eyes studied his companion.

Shafto carried the drinks back to the table and noticed Spencer's calculating stare.

"What's up?" he questioned anxiously. "What are you looking at me like that for? I've done good, haven't I? That stuff is what you wanted, ain't it?"

Spencer nodded, but made no reply. He was in fact considering whether Shafto's usefulness was at an end. Whether or not it was time for Shafto to be eliminated.

He smiled at the anxious, thin face. "You've done very well, Shafto. I'm pleased with you."

Shafto sighed with relief. "I'm fuckin' well glad to hear that, Spencer. I had that fat little bastard crying all over me pillows last night. Soaked 'um through, he did. And I had to screw him twice to cheer him up. But he went off back to school this morning wi' a smile on his chops."

He took a long gulping drink, and then asked, "Have I to keep on seeing him, Spencer?"

Spencer decided that Shafto and Julian Fothergill might still be of use. He nodded. And with that nod the death sentence on his companion was temporarily postponed.

He didn't touch his fresh drink, instead he stood up and told Shafto, "Keep the fat boy happy, buy him a present or something. Here . . ." He peeled off some banknotes from a thick wad and dropped them onto the table.

Shafto grinned delightedly and snatched them up. "Thanks, Spencer. Thanks very much."

"Remember now, stay off the scene," Spencer instructed. "I'll be in touch."

He walked away leaving the other man smiling happily.

Outside in the street it was drizzling, there were fewer pedestrians than earlier and the traffic was sparser. Spencer looked about for a taxi but could see none and, turning up his coat collar against the fine rain, he began to walk back to his hotel. He passed brightly-lit shop fronts and dimly-lit club entrances from which despite the lateness of the hour men and women issued invitations to enter.

Spencer was satisfied with the way his plans were progressing. The first instalments of his fee had been processed through various offshore accounts, and laundered successfully.

He intended to get in touch with Charles Hoffman in the next few days and finalise arrangements for the payment for the completion of the operation. But, first he was to complete the recruitment of his strike force and make arrangements for the helicopter.

He had also completed the necessary reconnaissance for his emergency plan which he would hold in readiness should Hoffman and his clients attempt a double-cross.

He pictured Shafto's anxious face, and briefly pondered how best to kill him when the time came. He had no personal malice against the man; it was merely a matter of tying up loose ends and leaving no traces behind. There would be other loose ends to be tied up and other traces to be erased both during and after this operation. And when that was done Spencer intended to disappear. After this operation there would no longer be a man named Spencer. Spencer would longer exist.

He suddenly noted two coloured youths, baseball caps worn back to front, standing in a doorway some distance in front of him, their heads constantly turning as they watched the street. Instantly his sense of danger alerted and he crossed over to the other side of the roadway, covertly watching for any movement on their part.

They remained motionless as he passed them but before he had travelled many yards further they were crossing the road to follow behind him.

Spencer's route to his hotel would soon take him out of this district and along quieter, more deserted streets. He briefly considered whether he should turn back to where there was still some safety of pedestrians and traffic. But then a savage anger suddenly swept over him. A fury of resentment that these two gutter rats should dare to hunt him. The lust to destroy became overpowering and he deliberately turned into a dark alleyway and hurried along its length searching about him for anything that he could utilise as a weapon.

The two pursuers ran into the alleyway behind him and were fast closing the distance between themselves and their quarry.

Spencer saw two empty milk bottles on a doorstep just ahead of him. The youths were now so close that he could hear their panting breaths. He suddenly darted sideways, snatched up a bottle in each hand, turned and hurled himself at his pursuers.

The speed of his onslaught caught both youths by surprise and before they could react he had smashed a bottle into the face of the foremost, then pivoted and swung his foot in a sweeping kick at the second youth's knee. The impact jarred up his leg as the youth was knocked off balance to fall sprawling. Spencer kicked again at the unprotected head and the youth cried out in pain and slumped face downwards. The first youth was bleeding, his face badly cut by the shattering bottle, but now he had a knife in his hand and he slashed out wildly. Spencer ducked back from the blade and threw the second bottle at his attacker's bloody face. The youth instinctivly lifted both arms to shield himself and Spencer's following kick took him squarely between the legs. He screamed, his knees sagged, the knife dropped to the ground. Spencer snatched it up and drove the blade deep into the youth's throat. Then he turned and ran. He rounded one corner, then another and then a third before slowing to a quick walk, his chest heaving as he sucked breath into his straining lungs. The street he was now on was empty of people, the only sign of life a cat arching its back to rub against a row of railings. The cat saw Spencer and with tail raised ran towards him. Spencer grinned and bent to stroke the purring animal. His breathing was easier now, and he experienced intense elation as he relived the brief moments of combat.

Then his seething madness roused from dormancy, and the cat clawed and spat and raced away. Images crowded Spencer's brain, dark faces screaming in terror, blood spurting from shattered bodies, tender thighs spreading in helpless, abject surrender. Sexual excitement coursed through him and his blood pounded, engorging his manhood into throbbing erection. Breathing harshly he hurried on through the streets, heading towards the area where he would find female flesh for sale.

The woman was fat, her flesh hanging in loose rolls stinking of sweat and cheap perfume, her breath acrid with ganja. Spencer paid the asking price without haggling. He took her standing against an alley wall. Ramming himself into her flaccid body, ignoring her protests at his roughness, until orgasm shuddered through him.

He turned from her without a word and walked away.

She stolidly watched his tall figure until it disappeared around the corner of the alley, then pulled down her tight skirt and wearily went back to wait for another customer to approach her.

Chapter Twenty-Six

ZORA Ahksar stared at the naked reflection of her voluptuous body in the full length mirror, and blessed the good fortune that had given her such a potent weapon. Even the strongest of men could be bent to her will by the lure of her flesh.

She thought of her besotted lover, Stanley Schellenburg, and her dark eyes flashed hatred. For long long months she had endured his insatiable ravaging of her body. He was a vicious satyr and the bruises and bitemarks on the satin skin of her belly and breasts and thighs were living testimony to his cruel lovemaking.

But her long purgatory was coming to an end. Soon Mehmet would be free, and on that joyful day she would extract a full payment for every bruise, every bite, every sexual degradation that Schellenburg had inflicted upon her. Before she had done with him, he would be begging for the merciful release of death.

Her thoughts turned to Charles Hoffman and she became uneasy in her mind. She was convinced that Schellenburg was sorely mistaken in his derisive contempt for Hoffman, whom he considered to be a weak, effete coward. She considered Hoffman to be more like a venomous snake, who like all snakes would try to avoid dangerous confrontation, but when attacked would strike back with deadly effect.

She visualised the lean elegance of Hoffman's man, Spencer, and a slight shiver ran through her body. She had seen the man only twice. Once in the restaurant and again at the Art Gallery. On both occasions that same shiver of dread had run through her body as she had suddenly remembered the terrifying childhood stories her Arab nursemaid had told her about the evil djin, '*Al Maut Shaitan*', 'The Death Devil'.

She had known many dangerous men in her life. Many killers. But all her instincts warned her that she had never before known such a natural born killer as this man Spencer.

Anger fired in her. Schellenburg had been contemptuous of Spencer also, asserting that he was just another hired thug. Schellenburg's arrogance was a wilful blindness, and his contempt for his fellow men was like a stupid, self-inflicted wound. A wound which would one day inevitably cripple him and render him helpless before his enemies.

Zora never made the mistake of underestimating her enemies' capabilities. Sometimes she was contemptuous of certain enemies, but she always bore in her mind the fact that they might well have the capacity to destroy her.

She began to dress, the wisps of white silk and lace underwear accentuating rather than concealing the sensual curves of her body. She drew sheer silk stockings onto her long slender legs, and then chose a simple white dress which contrasted strikingly with her olive skin and raven black hair and eyes.

Afterwards she brushed her long hair until it fell in shining waves to her rounded shoulders and examined her face in the dressing table mirror. Her complexion was marred by a scar which showed for an inch on her right temple and then disappeared among the thick black hair. Her fingers rested on the old wound and fierce hatred lanced through her. The scar had been caused by a blow from a rifle butt which had split her scalp wide.

She had fallen, stunned by the brutal force of the blow, and had recovered her senses to find herself being raped by the soldiers. One following another, jeering and urging each other on, and the savage violations had continued for day after day, night after night until the guerilla fighters of the Kurdish Liberation Front had stormed the Turkish army camp and freed her. But the rescue had come too late to save her mother and her sisters.

She had buried their bloody, ripped bodies and then had gone into the mountains with the guerillas. A fourteen-year-old girl carrying within her slender, immature body the growing seed implanted by her rapists.

All through that first bitter winter the helicopter gunships and jet fighter planes had strafed and rocketed the guerilla hideouts, killing and maiming, and the mountain troops of the Turkish Army had ruthlesly hunted for the survivors. Freezing cold, hungry, ill, the pregnant girl had carried her swollen belly through snow and ice and bitter biting winds, and miraculously had survived. Then, in the warmth of a spring afternoon, lying on the filthy ground in a ruined sheep-fold, alone and unaided, she had given birth to the rapist's child. And had cried her thanks to God that the baby was born dead.

She had buried the tiny corpse beneath a heap of rocks, shedding no tears, and from that moment on had become a dedicated, ruthless fighter with the Liberation Front, exacting a heavy toll from her Turkish enemies for the wrongs they had inflicted upon her. She had gloried in destroying her enemies, and had flourished physically despite the hardships of the guerilla life. Then she had met Mehmet Atabi, the young medical student who had risen to high command in the Liberation Front. They had become lovers and Zora had known great happiness with Mehmet.

She frowned unhappily. Mehmet had gone to America the previous year, sneaking into the country illegally to meet Kurdish-Americans and persuade them to aid their fellow countrymen's fight for a Kurdish homeland. The American authorities had arrested Mehmet and now he was in an American jail. The Turks were demanding that he be turned over to them, but Mehmet had applied for political asylum, and because his extradition to Turkey would undoubtedly end in his being executed as a rebel, various civil rights groups in the United States were challenging the extradition in the law courts. It had become something of a cause célèbre.

Zora did not believe that Mehmet would be granted asylum. She feared that the long-drawn-out legal wranglings would inevitably end in Mehmet being turned over to the Turks. In desperation she had gone to America herself and had realised that she would need powerful political allies if Mehmet was to win his case. Always a realist, Zora did not consider that disinterested altruism existed. She knew that there was always a price to be paid and was prepared to pay that price, no matter what it might be.

Her beauty had been her passport into Washington society, and for a few months she had listened and learned and watched for an opportunity. She had noted that Henry Cabot Macpherson was the coming man and that he wielded power and influence enough to have Mehmet set free, but he was very happily married and not at all altruistic. Then she had selected Stanley Schellenburg as her target.

Once she was sure that she had succeeded in emotionally enslaving the ageing politician to the extent that he was begging with her to marry him, she named her price for that marriage – Schellenburg's aid in gaining freedom for Mehmet Atabi. Schellenburg had agreed to use his influence to recruit other politicians to Mehmet's support. But to her despair no senior political figures wished to become involved in the Mehmet Atabi case. There were no votes to be gained in supporting a Kurdish guerilla fighter, and Turkey was a close ally of the United States, so any dispute with the Turkish authorities would not advance any politician's career interests.

Through Schellenburg, Zora had discovered the existence of Alexander Margrave. In desperation she had conceived the idea of kidnapping the boy, to bring pressure on his father to aid Mehmet Atabi. At first Schellenburg had rejected the idea out of hand, furiously berating her for even having thought of it. But she had persisted, and then had suggested to him how such an event might aid Macpherson's candidature for the presidency. The wave of support and compassion for the father that his son's kidnap would evoke in the American public would win millions of sympathy votes. Zora eloquently and continuously detailed all the advantages that would accrue to Macpherson's presidential campaign – the free publicity, the poignant spectacle of a strong man torn between duty and parental love; the countless opportunities for Macpherson to display strength and courage in the face of such terrible adversity. And best of all, everything would end well. Everything would end in triumph. The sheer pressure of public opinion would ensure that Mehmet must be released. Macpherson himself did not really need to use his own power and influence to gain that release. Public opinion would do it for him. And the sympathy vote would win him the presidency.

Stanley Schellenburg was too experienced and cynical a politician to be totally convinced by this hyperbolic scenario. But he could recognise the potential advantages to be gained by her plan. And he was completely besotted with her, and terrified of losing her if he did not help her. So eventually he had agreed and the plan was set into motion.

Now that Schellenburg had been obliged to return to the States with Henry Cabot Macpherson, it had been agreed that Hoffman was to report directly to her and give her the details of the kidnap plan. Following the actual kidnap Hoffman's man, Spencer, would keep the boy hidden while Henry Cabot Macpherson was given the ultimatum: his son's life in exchange for the release of Mehmet Atabi. The boy would be kept hidden until Mehmet had been set free and had reached a safe haven. Then, and only then, would the boy be released.

She applied the final touches to her lips and eyes. She used little make-up and wore only a few simple pieces of jewelry. As she completed her toilette she gave thought to the fact that after the kidnap of the boy, Margrave, she would have added two more nations to the list of her enemies – the Americans and the British would be trying to hunt down and punish the perpetrators.

Her dark eyes sparked with angry defiance. So what did it matter how many fresh enemies she made? The Kurdish people had never known anything other than enmity. Turks, Iraqis, Russians, Iranians, all were enemies. So what difference would adding the British and Americans to that list make to her? No difference at all! She and her beloved Mehmet would be back in their mountains, and from their hidden fastnesses they could defy the world.

Zora was suffering immense emotional stresses. She envisaged the outcry and resulting manhunt which would inevitably follow the kidnapping, and the long period of time which might elapse before the Americans agreed to free Mehmet. She was worried too that Hoffman and Schellenburg's nerve might fail them.

She did not trust Hoffman and thought him a treacherous man. And she was also doubtful about Stanley Schellenburg. He was besotted with her and presently malleable to her will, but she knew him to be a devious man in whom self-interest was paramount, and she feared that if the crunch came, self-interest would win out over any infatuation for a woman that Schellenburg might feel.

Although she doubted these two men, paradoxically she had no doubts concerning Spencer. His nerve would never fail. It could not, because he was not really human. He was a '*Maut Shaitan*', a 'Death Devil'!

Zora stood up from the dressing table and moved to the window to stand gazing out at the street below. This apartment was in Mayfair and was was one of the courtesy accommodations dotted around Central London which were retained by the American Embassy for the use of visiting VIPs. She was here by courtesy of Stanley Schellenburg but now that he had returned to the States she intended to vacate the apartment later that evening and move to an hotel.

Now she wanted to meet with Charles Hoffman and to find out what progress was being made towards the kidnap, but she would not use the phone in the apartment. She suspected that the rooms and phones in this place were bugged, and during their stay here she and Stanley Schellenburg had been very careful to guard their conversations. The fact that if the apartment were bugged then Schellenburg's grunting, foulmouthed, brutal lovemaking would be clearly heard by whoever was listening to the bugs she had fatalistically accepted as just another part of the price she must pay for Mehmet's freedom.

She decided to try and phone Hoffman from a public callbox and turning from the window went to the wardrobe for a coat, then left the apartment.

In the building block facing the windows of Zora's flat, a man laid aside the high-powered binoculars he had been peering through and used his personal radio.

"The subject is leaving the building."

After a short time the answer came back.

"I have the subject."

"Follow."

"Wilco. Out."

The binocular man stretched his arms wide and yawned, wrote down the woman's time of departure on his notepad and then once again settled to his intent vigil.

Chapter Twenty-Seven

STANLEY Schellenburg was a devious, manipulative, greedy man who all his life had wanted to both have his cake and eat it, and for many years he had been able to satisfy that greed by taking risks and keeping his nerve.

When Schellenburg had first met Zora Ahksar he had thought her to be just another 'Capitol Hill Groupie'. A breed which were all too common in Washington DC. Powerful politicians were like magnets for such women who traded their sexual favours for the kudos of being associated with the men of power.

She had been something of a mystery woman, speaking little about her life before she had suddenly appeared on the Washington scene. She claimed to be the widow of a rich Armenian entrepreneur, and that she was the only child of Lebanese Christian parents who had been killed during that country's civil war.

Ever wary, Schellenburg had used his contacts in the CIA to have her claimed background discreetly investigated. His contacts had only uncovered what she had already told him. The Lebanese Christian couple had indeed existed, and had had an only daughter named Zora, but she had been lost trace of after their untimely deaths. The Armenian entrepeneur had also existed, but nothing more was known about his marital affairs, except that he had once been married.

Although it was his lust for Zora Ahksar's physical beauty that had primarily ensnared him as their affaire progressed, he had become increasingly enthralled by her personality, and his initial purely physical lust had gradually metamorphosed into a much deeper and stronger emotion.

Schellenburg decided that he wanted this woman permanently in his life. He wanted to bind her to him, to make her his possession. He asked her to marry him and she refused.

This refusal only made him the more determined to make

her his wife. His desire to marry her became an obsession, and he constantly pestered and pleaded and badgered, but she remained obdurate in her refusal.

Then she began to cool towards him and in desperate fear that he was losing her, he swore that he would do anything she wanted, anything she might ask of him. It was at this point that she told him she wanted Mehmet Atabi set free. She told him that she had been a member of the Kurdish Liberation Front and that Mehmet Atabi had been her leader. She wanted the man returned to his people so that he could continue to lead them in their fight for freedom.

Atabi's freedom was the price for his, Schellenburg's, possession of her as his wife. When Atabi was freed, she would marry Schellenburg.

It had come as a tremendous shock to Schellenburg to recognise that she was just as devious, just as manipulative as he himself. But that recognition had perversely delighted him. It was the confirmation that she was his true soulmate. He felt that with this woman at his side there was nothing that together they could not achieve. Besotted as he was, he had agreed to pay her price.

Much of what Zora Ahksar had projected concerning the kidnapping of Alexander Margrave made sense to Schellenburg.

Henry Cabot Macpherson, although tipped as the front runner, was by no means a certainty for election in the present vagarious climate of public opinion. In fact, according to the latest opinion polls, Macpherson's ratings were slipping, as the powerful gun lobbies worked against him. The kidnapping of his son would undoubtedly gain Macpherson many millions of sympathy votes, and those extra votes could gain him the presidency.

All his life Schellenburg had sought to be the power behind the throne. He had realised at a very early stage in his career that the vast majority of Congressmen, Senators, State Governors and Presidents were directed by others who remained in the shadows, and that those people in the shadows wielded the true power.

Henry Cabot Macpherson's candidacy was the pathway to the ultimate ambition that Schellenburg had always hungered and striven to achieve. He knew that at his age he would never have such an opportunity again. If Macpherson became President, then Schellenburg would be the man standing in shadow behind him, directing his policies, wielding the true power, in the richest and most powerful country in the world.

Schellenburg recognised to the full the extreme dangers of the course he was now committed to. But the glittering prize he hungered to grasp was worth taking any risk for. He believed implicitly that triumphant victory could always be gained if a man had courage and nerve enough to take the necessary risks. And he possessed courage and nerve in abundance.

A triumphant exhultation exploded in his brain and he felt almost godlike.

I'll have it all, he told himself with fierce joy. Soon, I'll have it all . . .

Chapter Twenty-Eight

"GOOD evening, Charles. I trust you'll forgive my calling on you without prior appointment."

Hoffman smoothly concealed his surprise at this unwelcome visitor.

"Since when did an old friend need to make a prior appointment to visit me. Do sit down, and join me in a drink. The last I heard of you, you were in Ankara."

Sir Thomas Hamilton CBE did not accept the invitation to sit, however, but remained standing.

"This isn't a social call, Charles."

Hoffman feigned puzzlement. "Then what sort of call is it?"

"Let us say that I'm here in pursuit of enlightenment."

Hoffman did not like the way the caller was behaving and scented danger. He knew that Hamilton was in the Foreign Office, but he also knew that the man was connected in some way with MI6.

"Perhaps you should explain?" he invited with an sharp edge in his tone.

"As you wish." The other man nodded. "Zora Ahksar and Stanley Schellenburg. You've recently had several meetings with them, have you not? In fact you've had another meeting with Zora Ahksar earlier today."

Hoffman's brain was working with a lightning rapidity – he knew with absolute certainty that he was in grave danger.

"Yes I have," he admitted readily. "But I've recently had meetings with a great many other people. That's the cross I have to bear as a Member of Parliament. Boring meetings, with boring people."

"What was the reason for your meetings with Schellenburg and Ahksar?" Hamilton questioned bluntly.

Hoffman had too much respect for the other man's sharp intellect to try bluster or bluff. Instead, to gain a little time in which to think, he said, "Look here, I'm going to have a drink. Are you sure you won't join me?"

"Perfectly sure, thank you."

Hoffman moved to the ornate Second Empire cabinet on which the tray of drinks was set, and with his back to the other man slowly mixed a strong gin and tonic. Fear was building in him, but he knew that he must above all else keep his nerve and not give way to panic.

He turned, took a sip from the drink and then demanded sharply, "On whose authority are you asking me these questions?"

The other man smiled bleakly. "Now Charles, please don't waste my time. I can assure you that I am here on the very highest authority. I can assure you also, that if I consider it to be necessary, then we can hold this conversation elsewhere, in much less pleasant surroundings. But since we are old friends, I would prefer to conduct these enquiries in a civilised manner."

He paused, staring keenly at Hoffman's features, as if he were trying to read what thoughts lay behind that high patrician brow. Then he said, "Perhaps I will take that drink you offered me, after all, Charles. Then let's sit down and have a chat. We are behaving perhaps too formally for such old friends."

When both men were seated, with drinks in their hands, Hamilton was the first to break the tense silence.

"I'm going to lay some cards on the table, Charles. I would strongly advise you to look at your own hand very carefully, before making any play." He sipped his drink and then continued, "As you know for several years my main sphere of interest has been in the Middle East, particularly Turkey. The Turkish security people have been taking an interest in Stanley Schellenburg's affaire with Zora Ahksar, and they requested that we keep an eye on the couple while they're in the UK. So, naturally their meetings with yourself are of interest to us."

Hoffman feigned surprise. "What ever for?"

Hamilton raised his eyebrows in a pained look. "Do I really have to explain, Charles? I'm sure that you know that Ahksar is not what she appears to be."

"I only know what she has told me about herself," Hoffman asserted. "That she's a Lebanese national who was married to an Armenian businessman, and that she has been a widow for some time."

"My Turkish friends believe that Zora Ahksar has strong ties with a terrorist group, the Kurdish Liberation Front, and they suspect her of being personally involved in several murders of Turkish soldiers and policemen. They also believe that she was and is the lover of a man named Mehmet Atabi, a leading member of the Liberation Front, who is at present in prison in America. He is seeking political asylum, but the Turkish Government is demanding his repatriation to Turkey where he will stand trial for a multitude of offences, and will undoubtedly be executed. Of course the American civil rights groups, some ethnic groupings and the usual bleeding hearts are opposing Atabi's repatriation to Turkey, and at the moment it's something of a cause célèbre."

He paused and Hoffman told him, "This is all very interesting, Tom, but I hardly see how it concerns myself. I'm an old acquaintance of Schellenburg. He merely looked me up and introduced me to his lady friend."

Hamilton's weathered face wore a dismissive expression. "I hardly think that he merely looked you up to introduce you to his lady friend, Charles."

"Why do you doubt me?" Hoffman questioned.

"Because there have been some large sums of money passing through your accounts lately."

"Through my accounts?" Hoffman laughed aloud. "Coutts haven't informed me of any such transactions. I wish they had, because I could certainly use some extra cash."

Hamilton smiled acidly. "We know about your problems with Lloyds, Charles. But I'm referring to your accounts at Shapiro et Fils in Zurich, and the Carolinian International Investment Trust in Bermuda."

Hoffman's shock fleeted across his face and Hamilton noted that reaction, but pressed on remorselessly. "No one's discretion can be trusted in these days Charles. The betrayal of aliases is becoming quite a frequent occurrence in the banking world."

"I'm not alone in having offshore accounts, Tom," Hoffman protested.

Hamilton's attitude became warmer.

"Of course you're not. Frankly I've a couple of offshore

accounts myself. And I truly sympathise with the financial difficulties you have been facing of late. A sympathy shared by a great many other of your friends. You're one of us, Charles, and we don't enjoy seeing one of our own go to the wall."

He smiled in a friendly way and invited, "Now is there anything that you'd like to discuss with me, Charles? Any problems that I can perhaps help to resolve?"

Hoffman was beginning to feel a little less fearful, even though he could not decide if Hamilton actually knew anything about the deal with Schellenburg and Ahksar. Or whether this was just a 'fishing trip', and the other man was merely baiting the water to see what would rise from the depths.

Now he decided to use some bait of his own.

"Do your Turkish friends suspect that Zora Ahksar and Stanley Schellenburg are in some way acting against Turkish interests?"

Hamilton nodded. "Of course they do, because they know that Zora Ahksar always acts against Turkish interests. They suspect that she has inveigled Stanley Schellenburg into helping her."

"And our own people? What is their attitude concerning these Turkish suspicions?"

"Turkey is an ally, Charles. We are naturally concerned about anything that could be harmful to the best interests of a close ally." He paused and stared keenly at Hoffman. "At the same time we are also mindful that Stanley Schellenburg is a powerful and influential force in American politics. He is the close colleague and confidant of a man who might well become the next American president. Naturally we wouldn't wish to cause him any difficulties if we can possibly avoid doing so."

"So if I should by chance discover any information concerning Schellenburg and Ahksar, which might be of interest to your Turkish friends . . . ?" Hoffman delicately let the question hang in the air.

Hamilton's sharp blue eyes glinted with satisfaction. "That information should be given directly to me, Charles. The Turks would be most grateful, of course, and I'm sure that their gratitude would be expressed in a material way. There are some very promising potential investment opportunities under discussion at the moment concerning projects in Western Anatolia. Our people are very hopeful of getting in on the ground floor, so to speak. I'm sure that we could find a niche for you also."

Hoffman was beginning to sense that he was being offered a way out of his present dangerous predicament. And a profitable way into the bargain.

"May I pose a hypothetical question, Tom?"

"Please do," the other man encouraged.

"If that information concerning Schellenburg and Ahksar should be incriminating, and give rise to suspicion that I myself was in some way involved with them, then what would my own position be?"

Hamilton's weathered features smiled.

"Secure, Charles. I should say that your position would be secure."

"And any recent financial gains?" Hoffman pressed.

Hamilton considered that last question for some moments, then replied judiciously, "I don't think that your present assets would be diminished. Any financial increments gained latterly would be secure."

It was Hoffman's turn to silently ponder. Eventually he asked, "What guarantee can you offer for this security?"

"You have my word for it," Hamilton told him firmly. "You and I have known each other since our schooldays, Charles. We were at Cambridge together. You know that you can trust me. Haven't I given sufficient proof of that in past years? We have been in similar situations before, haven't we, when we have co-operated for our mutual benefit. This is just such another situation."

Hoffman thought deeply and the seconds lengthened into minutes, while his companion sat quietly waiting. Finally Hoffman nodded.

"Very well, Tom. We'll co-operate once again."

"Good!" Hamilton smiled bleakly. "You've made a very wise decision, Charles. Very wise indeed . . ."

When Sir Thomas Hamilton left Charles Hoffman's apartment he was deep in thought. As a youth Hamilton had been deeply influenced by a Jesuit tutor whose subtle teachings had developed to the full the Machiavellian potential of his pupil's character. Hamilton enjoyed intrigue for its own sake. He also believed that ends justified means.

147

He was confident that Hoffman had told him all that he knew concerning Schellenburg and Ahksar's motives for kidnapping the boy, Margrave. Personally he thought that Schellenburg was acting insanely for becoming involved in such a hare-brained venture. But Hamilton was a man with vast wordly experience and he fully subscribed to the view that there was no bigger fool than an old fool. Schellenburg was not the first man he had known who had lost his senses over a woman.

Now Thomas Hamilton had got to consider how best to turn what he had learned from Hoffman to advantage for both himself, and his country. Hamilton was passionately and unfashionably patriotic. He believed that if the current negotiations with the Turks concerning the commercial developments in Western Anatolia could be brought to a successful conclusion it would generate immense financial and political advantages for the United Kingdom. To uncover Schellenburg's plot would certainly gain kudos from the Turks, and might well help to bring the negotiations to a successful conclusion in favour of the British interests.

Yet Hamilton was fully aware that to discredit such a powerful American political figure as Schellenburg would gain him no kudos from the Americans. Quite the opposite. There would be much resentment against the British for causing the American Government such embarrassment.

Hamilton knew that he should report this matter to the highest authorities and leave it to them to deal with. But he despised his political masters, considering them to be bungling, cowardly, self-serving amateurs. He would deal with this matter himself. It was too important to be given over to the politicians.

Back at his office he summoned Hector Murchison, who was one of his closest and most trusted aides.

Murchison was a small, slender-bodied man whose hobbies included morris dancing and stamp collecting. Murchison was also a highly skilled and experienced operative who could kill with the cold and ruthless efficiency of a Mafia assassin.

Hamilton shared his information with his aide, then invited the other man's opinions on possible courses of action.

Murchison diffidently offered several possible alternatives.

"We could simply remove the boy from the College, sir, and put him under our protection.

"We could eliminate Zora Ahksar and the Anglo/Kurdistan Cultural Fellowship.

"We could discreetly let Stanley Schellenburg know that we're on to him.

"We could inform our friends in the CIA and let them handle it."

Hamilton considered each suggestion judiciously, signalling neither approbation nor rejection.

After Murchison fell silent, Hamilton frowned thoughtfully.

"This man, Spencer, does the name ring any bells for you?"

"He could be one of several profiles we have on file, sir."

"I wouldn't be happy to leave him running around. From what Hoffman has told me, he appears to be something of a wild card in the pack. Any solution to this problem must, I think, include the elimination of Spencer and his associates."

"Unfortunately I don't believe that we have the time to mount a full-scale search and destroy operation to deal with him. Therefore we must find some way of decoying him and his group to a suitable killing ground."

Hamilton silently pondered for several minutes. Then he offered, "Suppose we let it happen, Hector. We allow this man Spencer a free run to kidnap the boy. Then we simply move in and take them out. The boy as well. That would be a comprehensive solution to the problem." He smiled blandly. "By removing the boy and Spencer's group we please the Turks, because without the boy the Kurds cannot blackmail Macpherson, and at the same time we please Stanley Schellenburg because the boy's untimely and tragic death will undoubtedly gain Macpherson a huge number of sympathy votes.

"We shall, of course, very discreetly let it be known to the Turks and Stanley Schellenburg that each in their own way owes us a debt of gratitude."

He chuckled with cynical amusement. "Of course, in Schellenburg's case it may take him a little while to fully appreciate that we have saved him from his own folly. But I'm very confident that he will eventually come to an acknowledgement of the service we have rendered him."

He paused momentarily, then added with heavy sarcasm, "It should do wonders for the 'Special Relationship'."

Hector Murchison laughed aloud. He always enjoyed these displays of his superior's convoluted reasonings.

Chapter Twenty-Nine

THINGS had not gone well lately for Rod Cawson. Business was so slack it was almost non-existent. One of his two ageing helicopters had failed its last airworthiness inspection and was grounded. His bank manager was being extremely unpleasant about his escalating overdraft. He was four months in arrears with his house mortgage payments. This morning he had quarrelled with his wife, and she had threatened to take the three children and go back to her mother. And now to cap it all this tight-fisted bugger of a farmer sitting in front of him was carping about the price quotation that Rod had just given him.

"I wasn't thinking of paying that much. It's only fencing materials I want moving. Not bloody nuclear waste."

"Look, Mr Harper, I'll be flying across sheep pastures, so I'll have to take out extra insurance. The Welsh hill farmers like nothing better than to put in claims for damage to their flocks caused by low-flying aircraft."

"But it's not lambing time," the farmer argued. "You won't cause any damage. And most of the land you'll be flying over is mine anyway."

Rod fought down his accelerating irritation. Why was it that these bloody farmers always haggled about any price? With the subsidies that they were getting from taxpayers like himself, they could well afford double the quotes he gave them.

"Well, I'm sorry, Mr Harper. But my price is rock bottom as it is. I can't go any lower or I'd be losing money."

The farmer fingered the ugly birthmark that disfigured one side of his face. After some moments he grudgingly accepted.

"All right then. How soon can you start?"

"I'll have to register the flight patterns with the Ministry, in case there are any low-flying exercises planned. But hopefully I'll have clearance in a couple of days."

"All right." The other man accepted, then frowned doubt-fully. "Why do you need to have a loadmaster? Wouldn't it cost less to have one of my own chaps do it?"

"I need an experienced man, Mr Harper. The air currents can be tricky in the hills, and my own man knows what he's doing."

"Well, all right." The farmer frowned. "But I don't like paying men to sit around on their arses. He's not going to be just joyriding in my time, is he?"

For as brief instant Rod wanted to tell this sour, mean bastard what he could do with the job. Then he remembered his overdraft and forced a smile.

"No, Mr Harper. He'll be earning his wages, just the same as I will."

"He'll need to work hard then, the amount I'm having to pay." The farmer grumbled. "Now then, I'll want you to take me and my men down there as well."

Rod sighed resignedly. "All right. But if you want me to pick you up from your home farm you'll have to give me the map reference now. So I can file the diversion on my flight plan."

"We'll come here. I'm not having my cattle frightened by your machine."

After discussing the pick-up arrangements the two men said goodbye, and Rod Cawson watched the rusting Transit van drive away with mixed feelings. Although the cash deposit was more than welcome, Rod Cawson could not help but resent his hirer's surly, bombastic manner, and his insistence that the helicopter must be flown for working periods which would push it to the limits of its flight endurance time.

The job itself was one he had done before on several occasions: to transport fencing materials from the low ground up to the high barren wastes of the Cambrian Mountains. Rod Cawson did not anticipate any problems with the work. But he knew that he would have to resist the farmer's inevitable demands that each slung load be of maximum weight. In the tricky weather conditions of the high hills safety was para-mount. This was the reason that he always insisted on having his own loadmaster. On previous contracts some farmers had tried to exceed the payload while he was busy with the controls of the aircraft.

He fingered the wad of banknotes in his pocket, and felt happier than he had done for several weeks. This deposit would keep the wolves from the door, and might even win him a smile and a kind word from his irate wife.

His thoughts turned again to his hirer, and his smile was wry. The man must be a millionaire with all these farms dotted around the country, and yet he trundled around in a wreck of a van and dressed like a tramp.

I expect that's how he got rich in the first place. By not spending any money . . . Tight bastard!

Spencer drove sedately from the airfield, well satisfied with the morning's work. He would now complete the recruitment of his strike force, slot a few minor details into place, and then it would be all systems go.

He felt the pleasurable tinglings of anticipation that the prospect of violent action always stimulated in him, and was impatient to experience the wild exhilaration of facing danger and challenging fate yet again.

Chapter Thirty

REG Helling walked slowly across the pasture carrying the shotgun in the trail position.

A spring whanged and two discs went whirring across the sky.

In fluid motion Reg Hellings lifted the gun, aimed, swung and pulled the trigger.

The two explosions were practically simultaneous, and the discs shattered into tiny falling pieces.

The spring whanged again and two more discs soared high. The man moved with lightning smoothness, ejecting the smoking cartridge cases, reloading, sighting, aiming and pulling the trigger. Again the whirring discs were blasted to tiny shards.

Even as the shards tumbled towards the earth two more discs whirled skywards, only to shatter before they could reach the zenith of their flight.

"Not bad, Reg." The man operating the discharger came to stand by the marksman.

"No, not bad at all, Ron," the marksman agreed solemnly. "Mind you, that last couple flighted a bit awkward."

The operator chuckled hoarsely. "Ahh, so they did, didn't they?"

A stranger would have experienced great difficulty in telling these identical twins apart.

They were heavy-bodied, red-faced, slow-talking country-men and even their broad Worcestershire voices were similarly timbred, soft and low pitched.

"Who's that coming, I wonder?" Reg pointed down to the narrow winding lane that led to their ancient half-timbered farmhouse.

A shabby Transit van was travelling slowly between the thick hedgerows.

"It won't be Uncle George, will it?" Ron enquired. "It looks like his van."

"I shouldn't reckon so. He's going to Bromsgrove Mart today, aren't he."

Spencer braked in front of the farmhouse, and an old woman wearing a man's cloth cap on her mass of frizzled, dirty-grey hair, and an old army greatcoat tied with string across her bulging stomach, came to its open door and peered at him.

Spencer got out of the van and went towards her; three shaggy-coated dogs came barking around him, but made no attempt to snap at his heels.

The old woman examined this approaching newcomer closely. In his waxed Barbour jacket, moleskin trousers, green wellington boots and a cheescutter cap pulled low on his forehead, he looked like a gentleman farmer, but she didn't recall his face.

"Now then, Mester. Who are you?" she demanded suspiciously.

Spencer halted a couple of paces away from her and smiled.

"I'm an old friend of your sons, Mrs Helling."

She scowled and challenged. "How does you know who I am?"

"Like I told you, Mrs Helling. I'm an old friend of your sons. But even if they hadn't told me all about you, I'd have recognised the family resemblance."

"Phheww!" She expelled her breath in a noisy gust of derision. "Then you'm the only bugger who 'ud do, Mester. Because every other bugger I'se ever known always says that my lads takes after their feyther in looks."

"Where are they?" Spencer enquired. "I want to have a talk with them."

She waved her arm at the hillside. "They'm up theer, Mester. If you goes up that rise theer, you'll hear the gun. Just follow your nose then."

She screeched at the dogs, "Get away out on it, you buggers." And the animals went scurrying around to the back of the house, their tails between their legs.

Then she went back into the house without saying anything else to the visitor.

Spencer followed the path she had indicated, and walked steadily up the steep rising ground. As he crested the ridge he saw the men he sought coming to meet him. They moved with a ponderous slowness, as if the land was clinging to their heavy boots. Their faces were flat-planed and in appearance they resembled the simple-minded, harmless country bumpkins of fiction. But Spencer knew how deceptive that appearance was. He had seen both men breaking human necks with their great thick hands, as easily and dispassionately as they would snap the neck of a rabbit. And he respected the shrewd brains that lay behind the bucolic features.

Their flat red faces evinced no surprise at seeing him, neither did they express any curiosity as to why he had come. They merely greeted him.

"How bist, Spencer?"

"I'm fine. How are you?"

"Fair to middling, Spencer. Fair to middling."

"I've come to put some money your way," he told them.

"Ohh Ahrrr . . . Well that's always a useful thing to have, aren't it, Reg?"

"Ahhrr, it is that, Ron. We can always make use of a bit of extra, carn't us?"

The two pairs of light blue eyes gleamed with a peasant avarice.

"How much was you thinking of, Spencer?"

"A hundred thousand . . . each."

Ron ponderously lifted his clay-stained hand and rubbed his nose. Then he said thoughtfully, "I should reckon that he'd want a fair bit of work doing for that amount, 'udden't you, Reg?"

"Ohh Ahrr. I should think so," his twin affirmed.

They stood silently for some time, staring down at their massive hobnailed boots, and Spencer, knowing their ways, waited patiently.

Then Reg lifted his head and stared shrewdly at Spencer.

"I reckon you'd best tell us what the work is."

"Ahrr," Ron nodded. "And how long it 'ull take. Only we don't like leaving Mother here by herself for too long. She arn't so young as she used to be."

"I'm going to snatch a boy, and probably kill a few people to get to him." Spencer knew that these men required him to keep nothing hidden. If they suspected that they were not being given all the facts, then they would not take the job. But he had no qualms about giving them this information. They would guard it with their lives.

"The boy is the eldest son of Henry Cabot Macpherson. Do you know who he is?"

They both nodded, and Reg said, "Ahhrr, we'se been reading about him a lot lately. He's that Yank who'se running for President, aren't he?"

"When we take him there'll be all hell let loose. There'll be a lot of very sharp people looking for us." Spencer paused, then asked, "Are you still interested?"

The twins exchanged a look, then Reg chuckled hoarsely.

"The gamekeeper aren't been birthed yet, as could catch us, has he, Ron?"

Ron chuckled also. "No, he aren't, has he, Reg?"

Spencer grinned with satisfaction. He had recruited them.

"I reckon you could do with a cup of tay, couldn't you, Spencer?" Reg queried.

Spencer nodded.

"I reckon you could do with summat to ate, as well, couldn't you, Spencer?" Ron asked.

Spencer nodded.

Reg grinned broadly. "Right then, let's goo on down to the house, and Mother 'ull feed us. Then we'll have a talk."

Chapter Thirty-One

ONE section of the gloomy interior of the Helling brothers hay barn had been arranged to resemble a crude schoolroom. With several black boards ranged along one wall, and a row of hay bales placed like benches in front of them. Spencer finished chalking the last of several diagrams on the blackboards and turned to face the men seated on the row of hay bales – Terry Macrae and the Helling twins.

"Right, lads. This is the target area. Penfold House. Exterior surroundings. Interior ground floor. Top floor. Stairs. Rooftops."

He pointed to each diagram in turn.

"There is an armed policeman on twenty-four hour duty outside the house. They patrol for two hours between reliefs. There are closed-circuit surveillance cameras covering all approaches, but no cameras inside the house. The target himself is accompanied at all times by an armed bodyguard. The target is also tabbed.

"The surveillance control room is the College security office in the Old School Yard, approximately fifty yards distant from Penfold House, but with no direct visual line of observation.

"It's safe to assume that there are Armed Response vehicles on call, which can be in theatre within minutes of any alert. It's also safe to assume that there are arrangements for sealing off the access roads to the College. An alert will be triggered immediately there is anything suspicious happening. For example, any attempt to take out the cameras, blow the electricity supply, attack on the security office, Penfold House etc."

He smiled broadly.

"None of those measures will do them any good, because you will go in by chopper."

The seated men exchanged appreciative glances.

He pointed to another diagram. "This is a flat roof, with a sloping roof coming down to meet it. This is a dormer window in the sloping roof which lights the end of the top-floor landing."

He pointed to the diagram of the top-floor interior. "There's the dormer window opening onto the flat roof. Here's the target's room. Next door is the bodyguard. These are the other boys' rooms. I estimate that you can get into the house, snatch the target and be back on the chopper within a couple of minutes.

"Terry will keep the chopper at the hover, while you Ron and Reg do the snatch. Are there any questions at this stage?"

Ray Helling's soft voice sounded. "Well, I should reckon that that winder 'ull be barred off, wun't it?"

"We can count on it," Spencer agreed. "So you'll use a shaped charge and blow the sides in. That'll leave just a big hole."

"What about light to see where we're going inside?" Ron Helling asked. "Because when we blow the dormer off, we'll blow out the landing light bulbs as well?"

"Magnesium flares. You chuck a couple of flares to the end of the landing."

"What about the copper next door to the target?" Ron Helling wanted to know.

"You'll have to play it by ear. If he comes out, then shoot him. If he plays cagey, then a grenade into his room." Spencer chuckled. "That's how easy the actual snatch is going to be. A simple application of brute force, and if necessary, firepower. If anyone tries to stop you, simply blow them away".

The seated men were all smiling, but Spencer's next words wiped those smiles away.

"The hard bit is what happens next. How do we get away? How do we ensure that we all stay out of prison? Our target is not some nobody's son. His dad could well be the next President of the United States. We're going to have every policeman and security man in the world looking for us. They're never ever going to let up. They'll offer rewards, they'll offer an amnesty. They'll promise anything to get one of us to grass. Every snooping bastard in the world is going to be eager to earn that reward."

He studied their faces trying to evaluate the effect of his words, and was satisfied with what he saw. None of them had doubt dawning in their eyes.

He grinned with savage satisfaction – he had chosen his men well. He went on with confidence ringing in his voice.

"But we don't have a fuckin' thing to worry about. Because I'm going to get us all away and we all know that we can trust each other."

Now the smiles were returning to the faces before him.

"The getaway is always hard," he continued. "A lot of good operations have gone wrong during the getaway. This operation won't go wrong because I'll focus all the attention on the wrong place. The chopper will stay on station above the College for at least eight hours. It won't be going anywhere."

His listeners stared at him in bafflement, and he reassured them.

"Don't worry, none of us will be on it." He chuckled sardonically. "But our hostages will be."

Several more hours passed before the men left the barn. Several hours during which Spencer explained his plan in greater detail, and then made his men rehearse the actual kidnap. They laid out a rough mock-up of the top floor of Penfold House, and practised the sequence of movement over and over again.

It was dawn when Spencer drove away from the isolated farmhouse. Macrae was staying there with the Helling twins until the operation took place.

As he journeyed back towards London, Spencer decided that he would immediately put into motion his alternative plan.

Treachery was an ever-present factor, almost an integral part of Spencer's deadly trade. So he always prepared alternative plans into which he could instantly switch should the need arise. If those alternative plans necessitated that he should act treacherously himself, well that too was only part of the game, and it caused him no concern.

If anyone involved in this present operation were planning a double-cross of some sort, Spencer would be ready to counter it.

Chapter Thirty-Two

THE 'Atelier' was the very newest and trendiest gallery in London, specialising in the work of the most outrageous and avant garde artists. Currently it was showing the work of Bruno Higgins from Bradford, the latest sensation to come to the notice of the artistic world.

Lydia Margrave stood staring at the tangle of rusty barbed wire which rested on top of a mound of human excreta, and consulted her catalogue for its title.

'Married Sex'.

She sniffed disdainfully and the stench of the damp turds caused her to grimace in disgust.

"My own sentiments entirely. The artist should be buried in his own creation."

The male voice murmuring in her ear caused her to turn in shock.

"I'm so sorry. I didn't mean to alarm you. Please forgive me."

He was tall, lean and elegantly dressed, his close-cropped, iron-grey hair and moustache giving him a military air.

Lydia Margrave had always possessed an eye for quality clothes and she could instantly recognise that this man's clothes were of a very high quality indeed.

She smiled. "You didn't alarm me. I was startled, that's all."

He returned her smile and she noted his strong white teeth.

"It's the most awful rubbish, isn't it?" He gestured towards the exhibit and then widened his gesture to include the chattering crowd around them. "Whenever I see stuff like this, and hear people like these acclaiming it as great art, I'm always reminded of the story of the Emperor's New Clothes."

Then he paused, and chuckled wryly. "But perhaps I'm causing offence? Are you an admirer of Bruno's work?"

"Certainly not!" she stated forcefully. "I think it's absolute rubbish. I'm only here because my friend wanted to come."

"Your friend?"

"Estelle. Estelle Court. She's over there."

She nodded towards the fat, over-dressed, over-made-up, platinum-haired woman who was in the group of adulating admirers listening to the long-haired, ragged-jeaned Bruno ranting about his art in foul-tongued diatribe.

The tall man again chuckled wryly. "Thank God I didn't voice my opinions to the lady. She appears to be an avid admirer of the man."

He offered his hand. "My name is Rafe Glanville."

She readily took his fingers. "I'm Lydia Margrave."

"Is that Mrs, Miss or Ms?" he smiled.

"I think Ms." She suddenly began to feel quite flirtatious. She found him a very attractive man.

He made no attempt to lengthen their physical contact, but she detected the slight momentary increase in the pressure of his grip as he released her hand.

She saw the admiration in his face as he looked at her, and a warm glow invaded her. It seemed a long time since any man had stared at her with such uncalculating admiration.

"I've a confession to make, Ms Margrave. But I'm afraid that it may offend you." He became almost sombre in manner.

"A confession?" She was instantly intrigued. "A confession that might offend me?"

He nodded slowly, and then very seriously told her, "I was on my way to the Flemish Exhibition in Warners Gallery, and I happened to see you through the window there. I watched you for some time, and I knew that I had to meet you. It's not something that I've ever done before – introduced myself to a strange lady that I've only seen by chance. But it was an overwhelming impulsion. I really couldn't resist it. I truly hope that you're not offended by my approaching you in this way."

Doubt appeared in his expression. "Perhaps I'd better leave?"

Her hand moved involuntarily to detain him. She was charmed both by his explanation, and by the sudden diffidence.

"No. There's no need for you to go. I'm enjoying talking with you."

"Really?" Still doubtful, he sought further assurance, and she hastened to give it.

"Yes. Really. I'm enjoying talking with you."

He beamed delightedly at her, and impulsivly asked, "Would you like to come and see the Flemish Exhibition? There are some particularly fine Breughels, both the Elder and the Younger."

She frowned uncertainly and her eyes flickered towards Estelle Court, who was now talking volubly to the artist.

He followed the direction of her gaze. "Your friend seems to be perfectly happy, Ms Margrave. I'm sure she won't mind loaning me your company for a little while."

Lydia Margrave was very tempted to go with this attractive stranger, but still held back.

"I'm sorry. I'm being too forward." His voice was low, and there was a hint of desolation in its tone. "It's only that there are times when loneliness becomes a burden that's very hard to bear. I can look at a great painting and draw pleasure from its beauty. But without someone to share that beauty with, the pleasure is always sadly muted."

His words touched a responsive chord within her.

"Oh yes, Mr Glanville. I know exactly what you mean. I know that feeling so well."

She nodded at him. "I'll come."

"Shall I wait here while you tell your friend?"

Lydia laughed, and for a brief instant resembled the mischievous girl she had once been.

"She won't even notice that I'm gone. And not give a damn when she finds out." The urge to confide in him was momentarily overwhelming. "To be perfectly honest, I can't stand the woman. The only reason I came with her was because I was sick and tired of staring at the walls of my flat."

Giggling conspiratorially together they hurried out from the gallery.

For Lydia Margrave the hours that followed had a magical quality. Rafe Glanville was an erudite and charming companion, and had a sharp wit which made her laugh.

After leaving Warners Gallery they walked in St James's Park, talking constantly. One attribute which she found particularly attractive in him was that he also possessed the gift of listening, his gaze fixed intently upon her, his eyes warm and sympathetic.

When dusk fell they left the park and had dinner in a small, cosy restaurant. Mellowed by food and wine she felt ever more at ease with him, as if she had known him all her life; with that ease came the discarding of caution and their conversation became increasingly more personal, more intimate. She told him of her modelling days, her failed marriage and of her present loneliness, and in his turn he reciprocated her confidences, telling her about his army career, and his own failed marriage. About his wife, now living in Australia, and his two married daughters, both in America.

His smile was tinged with sadness when he spoke of his children, and grandchildren, and how much he missed them.

She covered his hands with her own to comfort him, and soon that comforting touch became a mutual caress, fingers stroking and clasping and entwining.

When the hour grew very late and tired waiters hovered and yawned, he stared at her with a yearning, unspoken question in his eyes, and she smiled and bobbed her head in assent.

In the hotel bedroom he took her in his arms and gently kissed her mouth, then whispered huskily, "I feel that I've spent all my life up until today waiting for you."

She thrilled to his words and when he crushed his mouth hard on her lips she met his kiss with a greedy hunger.

They stood in the darkness and slowly undressed, kissing and caressing each other's body as the garments were slipped off.

In lovemaking Lydia Margrave was as aggressive as any man, and it was she who pushed him backwards onto the bed and lowered herself on top of him, her mouth hungrily clamping on his lips, her hands searching his body. She raised up and sat astride his thighs, then cupped and gently squeezed his long hard manhood. She bent down and took the pulsing rod of flesh into her wet mouth, her tongue sucking and teasing and sucking until he groaned with the need for her, and forced her underneath him. Then it was his turn to take her jutting nipples into his mouth, and to press his lips to her belly and soft inner thighs. He entered her slowly, teasingly, not penetrating deeply and she moaned urgently.

"Don't tease me! Don't tease me!" And her fingers dug

into his lean hard buttocks and she pulled him deep into her flesh, pumping her hips and wriggling against him. No longer able to control his own desire he thrust faster and harder, and they gasped and panted endearments as they mindlessly drove on towards fullfilment. Their lovemaking ended in explosive simultaneous orgasm, and they stayed clenched tightly in each other's arms for long minutes.

Afterwards they smoked a cigarette, sharing it between them, and then made love again, only this time with a sweet gentleness, their bodies moving in tender unison.

The hazy contentment of physical satiation brought sleep quickly to Lydia Margrave. But her lover remained awake, sitting leaning against the headboard, smoking and staring into the darkness, his fingers tracing the long jagged scar that snaked across his muscled belly.

The woman stirred and muttered in her dreams, and Spencer glanced down at her defenceless face, and smiled in cruel satisfaction.

Chapter Thirty-Three

THE youthful pipers stood in a circle, cheeks bulging. Air swelled the bagpipes, drones keened, fingers moved rapidly on the chanters and the ranting notes of the Black Bear echoed across the parade ground.

Welsh Guards Sergeant Trevor Morgan strutted along the front rank of the Martyrs College Cadet Corps, pace stick held exactly horizontal under his left arm, his back ramrod straight, uniform immaculate, boots and badges glittering.

He came to a stamping halt and his black eyes glowered menacingly from under the vertical peak of his cap.

"What's your name, Cadet?" he hissed.

"Levy, Sergeant. Tobias Eliah Augustus Levy."

The sergeant's eyes bulged, his face purpled, and he threw his head back and bellowed at the skies.

"WHY GOD? WHY ARE YOU DOING THIS TO ME? WHAT HAVE I DONE TO DESERVE THIS? WHY ARE YOU PUNISHING ME?"

Broad grins and suppressed laughter travelled through the ranks.

The sergeant shook his head sorrowfully and in a pleading tone requested Toby Levy, "Will you please take six paces forward, Cadet Tobias Eliah Augustus Levy. In your own time, of course."

Trying not to laugh, Toby stepped forward six places and came to a clumsy halt.

"Thank you so much, Cadet Tobias Eliah Augustus Levy." The sergeant was very humble. "And now, would you be so kind as to turn round, so that the rest of the Corps can see your front. There's no need to make it a drill movement, Cadet Tobias Eliah Augustus Levy. Just face about."

Toby obeyed and stood at slack attention. He presented a very un-martial appearance. His tunic and trousers were stained and crumpled, his belt and badges filthy, his boots

166

muddy, his beret like a shapeless tea-cosy perched on top of his bushy mop of hair, and his spectacles, repaired with strips of sticking plaster, lodged perilously aslant his long nose.

Sergeant Morgan began to pace slowly in a circle around the youth, and as he moved he talked to himself in a conversational tone.

"In Martyrs College there are many ways in which a Collegian can spend his leisure time. He can go rowing, play rugby, play football, play cricket, play tennis, watch television, practise martial arts, read books, play chess or cards or draughts or any other bleedin' board game he chooses to. He can go to amateur dramatics, he can practise on the piano, he can lift weights, he can operate computers and he can also lie on his bed and wank himself to bleedin' death."

He suddenly halted and bawled up at the sky, "TELL ME, GOD, WHY WHY WHY WITH ALL THOSE OTHER THINGS HE COULD BE DOING, HAVE YOU SENT THIS WALKING DISASTER ONTO MY PARADE GROUND? I'M NOT A BAD MAN! I DON'T BEAT MY WIFE! I'M KIND TO OLD PEOPLE AND CHILDREN AND ANIMALS. I GO TO CHURCH AT LEAST TEN TIMES A YEAR! WHY ARE YOU TORTURING ME LIKE THIS? WHY GOD? WHY? WHY? WHY?"

By now the entire Corps were hooting with laughter, and in the centre rank Alexander Margrave was bent almost double. Toby Levy was grinning broadly, greatly enjoying being the centre of attention.

"GERROFF! GERROFF MY LOVELY PARADE GROUND!" Sergeant Morgan roared at Toby. "AND DON'T COME BACK UNTIL YOU LOOK AT LEAST AS SMART AS A BAG OF TURDS TIED UP IN THE MIDDLE! GERROFFFFFF!"

He chased the hapless youth across the parade ground, slashing with mock-ferocity at his buttocks with the pace stick while the Corps laughed and cheered and catcalled.

On the edge of the ground Tony Kilbeck was laughing as Toby Levy fled past him. Sergeant Morgan halted by the policeman.

"Did you see the state of that scruffy little bleeder?" he demanded with a broad grin. "Why should our country tremble with such men to defend her shores?"

"Got time for a smoke?" Kilbeck asked, and the soldier nodded.

"Yeah. I need a smoke after seeing Tobias Eliah Augustus Levy."

He shouted to the Corps to stand easy and took a cigarette from Kilbeck's proffered packet.

The two men were old acquaintances and they chatted easily.

"How are you finding this bodyguard business?" Morgan wanted to know.

"It's a pain in the arse," the policeman grumbled. "I'm bored out of my skull. And what makes it worse is that the boys don't like having me around, and the bloody adults look at me as if I'm something the cat dragged in. It's such a waste of time and money, as well. Nobody is interested in having a go at the kid. If the bloody High-Ups had any commonsense at all they'd know that."

"Well, I suppose they must think that he's in some danger, otherwise they wouldn't have put you here," the soldier argued.

"He's in no danger." Kilbeck was dismissive. "No more than any of the other lads. There's always a chance that some nutter might have a go at one of them because he thinks that they're too privileged or something. But in my opinion, if there is any danger to young Alex from a nutter, then it would have been better not to draw attention to him like this. Having him under surveillance marks him out from the crowd, doesn't it? It makes him a more easily identifiable target really, with a plod like me following him everywhere he goes. Tell you the truth, I'm letting him have a bit more time unescorted lately."

"You could be right." The soldier was non-committal. He took a last draw from his cigarette and flicked the butt away. "I better get back and give the little darlings some arms drill. If some bloody beak sees 'um standing around too long he'll report me for loafing. So long, Tony."

"So long, Trev."

"COMPANEEE SHUN! SLOOOPPPE ARMS! THE PARADE WILL ADVANCE IN REVIEW ORDER. BY THE CENTRE, QUUIIICCKKK MARCH!"

The corps marched fifteen paces forward and halted.

"COMPANEEE PRESENNNTTT ARMS!
SHOULDERRRR ARMS!
ORDERRRR ARMS!
FFFIIIIXX BAYONETS!
SLOOPPPE ARMS!
COMPANNEEE ABOUT TURN!
BY THE CENNNTRRE SLOWWWW MARCH!"

In the centre rank Alexander Margrave was enjoying himself. He took pleasure from the anonymity of the ranks. Here, he was not singled out as being in anyway different from his schoolfellows. As he sloped arms and ordered arms, marched and counter-marched he forgot his inner loneliness and became immersed in the close-bonded uniformity of drill. Many and various personalities fusing in pursuit of a common purpose. During these brief hours on the parade ground he could become what he desired above all else to be – just another face in a crowd.

He felt a sense of regret when the drill period ended and the sergeant dismissed the Corps. As he and Jamie Grenfell walked together from the parade ground in the middle of the mass of cadets he told his friend, "I'm going to join the Army when I leave here."

"Aren't you going to Uni?" Jamie was surprised.

"No, I don't think so. I don't think I could stand three more years of being under surveillance when I don't have to be. If I'm in the Army then there won't be any need for a bodyguard, will there?"

"No, I don't suppose there will be," Jamie agreed.

Fergus Cochrane came alongside the two friends. "Rupert and I are going into London next Saturday night after the Tattoo."

Alexander looked enviously at the older youth. "I wish I could come."

"You can if you want," Fergie told him.

Alexander shook his head. "How can I? Tony won't let me."

"There's no need for him to know." The tall youth's handsome face wore a conspiritorial expression.

"I've got something in my room that'll put him to sleep. Then, when he's snoring, you can come with us."

"What have you got?" Alexander was avid with curiosity.

"Extra strong knockout drops. Alaister Colquhoun made it in the chem lab. I tried it out last night and slept like a log for ten hours. Fergie grinned happily. 'Your pig will sleep like a baby when he's had a couple of spoonfuls of this. You'll be able to sneak out of your room and back into it without him knowing a thing.'

Alex was sorely tempted, but was worried about the sleeping draught. "It might harm him?"

"Of course it won't." Fergie was scathing. "Haven't I just told you that I took some myself. Do I look as if it harmed me?"

"How shall I give it to him?"

"That's easy. You do it after Final Assembly. He usually has a drink of something then, doesn't he? You just slip a couple of drops into his bottle or his cup."

The three boys checked their drill rifles back into the armoury and then returned to Penfold House.

Julian Fothergill passed them in the street, his gown drawn tightly around him, his head down.

"The Precious Jewel looks really ill, doesn't he?" Alexander drew attention to the teacher's pallid face and worried expression.

Fergie laughed carelessly. "He's probably just had confirmation that he's HIV positive."

Following some paces in their rear Tony Kilbeck also noticed Fothergill's drawn looks, and idly wondered what might be the cause. He had Fothergill marked as a homosexual and had taken the trouble to have the teacher's record checked, but there was nothing noted against the man.

Julian Fothergill was too engrossed with his own troubled thoughts to be aware of the notice being taken of him. He was almost sick with worry, unable to sleep at night, unable to eat, on tenterhooks every waking moment. He was dreading the time when Penfold House would be robbed. He was convinced that when it happened he would be unable to hide his guilt. Yet even in the midst of his dread, he could still wish that this terrible time of waiting would come to an end. That the robbery would take place soon and put an end to his torment. To compound his other worries, he hardly saw anything of Shafto. His lover had definitely cooled towards him.

Back at Penfold House Maggie Stevens met the returning boys in the hallway of the Boys' Entrance.

"Alexander, your mother phoned me earlier. She wants you to get in touch with her as soon as possible. Fergus, I want to speak with you privately."

She led the tall youth out of earshot of the other boys, and into the empty Assembly Room. He smiled charmingly as she halted and turned to face him, and she thought, I'm definitely going to have you, when Marcus leaves.

Aloud she told him, "Mary Jeffers found a packet of cigarettes in your room when she was cleaning it. You're lucky that I managed to intercept her before she could report to Mr Mollinson. Here." She gave him the packet. "Now hide them in a more secure place next time."

She smiled and caressed his smooth cheek with her hand. Then whispered, "I don't want to lose you, Fergie."

Despite his outward display of confident sexuality, Fergie was still a virgin, and though he lusted after this handsome, full-bodied woman, he was made nervous by this physical display.

Maggie sensed his nervousness, and it excited her, igniting a feverish heat of desire. Despite the risk of someone coming into the room, she could not stop herself from suddenly pulling his taut young body hard against her own and passionately kissing his fresh sweet lips.

The taste of her mouth and pressure of her breasts and belly fired Fergie's own desire, putting all nervousness to flight and he became instantly tumescent. They stood swaying, locked in each other's arms, mouths crushing and sucking, moaning with longing.

"Matron? Matron?"

"Oh shit!" Maggie swore in fury, and was forced to exert all her strength to break free of the excited youth's strong arms.

"Matron?" The big smeared lenses and carroty head of Phillip Gamage-Walker appeared around the edge of the door. And a knowing gleam came into his sly eyes as he saw the flushed faces of the couple, and noted their heavy breathing.

Maggie wanted to kill this sly little bastard. She wanted to grab his stalklike neck between her hands and tear his ugly ginger head from his scrawny scabby body. She wanted to hurl him through the window, she wanted to jump up and down on his body until it was crushed into a shapeless mass of bloody flesh and broken bones.

She smiled sweetly. "Yes, Phillip dear. What is it?"

"Mr Mollinson is asking for you, Matron." The sly eyes gleamed. "Shall I tell him that you're busy?"

"No, that won't be necessary, thank you, dear. I'll come directly."

She walked out of the room without a glance at Fergie, who was racked simultaneously with frustration and delight. Wild joy filled him. He was going to become the next "Favoured One". It was an absolute certainty. This brief encounter had confirmed it. He was going to share Maggie's bed when Marcus left. And although Marcus was a close friend, Fergie was wishing with all his heart that the other boy was leaving Martyrs this very minute.

When his mother answered the phone Alexander could hear a man's voice shouting in the background, and his heart sank. Her calling the College, coupled with this shouting, could only mean one thing – yet another of her love affairs was grinding to its inevitable ending, and he was again going to become the unwilling anvil on which she would hammer out her misery as she had done on so many other similar occasions

To his surprise she laughed gaily. "Oh, darling, I'm so glad you've called. I just wanted to let you know that I shall be coming down for the Tattoo thing next Saturday. I shall need two tickets. A friend will be coming with me. He's really looking forward to meeting you. We shall try to come early, so that we can spend the afternoon with you."

Alexander sighed heavily. On one weekend every month as a special treat, parents were allowed to come to the College and take their sons out for afternoon tea in Martyrs village. For Alexander these treats were always occasions to be dreaded. Inevitably his mother would bring her current man-friend, and almost equally inevitably he and Alexander would dislike each other on sight. The resulting afternoon would be a seeming eternity of utter boredom. His mother would attempt to fill the strained silences with inane chattering and forced bonhomie, and her current man-friend would either sulk or get blind drunk.

Since the introduction of the surveillance his mother's two

visits had been even harder to bear. She had treated Tony Kilbeck as if he were a hired servant, refusing to allow him to accompany the party to the tea shop, and the policeman's sullen resentment of such treatment only added to Alexander's embarrassed discomfiture.

Now he tried to sound suitably enthused by the prospect of her coming visit. "I shall look forward to seeing you, Mother."

"I should hope that you are looking forward to seeing me. Must fly now, darling. Take care of yourself. Mummy loves you."

"Goodbye, Mother." Alexander was speaking to an already empty line.

"Alex is very excited at the thought of meeting you," Lydia Margrave shouted to Spencer who was in the adjoining bedroom.

"That's good, darling," he shouted back. "I can't wait to meet him."

She stood looking out of the window and after a few moments he came behind her and put his arms around her, nuzzling the back of her neck with his lips, cupping and fondling her breasts with his knowing fingers.

"Oh, Rafe," she gasped and twisted her head to kiss him, and he urgently pulled her with him into the bedroom, his fingers already unbuttoning the front of her dress.

Chapter Thirty-Four

SPENCER was wearing dark glasses, casual clothing and a Breton cap when he and Charles Hoffman met at the Imperial War Museum. They strolled side by side through the busy halls, halting at intervals to examine various exhibits, but Spencer did not remove his glasses to read the explanatory texts.

He took a great interest in the actual fabric of the building, constantly crossing the floor to stare closely at different parts of the walls and doorways, until Hoffman was sufficiently intrigued by his behaviour to ask him what he was searching for.

Spencer chuckled. "I'm seeking traces of previous inhabitants, Mr Hoffman. Didn't you know that this was once the most famous lunatic asylum in the world? This was 'Bedlam'."

"I was aware of that fact." Hoffman's nervous tension made him pettish. The reason for that nervous tension was that strapped to his chest beneath his clothing a highly sensitive microphone was relaying the conversation to a tiny tape recorder in his inside pocket. "Are you ready? Is everything prepared?"

Spencer nodded casually, but behind his impassive facade a murderous fury was raging. Since he had begun talking with Charles Hoffman he had stood with his hands casually in his pockets, and in each pocket his fingers lightly held a metal box smaller in dimension than a cigarette packet. Strapped on his forearms were two seperate antennae wired to the individual boxes in his pockets.

The tiny box in Spencer's left pocket had suddenly begun silently vibrating as its antenna detected the energy field transmitted by the bias oscillator used in Hoffman's concealed tape recorder. Had Hoffman been concealing a radio transmitter then Spencer's other detector would have begun to silently vibrate when its antenna picked up the radio energy field.

Spencer knew that there could only be one reason for Charles

Hoffman recording this conversation – the man intended a double-cross.

Yet even in the heat of his fury Spencer acknowledged that this discovery, shock though it was, had not been completely unexpected. It was a confirmation of his previous strong suspicions.

To give himself time to think he questioned in his turn.

"Who are your clients?"

"That's none of your concern," the older man retorted irritably.

Spencer nodded his head. "Oh yes it is. If you want the details of my plan from me, then in return I want to know who you're working for. Otherwise . . ."

"Otherwise what?" Hoffman demanded aggressively.

"Otherwise, I walk out of here, and the operation is cancelled," Spencer told him coolly.

"You've always trusted me in the past'" Hoffman remonstrated. "Why can't you trust me now? You have nothing to gain by knowing who my clients are."

"In the past I've always worked for you directly. If there was any problem with the final payment, I knew where to find you. If there should be any problem with the final payment for this operation, how do I know who to look for? These clients could rip you off as well, Mr Hoffman. Have you thought of that?"

"If they try to cheat you or myself, then I should of course tell you their identities," Hoffman assured him pompously. "But there is no doubting their good faith in this matter. You'll get your final payment, Mr Spencer."

"Suppose something was to happen to you? A car accident perhaps, or even a heart attack? What guarantee do I have that your clients would make the final payment in such a case?"

Hoffman shook his head. "No. It's impossible. I cannot disclose the identities of my clients."

"Then in that case, Mr Hoffman, I shall content myself with the initial payment. The operation is cancelled. Goodbye."

Spencer swung about and began walking towards the main entrance of the building.

Hoffman was unsure whether Spencer was bluffing or not. But he could not risk calling that bluff. For reasons known only to himself Sir Thomas Hamilton had told him that the kidnap attempt was to go ahead as planned, and that Hoffman's own immunity depended on that.

He hurried after Spencer and caught up with him just outside the entrance.

"Wait, Mr Spencer."

When the other man halted, Hoffman nodded.

"Very well. I am working on behalf of the Kurdish Liberation Front. My contact with them is a woman named Zora Ahksar. If anything was to happen to me you could get in touch with her through the offices of the Council for Anglo/Kurdistan Cultural Fellowship. Their address is in the Directory.

Spencer nodded as if satisfied. The short respite had given him time to think.

"Very well, I'll do my part so long as I'm paid."

"You will be, I guarantee it." Hoffman could not help but show his relief. "Now it's your turn, Mr Spencer. What is your plan?"

"The target will be snatched from Penfold House next Saturday night, between eleven and midnight. We go in and out by chopper. We go across country, then abandon the chopper and disperse. I take the target with me and hold him until instructed to set him loose. It will be all very simple." He grinned at the older man. "Simple methods are always the most effective."

"Where will you abandon the helicopter?"

"Lambourn Downs."

"That's Lambourn Downs in Berkshire?"

"Yes, we land on the south side of Ewe Hill. I'll have a car waiting on the B4001 road a couple of miles from Lambourn village."

"Where will you keep the boy?"

"I've rented a house in Reading. Number Eighteen South End Crescent. Everything is prepared for him there."

"What about your men?"

"They're only employed for this single operation. They know nothing apart from the fact that we're going to snatch someone. They don't know my identity, or anything about the target."

"But what if they should talk afterwards? It might give the police some lead?"

"They won't talk," Spencer stated firmly. "I guarantee that."

Hoffman asked further questions, and made Spencer repeat the information he had already given several times over.

A nondescript man on the opposite side of the open space in front of the building was taking photographs of the two men through a zoom lens, cursing in frustration because Spencer had not removed his dark glasses or his cap, and so was still a concealed, anonymous face.

In the building itself, in a small room high up near the roof, Sir Thomas Hamilton was sitting at the window overlooking the museum forecourt watching the two men, and at intervals issuing instructions through his personal radio to other nondescript men scattered around the environs of the Museum.

Spencer and Hoffman's conversation ended and they bade each other goodbye.

"You won't hear from me again until the job is done," Spencer told the older man.

"Very well . . . good luck."

A brief handshake and they parted.

In the small room overlooking the forecourt Sir Thomas Hamilton hissed into his radio set, "Follow him."

Spencer strolled slowly towards the taxi rank. He thought it likely that Hoffman had taped the conversation for the benefit of some branch of either the American or British Security Service, and that being the case he, Spencer, could well by now be under some sort of covert surveillance. He did not waste any mental effort speculating about Hoffman's motives for turning traitor. Instead he devoted all his thoughts as to how best he could turn this discovery to his own advantage.

In the taxi he leaned forwards and passed the cabbie several banknotes.

"My girlfriend's husband is following me, and he's a big bastard. Do me a favour and help me lose him."

The cabbie looked at the notes, then stared at his passenger in his rearview mirror and gave him a salacious wink.

"You're on, Guv."

"I want you to stop outside some place that's got a rear entrance I can do a bunk through."

"I know just the one, Guv. The Red Griffon down Gladstone Place. You can walk in the front door, go downstairs to the lavatories and walk up the other stairs and come out in

Palmerston Street by the Tube. Unless you knew the other stairs was there, you'd never notice 'um. They're round the corner from the pisshouse in a sort of alcove. I've done a runner through there meself a few times, I'll tell you."

"Okay, just slow down when we get there, and I'll jump out while you keep moving."

Spencer settled comfortably back into the deep leather seat, making no attempt to see if he was being followed so as not to alert any pursuers that he suspected anything.

When the cab reached Gladstone Place there was no need for Spencer to ask the cabbie to slow down, the dense traffic was moving at a snail's pace. Spencer merely slipped from the moving vehicle and hurried into the entrance of the Red Griffon.

From two cars, one some twenty yards behind the taxi, the other three car lengths in front, men jumped out. They signalled each other with a wave of the hand, two stayed where they were on each side of the Griffon, the third and fourth men walked slowly to the Griffon entrance and entered.

Within a couple of minutes one of the men exited hurriedly from the Griffon and lifted his hands in an interrogative gesture. Then scowled and went back inside.

A short time later, back at the Imperial War Museum, Sir Thomas Hamilton listened to a radio transmission and swore beneath his breath, then told Hector Murchison, "They've lost him."

"He seems to be a tricky bastard, sir," the man observed.

Hamilton glowered and muttered grimly, "He'll find that I'm a trickier one, Hector. Hoffman's tape has already given me all that I need."

Murchison noted his superior's glowering expression and wisely made no comment.

Spencer was sitting in a small cafe several streets away from the Red Griffon, toying with a cup of coffee. He had much to think about. Now that he was certain that Charles Hoffman was going to double-cross him in some way, he could simply disappear, abandon the kidnap of Alexander Margrave and take the money he had already been paid. That would be the logical, realistic thing to do. But Spencer was not a man who had ever been dominated by logical realism.

By attempting this double-cross, Charles Hoffman had now placed himself very firmly among the ranks of Spencer's enemies. Spencer saw this treachery as a personal challenge, a gauntlet thrown down at his feet, and he was more than willing to take up that gauntlet and accept that challenge.

Spencer took a drink of the strong sweet coffee and exhilaration burgeoned in his mind. He would still kidnap Alexander Margrave, but now he would dictate the disposal of the boy.

Spencer ordered and drank several more cups of coffee while he pondered on the necessity of altering certain aspects of his plans.

Speed of action had now become paramount. Loose ends must be tied off earlier than he had anticipated. If the British or American Security Services were now involved, then Spencer knew that he must strike quickly and keep them off balance.

His dark-grey eyes glowed with an unholy glee as an idea occurred to him, an idea which afforded him immense pleasure. He could tie off one loose end, and extract a sweet revenge at the same time. He instantly rose, paid his bill and left the cafe.

Chapter Thirty-Five

THERE was no reply to the ringing of Shafto's front doorbell, and Spencer scowled as he glanced at his wristwatch. It was eight o'clock.

He went back downstairs and out into the street. The evening was fine and clear and the Soho pavements thronged with people in search of entertainment. There was a holiday atmosphere and smiling expectant faces, and Spencer in his dark glasses, Breton cap and casual clothes attracted no attention amongst the colourful clothing and extravagant fashions that surrounded him.

He spent the next hours searching for Shafto, moving from club to club, bar to bar, and at last in a small, seedy shebeen near King's Cross he ran his quarry to earth.

Shafto was sitting at the bar in company with a frail-looking young boy, he had one arm around the boy's shoulder and his free hand was fondling the slender jean-clad thighs. He looked to be half-drunk, his painted face haggard and unshaven, his clothes creased and untidy.

Spencer moved to his side and whispered in his ear. "I want to see you outside. Get rid of the chicken."

Shafto's head twisted round and his face filled with alarm. He opened his mouth to speak, but Spencer laid his forefinger across the scarlet lips.

"Shhhh! Outside!"

He slowly strolled along the pavement and heard Shafto's panting breath as the man ran after him, the frightened sentences tumbling from his mouth.

"It's the first time I've been back on the scene, Spencer! Honest it is! I just got real fed up hanging around in me flat wi' nowt to do. I was going up the fuckin' wall, I was. Honest, it's me first time back."

Spencer put his arm around the small man's thin shoulders and hugged him affectionatly.

"That's all right, Shafto. You don't have to explain. I don't mind you having a night out."

Shafto physically sagged with relief. Then he questioned curiously, "What do you want, Spencer? Have you got another job for me?"

"Yeah, and it's a good one. It'll pay well," Spencer told him. "Let's go to your place and I'll tell you all about it. Then you can get back to that chicken."

With his arm still around the small man's shoulders Spencer smiled down at the painted face.

"You deserve a night out, Shafto, but business has to come before pleasure, doesn't it?"

"Oh yeah, Spencer. Yeah, it does. Every time," Shafto agreed fervently and went willingly back to his flat.

The House was sitting late, and Charles Hoffman had just gone into one of the bars for a refreshing drink when the Messenger came to him.

"There's a call for you, Mr Hoffman. The gentleman said his name was Sir Thomas Hamilton. He said it was an urgent matter, and he's holding. He's on line 230, sir."

"I see, thank you." A frisson of anxiety shivered through Hoffman, and he hurried to the nearest phone and obtained his connection.

"Hello, this is Charles Hoffman."

"I have to see you urgently, Mr Hoffman."

Hoffman frowned as he recognised the voice, and demanded angrily, "What the hell are you playing at? I was told that Tom Hamilton was calling."

"And so he is, Mr Hoffman," Spencer chuckled amusedly. "It's more convenient that he should make this call."

"What is it? What do you want?" Sudden tension gripped Hoffman and he questioned urgently, "Is it the job? Surely you haven't done it yet?"

"No." All suggestion of levity abruptly disappeared from Spencer's tone. "I have to see you straight away."

"But that's impossible." Hoffman protested. "I'm expecting the division bell at any moment."

"I don't care if you're waiting for the Last Trump, Mr Hoffman," Spencer told him harshly. "I said I need to see you straight away. Come to this address: Flat two, Twenty-Three

Terrow Court off Tottenham Court Road, and take dammed good care that no one follows you."

Hoffman seethed at the other's tone, and still protested. "But I have to vote tonight. Can't you understand? It's a matter of urgency for the Government."

"And I want to see you about a matter of life and death, Mr Hoffman." Spencer hissed the words. He re-stated the address of Shafto's flat. "Have you got that? Now get here immediately."

Hoffman stood silently scowling with impotent anger, and Spencer demanded harshly, "I said have you got that address?"

"Yes, I have it," Hoffman gritted out.

"Get here now!" The line went dead.

Hoffman slammed the handset back into position, and vowed, I'll make you pay for your insolence, Spencer. I'll make you dammed well pay for speaking to me like that.

For a brief moment he toyed with the idea of disregarding this arrogant summons. But he knew that he had no real choice.

He beckoned to a passing fellow Member.

"Jeremy, could you do me a favour? I'm feeling quite ill, and I'll have to go home. Please explain the reason for my absence to Tony, will you?"

The other man raised his eyebrows quizzically. "I have to say, Charles, that you present a picture of rude health to me."

"Please, Jeremy, I'll owe you one in return. In fact, I'll owe you two."

The other man grinned. "Fair enough. I shall hold you to that. Off you go before Tony catches sight of you. He won't be so accepting of your illness as I am."

Within scant minutes Hoffman had left the House and was in a taxi heading for the Tottenham Court Road.

The narrow Court was shadowed by its tall tenement blocks, and from the window of the flat directly opposite the entrance to number 23 a cacaphony of music, shouting, drunken laughter and shrieking drowned out even the roaring traffic noise from the Tottenham Court Road.

Charles Hoffman entered the urine-reeking hallway of number 23 and slowly mounted the ill-lit stairs to the second landing.

He peered at the number on the door, barely able to decipher it in the gloom.

Spencer opened the door to the first ringing of the bell. He smiled and beckoned.

"Do come in, Mr Hoffman."

As he entered the small flat Hoffman's fastidious nose wrinkled at the mingled stench of human sweat and sweet cloying perfume. He glanced around at the cheap garish furnishings of the room and his face mirrored his distaste.

Spencer noted the other man's expression and grinned. "Not to your taste, Mr Hoffman?"

"Frankly, no," Hoffman snapped, and the rancour that had been festering within him burst its bonds. "I tell you now, Spencer, that I will not tolerate being spoken to as you have spoken to me tonight. You are forgetting, I think, that I am your employer."

Spencer smiled and shook his head slowly, and Hoffman stared in puzzlement.

"No, Hoffman, you are not my employer," Spencer said softly. "Not any longer. I've just terminated our contract of employment."

"What the hell do you mean?" Hoffman demanded truculently. Then his eyes widened with shock and fear.

Spencer rammed the barrel of the handgun hard against the older man's temple.

"Who else are you working for, Hoffman?" He still spoke softly, but now there was deadly menace in his eyes. "Who have you given the tape to?"

"Tape? What tape? I don't know what you're talking about . . ." Hoffman bluffed desperately.

"Don't give me that shit!" Spencer hissed contemptuously. "You were taping me this afternoon at the Museum. Now, for the second and last time of asking . . . Who are you working for? Who did you give the tape to?"

Hoffman's mouth opened and closed like a fish gasping for air, but he could emit no words.

"I'm going to count to three, Hoffman," Spencer told him pleasantly, "and then my patience will have become exhausted, and I shall pull the trigger and blow a large hole in your head . . . One . . . Two . . ."

Sheer terror flooded through the older man and he managed to gasp out.

"No! Please, no! Wait! Please wait!" Haltingly he told Spencer, "It's a man . . . an old schoolfellow of mine . . . his name is Hamilton . . . Sir Thomas Hamilton . . . I don't know who he is with . . ."

The pressure of the metal circle against his temple brutally increased.

"Please! Please don't shoot me! I'm speaking the truth . . . I don't know who he's with . . . Some sort of intelligence department . . . but I don't know which . . . That's the truth, Spencer . . . I'm speaking the truth."

Spencer questioned the terrified man at great length, forcing him to repeat himself over and over again, until he, Spencer, was satisfied that he had extracted all that the other man knew concerning Sir Thomas Hamilton.

Then he ordered, "Take off your clothes."

"What?" Even in the depths of terror, Hoffman's dignity could still be affronted.

"Take off your clothes. All of them," Spencer repeated, and the pressure of the metal circle again increased sharply.

"All right. Keep calm. Please keep calm." Hoffman was pleading now.

"Do as I tell you, Hoffman, and you'll live."

"I'll do whatever you say. Yes. Anything you say." Hoffman was babbling as he fumbled out of his clothing.

All of his patrician dignity departed from him with his discarded clothing. He stood shivering, pot-bellied and flabby fleshed, his muscleless arms wrapped around white mottled skin, his spindle shanked legs thick with varicose veins.

"Fold your clothes neatly and stack them on that chair there," Spencer instructed.

Hoffman obeyed.

"Come on." Spencer jerked his head and stepped away from his captive, but the barrel of the gun stayed aimed at the other man's head.

He made Hoffman step into the bedroom which was in darkness with its curtains drawn.

Hoffman fumbled his way forwards until his knees collided painfully with the edge of the bed. He cried out in shock, then Spencer was again next to him and the hard circle of metal was once more digging hard into his temple.

"Get on the bed," Spencer hissed.

Hoffman leaned forwards, lifted one leg and crawled onto the bed, then his fingers landed on human flesh and he shouted out in fright.

Spencer's hand gripped the back of the older man's neck and with brutal ease he forced him down upon the still warm flesh of Shafto's corpse.

Hoffman wailed pitifully and then the length of thin rope bit deeply into his scrawny throat and choked off his cries.

His struggles were mercifully brief.

Breathing hard, Spencer straightened and moved to switch on the light.

Shafto was lying on his back. He was naked, arms outstretched, eyes wide and staring, a black trickle of drying blood running down into his close-cropped hair from the bullet hole just above his right ear. The old colt revolver from which the bullet had been fired was lying on the floor beside the bed beneath Shafto's overhanging hand. Shafto's palmprint and fingerprints were on the revolver. Spencer had wiped his own from the gun after executing Shafto, and had then carefully positioned the gun in the dead man's hand, before allowing it to drop naturally to the floor.

He studied the two corpses for a few seconds and then made some adjustments to their positions, so that they were laying in intimate embrace. He smiled with satisfaction at the completed tableau.

"Romeo and Juliet. Two star-crossed lovers. That's what people will say when you're found," he told the bulging, blood-reddened eyes of Charles Hoffman. "They won't be able to decide whether it was a lovers' quarrel, or a bit of rough sex that went wrong, will they?"

He switched off the light and went cautiously from the flat.

Down in the court he met a bunch of noisy drunks coming from the main road, and he quickly pulled his cap low and replaced his dark glasses.

"Hey, man, where's the party?" one of the drunks yelled.

Spencer turned and pointed to the source of the deafening noise.

"Are you leaving? Ain't it any good?" the drunk demanded.

Spencer laughed and told him, "It's been a great party, man. Only I've got to get up for work in the morning. Enjoy yourselves."

He pushed past the drunks and went on into the busy, brightly-lit main road.

Chapter Thirty-Six

"WHAT do you mean, he's gone missing?" Thomas Hamilton demanded acidly.

"Well, sir, he's not at his home, and his man has no idea where he is. He left the House of Commons at approximately eleven forty-five on Thursday night and he hasn't been seen since. He apparently received a phone call from someone giving your name and then left the House almost immediately after that," Hector Murchison explained.

This news of Charles Hoffman's disappearance following a phone call purported to be from himself disturbed Hamilton.

Of course there could be several innocent explanations for the man's absence. Hoffman could be with a woman, or taking a freebie trip, or even visiting friends, but Hamilton feared that there might be a more sinister explanation.

"Zora Ahksar?" he questioned.

"She's still staying at the same hotel, sir. Spending nearly all of her time in her room. She's received no telephone calls, visitors or mail, and all we're picking up from her rooms is normal stuff, the TV, and radio, and she sings to herself sometimes. Bloody awful voice, she's got, sir."

"We're not holding auditions for the bloody opera, Murchison, I'm not in the least interested in the quality of her singing voice," Hamilton snapped impatiently.

"Sorry, sir."

"Go and get yourself a cup of tea, or something," Hamilton instructed. "Then stand by."

When he was alone, Hamilton leaned back in his chair and considered the possible implications of what he had been told.

Had Charles Hoffman lied to him all along concerning the projected kidnapping of the boy, Margrave?

Had Charles Hoffman simply fled the coop?

Hamilton's thoughts turned to the coming night. If Hoffman

had fled, then it seemed very likely that the story of the kidnap attempt might simply be a farrago. Something cooked up by Hoffman to keep him, Hamilton, happy, while Hoffman made his preparations to flee.

Hamilton's lips tightened angrily. He'd look a damm fool if he deployed his men on false information. On the other hand, he'd look an even bigger damn fool if he did not deploy his men and the kidnap attempt was made.

Was the man, Spencer, implicated in Hoffman's disappearance? And who was Spencer?

Despite an extensive search over the last 48 hours Hamilton's team had discovered no previous file or record for Spencer, although there were several possible profiles which could be him to be found among the ranks of international terrorists and mercenaries.

"God blast it! I should have put Hoffman under close surveillance." Hamilton was angry with himself, yet at the same time acknowledged that he had no reason to doubt Hoffman's willingness to co-operate. The man had everything to gain by co-operation, and had known from previous experience that he could trust Hamilton to fulfil his part of their bargain. It was because of these factors that Hamilton could not fully accept that Charles Hoffman had fled to escape him. He could not believe either that Spencer had somehow found out about Hoffman's treachery and disposed of him.

"He had no such opportunity. If he had contacted Hoffman again after the meeting at the museum, then Hoffman would surely have informed me immediately."

Almost an hour passed, while Hamilton mentally examined various scenarios. Eventually he decided that he would adhere to his original plan. His best marksmen, armed with snipers' rifles and night sights would lay an ambush at Ewe Hill, Lambourn Down. The kidnappers and the boy would be disposed of. The boy's tragic death attributed to the terrorists who had kidnapped him. Hamilton would have another man in the environs of Penfold House, to act purely as an observer, who would relay the news of the kidnap to him. Hamilton decided that there was still no need for him to inform anyone in higher authority. If no kidnap attempt was made, and if the deployment to Lambourn Down became known, it could be passed off as a training exercise. If the kidnap attempt was made, then he could garner all the kudos.

He buzzed the intercom, and ordered, "Murchison, come here please."

When his aide appeared he ordered, "We'll adhere to our original scenario for tonight. You'll take the ambush team down to Lambourn Down. Harris will act as observer at Martyrs College. In the meantime tell Swinton that he is to deploy all available operatives to track down Charles Hoffman. When Hoffman is found, he is to be brought here to me immediately. If he refuses to come, then use whatever force is necessary to get him here."

"Very good, sir."

Hamilton glowered and his fingers tapped a staccato rhythm upon the desktop. If Charles Hoffman had tried to fool him, then Charles Hoffman would pay a heavy price for it.

Chapter Thirty-Seven

ROD Cawson was having a wonderful dream. A beautiful young girl was lying next to him on a sunlit beach. She had nothing on but a tiny bikini bottom, and her pert breasts were luciously firm yet tender to his touch. He gently removed the wisp of bikini, then turned her body so that she lay on her back with her thighs opened invitingly. He moved on top of her, nestling between those silky-skinned spread thighs and tried to enter her. But found he could not penetrate her warm wet flesh. There was an invisible barrier interposing itself between him and paradise. He tried again and again to enter her, his frustration almost driving him insane, yet still that impenetrable barrier held firm.

"Get off me!"

The strident female voice awakened Rod and he opened his eyes and saw only, inches from his face, the angry features of his wife, Julie.

"I said, get off me."

The staleness of morning breath gusted against his nostrils, and it's foulness instantly shrivelled his erection into flaccidity.

Sighing with bitter disappointment he rolled from her and pushed back the bedclothes so that he could get out of bed.

The sight of his depressed face and bent shoulders touched a chord of contrition in his wife, and she offered, "We wouldn't have had time to do it anyway, Rod. You've got to be at the airfield by half-past seven, remember. I'll do you some breakfast, shall I, while you get ready.

"Okay, thanks. I'll just have some scrambled eggs." He accepted the proferred olive branch.

While he showered and shaved, his low spirits began to perk up and he found himself enjoying the feel of the fresh razor blade gliding across his jaw and cheeks and throat. He slapped on aftershave, hissing at the sharp bite of the alcohol. Then he dressed and came downstairs to the break-fast table.

His wife came to him and kissed him lightly on his cheek. She had gargled with mouthwash and sweetened her breath, and he felt a stirring of sexual desire. Even after having birthed three children her body was still shapely and slender, and her face framed by sleep-tousled hair looked young and pretty.

"Let's go back upstairs," he said, only half-jokingly and she giggled.

"We haven't got time. You'll have to wait until you get back from this trip. How long do you think you'll be away?"

He pursed his lips and thought briefly. "About five days, I should think. From what Harper told me needed shifting."

"You'll phone me, won't you?" Julie sought confirmation.

"Yeah. But sometimes it's difficult to get through on a mobile from the mountains. So if you don't hear from me for a couple of days, don't worry."

On these types of field trip Rod always bivouacked on site, sleeping in his ageing Westland Wessex Mk2, ex-RAF helicopter.

"Have the extra fuel tanks been fitted?" Julie asked.

"Yeah. Worse luck!" he mock-grumbled. "They'll give me about eight and a half hours endurance, so I expect that mean sod will have me airborne all day and every day."

"Are you picking Billy up?"

"No, he's using his own car."

He finished eating and got up to leave.

"Aren't you going to say goodbye to the kids?"

"No, let them sleep. They were up late last night. I'll bring them something back from Wild Wales."

He kissed his wife and left the house.

Outside the air was fresh and cold and only a spattering of cirrhus marred the clear skies.

Rod stared appreciatively upwards. The weather forecast was favourable, so he wasn't anticipating any lost time on this job. He breathed deeply of the cold air and his spirits were high. This could be the end of the bad times and the beginning of the good. From now on his business might start to thrive.

Whistling happily he got into his car, waved to his wife who was watching him from the window and drove away.

Julie yawned and glanced at the clock. She could steal

another two hours of sleep before she needed to wake the children. She smiled contentedly. It was so good to see Rod happy again and she silently blessed the farmer who had hired him.

There was something about these men that made Billy Golding feel uneasy. They were all too silent, sitting in a row on the greasy bench in the shabby office, their dour faces staring straight ahead.

Their boss, Mr Harper, had been civil enough, but Billy was a gregarious man who enjoyed a chat and a laugh, and if he was going to be spending the next few days with these strangers, then he would have preferred that they didn't remain as strangers. He had introduced himself to them the moment they had debussed from the rusting old Transit van, but they had not returned his friendly greeting. He had cracked a couple of jokes, which had been met with stoney faces. Then he had offered to make them a cup of tea which had been declined with silent shakes of their heads.

Mr Harper, the one with the ugly birthmark down his chops, had politely asked where Rod was, and what his, Billy's, name was, and had then lapsed into the same sullen silence as his workmen.

It was the look of the workmen that Billy didn't really like. They were three big, tough-looking buggers, with cold eyes, who all looked capable of kicking him to death if they felt like it.

I'll be glad when this job's over and done with, he decided.

Spencer went out from the office and had a closer look at the cluster of buildings which comprised the airfield. The place was a tumbledown, half-abandoned legacy of the Second World War, which had been refused planning permission to expand, and had gradually become increasingly rundown and moribund. All that operated from here now was a small glider club, and Rod Cawson's helicopters, plus the occasional weekend parachutists and skydivers.

Spencer wandered around the edges of the grass landing strip, enjoying the freshness of the morning, his mind and body relaxed. He felt no anxiety about the impending action, only a sense of anticipatory relish for the coming of violent excitement.

It was during the times of greatest risk and danger that Spencer felt most vibrantly alive.

He looked at his wristwatch – it was seven o'clock. Cawson should be arriving in about thirty minutes.

Terry Macrae came out of the office to join him. The big Australian appeared tense and nervous.

"I'd better get a look at the chopper, to see if it's been modified at all."

"Okay." Spencer led him to the hanger where the aircraft was kept.

Macrae climbed into the fuselage and painstakingly checked the interior and then the controls. When he finally reappeared he was grinning.

"She'll be right. I can fly her with me eyes shut. There's been nothing modified."

"Hey, what are you doing in there?" Billy Golding shouted from outside the hangar door, and came hurrying towards them, his face angry. "You're not allowed in there. Mr Cawson don't let anybody mess about in the chopper."

Spencer ignored the oncoming man and asked Macrae. "You're positive that you can handle it?"

"Too bloody right, mate. Like I said, with me bloody eyes shut."

"Okay."

"What were you doing inside the chopper? Have you messed about with any of the controls?" Billy Golding reached them. "You ought to know better than to let your men mess about like this, Mr Harper."

"What's going on?" Rod Cawson now hurried into the hangar, and joined the trio. "What's up, Billy? Mr Harper?"

Spencer turned to face the two men who were standing side by side. "There's been a slight change of plan, Mr Cawson," he informed him quietly. "I shan't be requiring your services after all."

Spencer put his hand inside his donkey coat, pulled out a pistol with a silencer fitted on its barrel and calmly shot both men through the centres of their foreheads.

Both men dropped dropped, blood jetting from the small holes. Golding stayed motionless, but Rod Cawson's heels drummed against the concrete and his body jerked and flapped like a landed fish.

"It's strange how headshots create these differing reactions, isn't it," Spencer remarked casually to Terry Macrae. "The twins can give you a hand to chuck them into the chopper. I want you to take it up for a trial run and we'll do a radio check as soon as you're airborne."

Macrae's ruddy features had paled, and he was staring at Spencer as if he were awestruck.

Spencer smiled at him banteringly. "You look like a virgin whose just lost her cherry."

The Australian expelled his breath in a noisy gust. "I'd forgot what an evil bastard you can be, Spencer. I warn't expecting you to top 'um like that."

Speculation gleamed in Spencer's eyes. "I hope that you're not going soft on me, Terry. Perhaps you've been away from the action for too long? If you want out, then now's the time to say so."

"Jesus, Spencer, give me a break," the Australian protested. "I'm on for it, all the way. It was just that I warn't expecting you to top 'um like that. It give me a bit of a shock, that's all. I'm on for it all right."

"Okay." Spencer nodded and turned and left the hangar. He sent the twins to join Macrae, then carefully searched the office. He and his men were all wearing thin leather gloves so there would be no fingerprints to be found. He wanted to make sure that there were no documents or notes written by Cawson which might give an investigator some sort of lead to follow up. Once satisfied that the office was clear, he closed the door and locked it, then drove the Transit van into the hangar.

In the van were army camouflage suits and accoutrements, and Macrae and the Hellings changed into the military gear. They transferred explosives and weapons into the helicopter, and Spencer told them, "Reg and Ron, find something to cover that blood up with. Old sump oil will be best. Terry, take the chopper up and we'll do a radio check, then pick up the lads and move to the staging area. You've got the timetable, make sure you stick to it exactly. Now synchronise watches. I won't bother wishing you good luck. Stick to the plan and luck won't come into it. You do your part, and I'll do mine, and we'll all be rich."

He drove the van away from the airfield, and parked about two miles down the road. The helicopter was already airborne and Spencer made radio contact. Reception was excellent, and satisfied Spencer went off air and drove on.

He wondered what preparations the mysterious Sir Thomas Hamilton was making to guard against tonight's kidnap attempt, and smiled . . .

Chapter Thirty-Eight

HUBERT Mollinson used a red crayon to write on the whiteboard, then turned to face the class.

"Baring?"

"Sir?" The youth, who had been gazing out of the window, instantly assumed an expression of alert interest.

Mollinson's skull – like features twitched in a rictus grin. "Please do not assume an enthusiasm that you do not feel, boy. I know that the study of the French language is a matter of supreme indifference to your good self."

Muffled chuckles came from the other boys.

"But I am enthusiastic about the French language, sir," Baring asserted.

"Then in that case I shall ask you to read what I have written on the board."

The youth's long hair flopped across his smooth brow and he flicked it back with his hand.

"But it's English, sir," he protested.

"How perceptive you are today, Baring," the master said admiringly. "Now stand up, so that we may all see and appreciate your masculine beauty, and read what I have written on the board."

Grinning broadly, the youth stood and read aloud. "First of all, thank you for your letter, which gave me great pleasure."

"Excellent!" Mollinson applauded sarcastically and told the rest of the class, "You may express your appreciation for Baring's reading ability in the traditional manner."

They cheered and thumped their desktops for a few seconds until silenced by a wave of the master's hand.

Grinning broadly Baring sat down, but then Mollinson frowned and gestured for him to stand up again.

The youth's grin faltered as he realised that the formidable man in front of him was poised to strike.

"Now Baring, I'd like to hear the translation."

The youth hesitantly stammered, *"Tout d'abord pour votre lettre, que pour moi était un plaisir . . ."*

"SILENCE, YOU BLOCKHEAD!" Mollinson roared, and the sudden bellow caused everybody in the class to jump. "YOU HAVE NOT DONE THE TASK I SET YOU LAST WEEK, HAVE YOU, BARING?"

The youth's fresh face reddened guiltily, and he protested weakly. "But I have, sir. It's just that I find French very difficult."

"NOTHING IS DIFFICULT IF YOU WORK HARD ENOUGH, BARING. EVERYTHING IS RENDERED EASY BY HARD WORK," Mollinson bellowed and then his voice dropped to a normal conversational tone.

He half turned so that he could point at the red-lettered sentence, and translated fluently.

"Je te remercie tout d'abord de ta lettre qui m'a fait très plaisir." Then told the youth, "You will report to me at two o'clock this afternoon, Baring."

"Oh but, sir, it's Saturday!" Baring exclaimed in dismay.

"Thank you, Baring, for imparting that item of interesting information." Mollinson was silkily sarcastic now. "I shall make a note in my journal that today is Saturday."

"But, sir . . ."

"SILENCE! SIT DOWN!"

Baring slumped sulkily into his seat, muttering beneath his breath.

The bell in the corridor began ringing to signal the ending of the period and Mollinson tucked his hands behind him beneath the long gown and swept from the classroom.

"Fucking hell!" Baring swore feelingly. "Why couldn't that fucking bell ring before fucking Famine picked on me. I was going to go into Sloughton this afternoon and meet my girlfriend."

Alexander Margrave felt genuinely sorry for the other boy, but Jamie Grenfell was less sympathetic.

"I'll go and meet her for you, if you like, Baring. I haven't met her before, but she'll be easy to recognise with that wooden leg she's got."

"No, Jamie, you're mistaken. Baring's girlfriend is the one who's disgustingly fat," another boy chimed in, and there was an instant hubbub of voices.

"No, she isn't the fat one. She's the other one who's breath is so bad that she's always surrounded by dead flies."

"That's not her. Baring's woman is the one who keeps on beating up the oiks! The one with the broken nose and cauliflower ears."

"Oh, that one. She's lovely, isn't she!"

"Yes, when Baring introduced her to his people, his father offered to arrange a match for her with Nigel Benn."

"It would be impossible for the referee to tell them apart!"

"Is she a Yoruba, Baring?"

"I think she's an Ashanti."

"You're all wrong. She's a Kalahari Bushwoman. You can tell that by the size of her arse!"

"It's not her arse, it's her hump. It slipped last year."

"BASTARDS!" Baring threw himself at his tormentors, and laughing and jeering the boys joined in a general mêlée, tumbling out into the corridor, struggling furiously along its length and out through the street door.

Tony Kilbeck was standing across the street when the doors burst open and a clump of struggling boys spilled out onto the roadway. He saw Alexander in the middle, wrestling with a much larger boy, and for a brief moment wondered whether or not he should intervene to save his charge from any physical damage. The next instant a shouting master was among the group and the boys separated and straightened their dishevelled clothing, laughing with excited pleasure.

Even though he had witnessed it so many times before in the College, Tony Kilbeck could still be impressed with the high standard of discipline that was exerted so apparently effortlessly by the masters. He could not help but compare the outward good manners and obedience to authority of the Martyrs pupils with the behaviour and attitudes of less gilded youth, to the latter's disadvantage. While he resented the arrogance of Martyrs College, he was still forced to admit that the good manners which were the norm here made life much pleasanter.

"Hello, Tony." Alexander had come to speak to him.

"Hello, Alex. Are you ready for the big parade?"

"Of course," the boy replied gravely, but his eyes were dancing with pleasurable anticipation.

This coming evening's Tattoo was the big occasion for the Cadet Corps. It was to be staged on one of the playing fields before an audience of parents and dignitaries. The Corps would parade in full dress and give a drill display. The Pipe Band would perform, and the Drum and Bugle Corps would beat retreat. There was to be a demonstration of senior cadets abseiling from a helicopter of the Army Air Corps, and then a mock terrorist ambush and hostage rescue, in which a Scimitar reconnaisance tank of the Household Cavalry would take part.

Alexander was to be in the drill display and had spent many hours spit and polishing his parade boots, and preparing his full dress uniform.

"Where to now?" Kilbeck wanted to know.

"That was my last class for today. I think I'll spend some more time on my boots, while I'm waiting for my mother to come," Alexander told him.

"That's the afternoon free for me then." The policeman grinned wryly. "Your Ma can't stand the sight of me."

Jamie Grenfell came to join them.

"Toby Levy said that there was a phone call for you earlier from your Ma, Alex. She said to tell you that she and Rafe were on their way."

Alexander's face fell and the eager anticipation for the coming evening suddenly drained away, leaving him feeling flat and depressed.

"Is she staying for the Tattoo?" Jamie wanted to know.

Alexander nodded. "Yes, apparently her new boyfriend was in the Army, and he wants to see the Tattoo. I'm to spend the afternoon with them."

"Do you know him?"

"No."

Jamie grinned lightheartedly. "Well, he can't be any worse than that specimen she brought down with her on Foundation Day. He was a bloody awful oik, wasn't he? We all wondered where on earth she'd dug him up from."

Alexander experienced a burning sense of shame and wished with all his heart that his mother would stop inflicting her boyfriends upon him.

Tony Kilbeck saw his charge's troubled eyes and pity for the boy whelmed over him.

Poor little bugger, he thought. Money can't buy everything, can it?

When they reached Penfold House Tony Kilbeck went

upstairs to his room, but Alexander was instantly accosted by Fergie Cochrane who drew him aside to whisper.

"It's all set for tonight, Alex. My brother is going to pick us up at eleven o'clock on the rear road. Then we're going to the club in Wandsworth. Here." He pressed a small corked bottle into Alexander's hand. "There are the knockout drops. Make sure that you give your pig a good dollop. We don't want him waking up when we're clubbing it, do we?"

Alexander felt troubled and doubtful. "I don't know if I should do this, Fergie. I feel very uncomfortable about it. Suppose something goes wrong and it harms him?"

"Nothing can go wrong!" The tall handsome youth assured vehemently. "It will only send him to sleep, that's all."

Still Alexander hesitated and with an exclamation of annoyance the older boy snatched the bottle from him.

"If you're chicken, then I'll do it for you."

Before Alexander could protest Fergie had gone from sight.

Elsewhere in the house the domestic staff were going about their various duties.

Maggie Stevens was doing paperwork in her office.

Reena Brown was making the junior boys' beds and daydreaming about the coming night.

I'm sure to meet a man tonight, she kept telling herself and mentally visualised what he might look like.

Theresa Sweeney was also making beds and greedily anticipating that first glorious taste of Guiness that she would enjoy the moment she finished her work.

Beryl Murphy was washing up the mugs and plates of the morning elevenses and praying that her husband would not come back from the Crown and Anchor vicious with drink.

Dermot Murphy was in the Crown and Anchor getting drunk and quarrelsome.

And Mary Jeffers was doing what she enjoyed above all else – Searching through someone else's personal belongings.

Maggie Stevens had told her to clean Julian Fothergill's quarters, and it was the first time that Mary Jeffers had been inside his rooms. Normally Beryl Murphy cleaned them.

Her adenoidal breath fluttered in her nostrils as she locked the door so that nobody could burst in upon her without warning. Then she took a visual inventory of the room's contents. The sitting room was sparsely furnished and austere in decoration, as befitted a bachelor master. But the bedroom presented a picture of startling contrast. Its perfumed draperies and pastel shadings of colour could have suited the bedroom of a woman. Mary Jeffers' flat features twitched as if she was scenting prey. Carefully, but with the speed imparted by long practise, she began to search through drawers and cupboards. She found many articles of flimsy silken female underwear, and behind the thick lenses of her glasses her eyes gleamed moistly.

It's true then. The rumour about Fothergill. He must be a queer to wear this sort of stuff, she decided.

Her excitement increased when she discovered that the bottom drawer of the tallboy was locked. She had long since learned how to defeat the flimsy locks of the College furnishings. She pulled out a lockknife and with practised ease forced back the tongue and freed the drawer. Inside were bundles of letters, two photograph albums and some video casettes.

She stared down at the articles with delight. It was like discovering a treasure trove. Quickly she scanned through the letters and photographs, giggling nervously as she saw their pornographic contents. Pictures of naked young men indulging in all types of sexual deviations, and in the letters torrid passages of explicit details about homosexual love. Like a child in a sweet shop Jeffers constantly switched from one goody to another before taking up the video casettes.

There was a television set and VCR in the corner of the bedroom, and Jeffers inserted the first casette and stared eagerly. A dark-hued picture appeared on the screen and she was forced to move closer to the set to distinguish it clearly. There were two men in the picture, one mounting the other like a dog. Then the man underneath lifted his head and stared straight into the camera lens and Mary Jeffers cried out in excited recognition.

"Fothergill! It's Fothergill! A man's shagging Fothergill!"

She clapped both hands to her mouth, and giggled wildly, rocking her body backwards and forwards in unconscious counterpoint to the thrusting rhythm of the man on the screen.

"It's somebody shagging Fothergill." An hysteria was rapidly rising in the woman's mind and she began to hyper-ventilate, her lips wet with saliva, her breath rasping harshly. "It's Fothergill getting shagged! Getting shagged! Getting shagged!"

*   *   *

"The Lower Master has asked me to have a word with you, Mr Fothergill." Hubert Mollinson indicated the chair in front of his desk. "Please be seated."

Julian Fothergill, tense and extremely nervous, stiffly sat down and clasped his hands tightly before him on his lap, his fingers tugging and kneading in writhing embrace.

Mollinson frowned severely. "It has been noted that you appear to be somewhat stressed of late. Normally that would of course be a personal matter for yourself only, unless you chose to seek guidance or advice from a senior master. But your work is suffering, Fothergill. Your classes are becoming increasingly rowdy and undisciplined. So much so that the matter has come to the attention of the Lower Master. Since you are my assistant, then your conduct naturally falls within the area of my direct responsibility. This being the case the Lower Master has asked me to have a word with you." He paused, his gaunt features wearing an expression of derisive contempt. "Is there anything that you would like to discuss with me, Fothergill? If you are in some sort of difficulty, then I stand ready to help you, if I can."

Lying bastard! You'd hang me up by my balls if you could, Julian thought bitterly. Aloud he said only, "No, Mr Mollinson. I'm not in any sort of difficulty."

"Then why is your work suffering, Fothergill?" Mollinson demanded truculently. "You know that we demand high standards in this college, and that anyone who fails to meet those standards faces dismissal."

"I've been ill," Fothergill flustered defensively. "That's why my work hasn't been too good lately."

"Have you consulted your doctor about this illness?" Mollinson's manner was plainly disbelieving.

"No, not yet. I thought it might pass."

"Of what nature is this illness?" the older man asked pedantically, then sneered, "is it infectious, I wonder?"

Julian Fothergill shook his head. "No, Mr Mollinson. It's not infectious."

Mollinson raised his eyebrows, and queried silkily, "Not infectious? Come now, Fothergill, if you know that your illness is not infectious, then you must also know what it is that ails you. Be good enough to tell me. I have the boys to consider."

"It's a private matter." The young man asserted doggedly.

Mollinson slowly shook his head. "No, it is not a private matter. I am the guardian of fifty boys. Their welfare is my responsibility. I must insist that you tell me."

The blood pounded in Fothergill's head; he felt that he could not endure a single moment more of this inquisition. All the guilty shame of an entire lifetime crowded in upon him and he wished that he were dead. Desperately he fought for control, but the pressure upon his over-strained nerves was too much to be borne and he suddenly burst into tears.

Shocked and appalled Mollinson could only stare silently at this spectacle of helpless misery. Then the softer, kindlier side of his nature asserted itself, and he rose and went round his desk and put his hands on the bowed, shaking shoulders.

"Come now, Fothergill, try to control yourself," he soothed gruffly. "This won't serve any useful purpose. You must tell me what is troubling you. I'll do my best to help you. I promise you that I will do my very best for you."

This totally unexpected kindness completely swept away any remaining constraint in Julian Fothergill's mind, and he turned to clutch at his senior, like a small distressed child clutches at a comforting parent.

He began to babble out his guilty secrets, the words pouring out in jerky, gasping haste. He held nothing back, confessing all. His homo-sexuality, his affair with Shafto, the blackmail which had followed.

Mollinson listened silently, grim-faced with anger, yet without any great sense of outrage or disgust. He was a pragmatic realist, who had long since accepted that the ancient public schools, like the great religions, had always attracted homosexuals into their service, and always would do so. Although he despised this sobbing creature, he did not utterly condemn him. He considered that the man could not be held to blame for his deviant sexuality, any more than a cripple could be held to blame for his bodily deformity.

He believed Fothergill's repeated assertions that he had never attempted to seduce or corrupt any of the boys in his charge, and the anger he was now feeling was as much self-directed, as otherwise. He should have recognised what Fothergill was, and have taken steps accordingly. Mollinson blamed only himself for this failure.

"I'll resign immediately," Fothergill offered chokingly. "I'll leave here today!"

"No, you will not!" Mollinson said firmly.

Fothergill's tear-wet face stared up in amazement. "But I must!" he protested. "I must!"

"Be quiet!" Mollinson ordered brusquely, and his thoughts were racing. He could visualise the tabloid headlines if they got hold of this information. He could visualise also the damage that such headlines could do to the College.

Hubert Mollinson loved the College with a passionate fervour. He had given it his devoted service and allegiance ever since he had first set foot inside its ancient precincts. He would dare anything, do anything, risk anything, sacrifice anyone or anything to defend his school and its good name.

He fully accepted the unpalatable fact that this fool had created the potential to do a great deal of damage to his school. He must now set his mind to find ways and means of damage limitation.

He scowled down into the tear-wet face beneath him. "Listen to me, Fothergill. I shall try to save you from your own folly. For your part, you must give me your solemn oath that you will do exactly as I tell you. Do you agree to that?"

Hardly daring to hope that he was being offered salvation, Fothergill assured vehemently, "I'll do anything, Mr Mollinson. I swear it! I'll do anything that you say."

"The first thing you will do is to break off all connection with this man, Shafto, and for your remaining time here you will abstain absolutely from any sexual relationships. You will give me the incriminating material, and anything else that you might have which could be deemed deviant and I shall destroy it in your presence. Do you agree to this?"

Fothergill nodded vigorously.

"Very well," Mollinson accepted. "Now as to any robbery or burglary of these premises, I think that we can safely discount that possibility. The information that these ruffians have extracted from you is of no real use to them if their purpose is to steal from us. We have a sophisticated security surveillance system in place, plus an armed police presence.

"Your poor work we shall explain as resulting from simple illness, which you very courageously, if unwisely, sought to conceal from me in order that you might continue with your duties here. I am going to confine you to your quarters for a week or so. You will play the part of a convalescent and my wife will care for you, bring you your meals etc. etc. You will of course have no direct contact with the boys or any other member of staff during that period."

Again he paused, as if inviting comment, and once more Fothergill nodded vigorously in agreement.

"Good, you are being very sensible, at last, Fothergill. Now these measures should suffice for the short term, but of course your long-term future cannot any longer rest here. Have you ever considered working abroad, Fothergill?"

The young man's shock at this question showed clearly, but Mollinson pressed on remorselessly.

"You must realise that it is in your own best interests, and in the best interests of the College, that you pursue your teaching career elsewhere, Fothergill, preferably abroad. I'm sure that one of the Gulf States would suit you admirably. The Arabs after all are noted as being amenable to your type of sexual proclivity. I have an old friend in the British Council in Abu Dhabi who is frequently in need of experienced teachers. Would you like me to write to him on your behalf?"

Fothergill stared into the hard eyes of the older man, and knew that this request was in fact a command. He stayed silent for some moments, and unaccountably his spirits perked up a little. It was true what Mollinson said. The Arabs were not averse to homosexual practises. Life might be quite good out in the Gulf. Lots of sunshine, tax-free salary, dark-eyed, lissom-bodied young Arab men . . . He nodded, and a hesitant smile came to his lips.

"That might suit me very well, thank you, Mr Mollinson."

"Good!" Mollinson smiled grimly. "You will of course finish the term here and give suitable notice when it is your intention to move to the Gulf."

"Very well, Mr Mollinson. "Fothergill agreed submissively.

"Go to your quarters then, Fothergill. And rest yourself for a week or so. Put this unhappy episode firmly behind you."

"I will, Mr Mollinson. And thank you again. I am truly grateful to you. I'll never forget the kindness that you've shown me."

The young man really was grateful. This sour, miserable man before him had proven himself to have a good and kind heart.

"Say no more, Fothergill."

Mollinson picked up his phone and dialled the Matron's number. When she replied he ordered, "Will you come to my study when you have time, please, Mrs Stevens."

And told Fothergill. "I shall give Matron the necessary instructions concerning your privacy. That will be all for the present."

He bent his head over a sheaf of papers and the young man exited the study.

At the door of his quarters he met Mary Jeffers coming out. She looked at him with a peculiar expression of furtive glee.

"Matron told me to clean your rooms, Mr Fothergill."

He nodded. "Thank you, Mary."

In his bedroom he lay down on the sensually coloured coverlet and gave way to soft tears of utter relief. His nightmare had finally come to its ending.

On the top floor of the house, Fergus Cochrane moved cautiously to the door of Tony Kilbeck's room. From other rooms there came to sounds of voices and laughter as some of the boys put the final touches to their boots and accoutrements. Fergus knew that the policeman was downstairs talking to Maggie Stevens and that Alexander Margrave was walking in the college campus with his mother and her new boyfriend.

He slipped into the room and quickly scanned the contents. A half-empty bottle of Scotch whisky together with a glass tumbler stood on the bedside locker. Fergus took the bottle of knockout drops from his pocket and poured a generous measure from it into the whisky bottle.

Smiling he crept out of the room and went back downstairs.

It was a good half-hour later that Tony Kilbeck returned to the top floor. He poked his head into Alexander's room and saw that the boy had not yet returned from his mother's visit.

In his own room he sighed exasperatedly. It didn't matter how much charm he exerted, how hard he tried, the delectable Maggie Stevens never did more than flirt teasingly with him.

Still, I might as well keep on trying, he decided ruefully. There's fuck all else to do around this place. And who knows, I might get to crack her one day.

His thoughts still filled with the lush breasts and hips of Maggie Stevens, he opened the bottle of whisky and poured himself a half tumbler full of the spirit, which he tossed down greedily, gasping as its fire burned through him. Then poured another half-tumbler and lay back on his bed, sipping it. The powerful sedative combined with the alcohol to devastating effect, and within half an hour the policeman was in a drugged coma from which he would not awake for many many hours.

Chapter Thirty-Nine

"DO you ever try to visualise these men as they were when they were here?" Spencer asked Alexander Margrave as they stood side by side reading the lists of scrolled names on the great bronze plaques which memorialised the war dead of Martyrs College.

"I do sometimes, Mr Glanville." The boyish features were solemn. "I always suppose that apart from their dress they looked very much like the boys who are here now."

"There are so many names here and this section is only for the First World War. I dread to think how many Old Collegians have died or been wounded in all the other wars since this place was founded." Spencer found that he was genuinely impressed by these silent records of sacrifice. "What a pity it is that all these gallant men and boys had to die while the worthless shirkers who were too frightened to risk their own skins stayed at home and profited by the War."

"You were a regular soldier, weren't you, Mr Glanville?" Alexander was greatly taken by this tall, quietly-spoken man, who was so totally different from previous men his mother had brought down to the College with her.

"I was indeed, Alex, for twenty-seven years."

"What regiment were you in, Mr Glanville?"

"The Grenadier Guards. But I spent a considerable time on secondment to the Parachute Regiment and other formations."

"Were you in action?" the boy questioned eagerly.

"I served in the Falklands Campaign and the Gulf War, and did several tours in Northern Ireland. But I saw nothing that would remotely compare with what these poor chaps saw and went through."

"Will you tell me about it?" Alexander's eyes shone with excitement.

Spencer chuckled and in a fatherly gesture patted the boy's shoulder. "Some day, I will, Alex. But now I think that we'd best rejoin your mother. I don't think that she shares our interest in old wars."

Lydia Margrave was impatiently pacing the cloisters, and when the pair rejoined her she snapped irritably, "Thank goodness. I thought that you were going to spend the rest of the day looking at those boring lists."

"Those lists represent all that is best about this country, Lydia. I don't find them in the least boring. They fire one's imagination," Spencer told her sternly and Alexander was pleased that his new-found friend shared his own opinions concerning the records of brave men.

They walked back to Penfold House and parted at the boys' entrance. Alexander was reluctant to say goodbye to his mother's new friend, and said sincerely, "I've really enjoyed meeting you, Mr Glanville. I do hope that we shall meet again."

"We shall certainly meet again, Alex, if I have anything to do with it," Spencer replied warmly.

"What was he like, your Ma's new bloke?" Jamie Grenfell wanted to know when he met Alexander on the stairs.

"He's a good guy. I hope to meet him again. He was in the Army. He's been in action as well," Alexander told him enthusiastically.

They moved upwards and Fergus Cochrane came leaping down the stairs from the top floor, his handsome face flushed with excitement.

"It's all clear for tonight." He grinned triumphantly and punched the air. "Yeah, Man! Warehouse here we come!"

"Have you done it?" Alexander asked, and could not help but feel nervous.

"Too true," Fergus told him. "Your pig is snoring like a trumpet. He won't wake up 'til early next week. So, tonight we all hit the town!"

Alexander and Jamie Grenfell exchanged a long look, then Jamie's face split into a huge grin and he whooped joyously, and after a moment Alexander grinned and whooped as well.

Chapter Forty

A ripple of applause sounded from the spectators as the band shambled onto the field. In the crowd a fond mother nudged the stranger next to her and informed her proudly, in a broad Lancashire accent, "My Phillip's in the band, you know. There he is there. He's playing that, whatdyemacallit."

The Dowager Lady Erskine leaned away from the sharp impact of the Lancashire lady's elbow and accused her husband next to her, "I told you that we shouldn't have come! The College isn't what it was. The place is being swamped by the nouveaux riches, these days."

On the saluting dais in front of the tiered rows of spectators the plump-bodied guest of honour, Prince Mohammed bin Sultan of Saudi Arabia, stifled a yawn and wished that the hours might pass swiftly. He had a pressing assignation with a particularly attractive escort agency girl in London.

"Your uncle, Prince Faisal was very impressed with our cadet band when he was last here, Your Highness," the Headmaster, Doctor Miles Hinde-Smythe smiled at him, as if inviting comment.

The prince inclined his head and lied graciously, "As I am impressed myself, Headmaster. They present a most martial appearance."

The band blared forth the rousing strains of "Imperial Echoes", and the quality of their musicianship was fortunately far superior to their martial bearing.

At the far left edge of the banked rows of spectators Lydia Margrave surreptitiously caressed the muscular thigh of her escort.

"Are you trying to drive me mad, darling?" he whispered in her ear, and she giggled girlishly.

"Well, you've succeeded," he told her. "We're going to find a quiet corner."

"Oh no, Rafe." She laughed in soft delight.

209

"Oh yes, Honey." His eyes narrowed, and cruelty glimmered in their dark depths.

She felt his warm breath in her ear and she shivered with delight as she allowed herself to be led to the dark rear of the tiered benches.

His hands were roaming over her body, he was whispering to her, his lips teasing her mouth. They moved in close-locked embrace across the greensward towards the serried rows of cars parked in the black shadows of the trees. When they reached Spencer's Bentley she whispered, "Shall we do it on the back seat, darling?"

The terrible lust that had been pullulating in his brain abruptly engulfed Spencer and he was suddenly transformed into a ravenous animal. He slammed her back across the bonnet of the Bentley, his fingers lifting her skirt and tearing aside her flimsy silken panties.

She cried out as he rammed himself brutally into her body, his mouth silenced her protests and the seething images of madness crowded his brain. The soft breeze carried the wild skirlings of the bagpipes across from the playing field, but Spencer could only hear the cacaphonic screams of terror issuing from gaping mouths in dark faces, and see the crazed eyes of horror as blood spurted from the wreckage of human flesh.

The pounding of his body reached a crescendo, he grunted deep and gutturally in his throat, as his hands gripped the woman's neck and jaw and savagely twisted, heaved and jerked, a sharp cracking of bone sounded audibly, and Lydia Margrave died even as her insane lover's semen spurted.

The madness ebbed slowly from his mind, and he blinked as if awaking from sleep. He stared through the gloom at the dead face only inches from his own, and as he withdrew himself from her body and stepped back she slowly slipped down onto her knees and fell face forwards onto the ground. The soft wind soughed once more carrying the plaintive strains of the "Flowers of the Forest" across the dark landscape from the floodlit playing field.

Spencer cursed sibilantly and quickly checked around him to make sure that no witnesses were in the vicinity. He had not intended the death of Lydia Margrave at this point in time. She would have been more useful to him alive but he did not indulge in self-recrimination. This was not the first time he had killed in momentary loss of self-control. He was only thankful that no one had come upon them as it happened. But now he must make the instant adjustment to his plans that this untimely killing had necessitated.

He unlocked his car doors and, lifting Lydia Margrave's limp corpse, he carefully placed her upright on the back seat, arranging her body so that to a casual onlooker she would appear to be sleeping. He checked his wristwatch. He must make his next move somewhat earlier than he had anticipated. Calmly straightening his clothing and tidying his appearance, he strolled back towards the playing field.

"You did very well, considering," Sergeant Trevor Morgan told the drill team. "Only a couple of mistakes." He grinned broadly. "You're not quite ready for Buck House Guard, but I wouldn't mind taking you on Windsor Castle relief."

Alexander Margrave experienced a warm glow of pride. He had gloried in every moment of the precisioned drill. His pride was shared by the other members of the drill team, and when the sergeant told them to stand easy, and break ranks, they clustered together excitedly discussing their display.

"Sergeant?"

Trevor Morgan turned to the man who had addressed him. His practised eyes instantly evaluated the soldierly bearing, the Saville Row suit, the close-cropped grey hair and moustache, and above all else, the Brigade of Guards tie.

"Tonight was one of the best Corps drill displays that I've seen, Sergeant. Please allow me to congratulate you."

"Thank you very much, sir." Trevor Morgan was sincerely gratified.

"Could I have a private word, Sergeant?"

"Certainly, sir."

The two men drew aside and talked in low voices.

"I need to speak to Alexander Margrave, Sergeant. I've come here with his mother, and she's feeling unwell. I'm going to take her back to her home, but she very much wants to have a word with her son before we leave. Could you release him for a few minutes?"

"Of course, sir. Is there anything I can do to help?"

"No, thank you, Sergeant. She's sitting down in the car now, and I'm sure that it's nothing too serious. Might I have a word with the boy?"

"Certainly, sir . . . CADET MARGRAVE, REPORT TO ME! AT THE DOUBLE!"

Alexander ran to the two men and Spencer smiled reassuringly.

"It's your mother, Alex. She's feeling rather poorly. She wanted to have a word with you before I take her home. The sergeant has very kindly given permisson for you to come and see her if you wish."

The sergeant nodded. "Off you go, Cadet Margrave. Report back here to me as soon as you've seen your mother."

"Yes, Sergeant." Alex felt no real anxiety for his mother. He was well used to the feigned headaches and fainting attacks which she used to get her own way if ever she was thwarted. He assumed now that she was merely pretending to be feeling unwell to gain Rafe Glanville's sympathy.

"Your mother's resting in the car, Alex. I'm sure that she'll be alright once she's had a good night's sleep." Spencer smiled kindly at the boy. "But she's anxious to say goodbye to you."

They walked off side by side.

"Where's your policeman friend?" Spencer was concerned by the man's apparent absence, and wondered if he might be watching them from a distance.

Alex experienced a hot flush of guilt. Fergie Cochrane had sent one of the boys back to Penfold House to check on Tony Kilbeck and the boy had reported that Tony was still snoring away in his room.

"He's taking a few hours off, Mr Glanville," Alex lied somewhat shamefacedly. "He says that there's no need for him to be with me when I'm surrounded by the Corps."

"No, I don't suppose there is," Spencer laughed easily. "You're perfectly safe with a hundred of these bloodthirsty young scoundrels around you, I'm sure."

As they walked they talked companiably about military subjects and Alex found that his initial liking for this man was being considerably reinforced every moment that he was in his company. He wished fervently that this latest boyfriend of his mother's might stay with her and perhaps eventually even marry her. Alex thought that he would very much like to have Rafe Glanville for his stepfather.

They skirted the playing field and passed the Scimitar reconnaissance tank which was parked on the perimeter road, it's three-man crew lounging by its side.

Spencer noted the boy's interested stare, and told him, "It's a fine vehicle, Alex, but within a few years it will be a virtual museum piece."

"Why do you say that, Mr Glanville?"

"Because the helicopter is the future master of the battlefield. It can move at speed over any type of terrain, and even with the present missile systems it can take out a tank at three thousand metres.

"Of course there will always be a role for some type of armoured vehicle, but if you'll take my advice you'll specialise in helicopter warfare when you join the Army.

"I've recently had some interesting material about the projected role of helicopter assault in the next century, sent to me by a friend who's serving at the American Tactical Combat School in North Carolina. I'll pass it on to you, if you'd like it."

"Yes please, Mr Glanville. I'd like that very much." Alex felt a warm glow of gratitude towards this pleasant, generous man and wished even more strongly that he would forge a permanent relationship with his mother.

They left the floodlit area and approached the rows of parked cars beneath the high-branched elm trees. Spencer peered into the darkness ahead, searching for any sign of movement. A sense of exhultant triumph was already burgeoning within him. Everything had gone with such ease and smoothness that it seemed that the Gods of Chance were on his side.

Then he saw the long lancing beam of a torch switching from side to side, striking shards of reflected light from the highly polished windscreens of the luxury cars. He realised that the torchbearer was moving along the row in which his Bentley was parked. His Bentley, with the dead body of Lydia Margrave seated on the back seat.

Ex-Company Sergeant Major Barry Snagg was feeling distinctly dis-chuffed. Totally pissed off, in fact. The fucking Bursar, Doctor Terence fucking Bairstow, PH fucking D, Hons, Cambridge, had once again stuck his long nose in where it was not wanted, telling the Headmaster that the budget did not allow any cash for employing any extra security men for tonight's Tattoo, and as a result Ex-Company Sergeant Major Barry Snagg was having to spend his valuable time acting as a bloody car park attendant, instead of being where he should be, at the nerve centre of operational security directing his team.

Barry Snagg swore long and heartily as he contrasted his twenty-five years arduous and at times dangerous service in the Airborne Forces with the easy, soft years spent by Doctor fucking Bairstow in the sheltered comfort of academic life.

And I'm having to take orders from that stupid, gutless pillock, who wouldn't have the bottle to jump off a bloody pavement. There's no fucking justice in this life, and that's a fucking fact! he complained bitterly to himself.

Spencer guessed that the torchbearer was a patrolling security man, and didn't hesitate when he realised that the man was approaching his car.

"Hey, you there! What are you doing?" He bellowed and told Alex, "Stay behind me, son, that could be a prowler."

He began to run towards the lancing beam of light and after a moment the startled boy followed.

Barry Snagg heard the shout and came to a standstill, swinging his light to try and pick out his challenger.

The light caught the running figures and Snagg chuckled wryly, "Some parent and his boy thinking they've caught a thief."

He moved to meet the oncoming pair, passing Spencer's Bentley, unaware of the pale blob of Lydia Margrave's features in its rear seat.

"It's quite all right, sir. I'm the Chief of College Security," he shouted.

Spencer instantly slowed. "Oh, I'm sorry. I do apologise. I thought for a moment that you were a prowler."

Snagg briefly shone his torch onto the tall man's face and on that of the boy by his side.

"No need to apologise, sir. I wish that more people would have a go when they see something suspicious going on. It 'ud make my life a bit easier, I can tell you."

"Is the gate open?" Spencer enquired. "I have to leave now."

Snagg had placed this man as an ex-officer. "It's locked, sir, but I'll go and open it for you directly."

"Thank you very much indeed, Mr . . . ?"

"Snagg, sir, the name is Snagg."

"Thank you, Mr Snagg, that's most kind of you."

Snagg saluted. "Not at all, sir. You're welcome." He marched smartly off towards the gate some hundred yards distant, which opened onto the main road leading to Sloughton.

Alexander was looking at Spencer with great respect. He had been amazed at the speed and fitness displayed by him and very impressed with his courage. He had gone forward to tackle that prowler without a moment's hesitation. A dawning hero-worship was blossoming fast in the boy's heart.

They went on toward the Bentley and Spencer said, "I think your mother is sleeping, Alex."

The boy peered at the pale blob in the rear seat. "Perhaps I shouldn't wake her up."

Spencer glanced about him. From the floodlit glow of the playing field the crackling of blank ammunition and the bangs of thunderflashes echoed across the greensward.

Alex leaned forwards to look into the rear of the car, and Spencer raised his hand and chopped down savagely into the base of the boy's skull.

Alex fell without a sound. Spencer stepped over him and opened the boot of the car. He took out a roll of thick masking tape and in a few seconds trussed, gagged and blindfolded the fallen boy. He ripped the alarm bleeper from the slender wrist and tossed it into the darkness. Then he bundled Alexander's senseless body into the boot and got into the driving seat.

He motored sedately towards the gate, and as he exited he smiled and waved at the saluting Barry Snagg, winding down his window to tell him, "Thank you very much for your help, Mr Snagg."

Snagg grinned his appreciation for the courtesy of this officer and gentleman.

"You're welcome, sir." He got a quick glimpse of the lady asleep on the rear seat as the car passed.

As he drove towards Sloughton, Spencer considered his next move.

Because he had seen and seized his opportunity, this operation had succeeded earlier than he had anticipated. But this success meant that Terry Macrae and the Helling twins had now become superflous to requirements.

He pulled into a secluded lay-by, and took his powerful radio transmitter from the glove compartment. He stepped out of the car and transmitted.

"Legion, over. Legion, over."

Almost instantly Cesar Perales replied, "Legion receiving. Legion receiving."

"Sunburst, Sunburst, Sunburst. Over."

"Legion, received and understood. Out."

Spencer changed frequency and transmitted, "Pegasus, over. Pegasus, over."

He was forced to repeat the call several times before Terry Macrae replied.

"Pegasus receiving. Pegasus receiving. Over."

"Pegasus, Strike, Strike, Strike. Over."

"Pegasus, received. Pegasus, received. Out."

Terry Macrae switched off his radio and told the Helling twins. "Off we jolly well go."

"It's a bit early, aren't it?" Ron Hellings queried.

"Yeah, it is," the big Australian conceded. "But Spencer knows what he's doing."

"Ohh ahhrr, he always does." Reg Hellings grinned.

Within seconds the helicopter rose from the distant woodland clearing and flying low, headed towards Martyrs College.

Spencer gazed up at the clear moonlit sky, and smiled contentedly, then looked into the drainage ditch that flanked the lay-by. It was deep enough.

He took Lydia Margrave's corpse from the rear seat and gently lowered it into the ditch. She could not be seen in the darkness, and only in daylight if someone were to stand directly above her. Spencer was satisfied that she would remain undiscovered for the few hours he required.

He unclipped the false number plates covering the original plates at front and rear of the car and threw them in with the dead woman. He re-entered the car, took a small package from the glove compartment and switching on the interior light used his rear mirror to guide him, as he changed his appearance from debonairly handsome Rafe Glanville, to elderly, ugly, brown-teethed James Arnold.

Once satisfied with the transformation, he began his journey back to his Cotswold house.

*   *   *

On the western side of Martyrs village, a mile distant from the College, the rusty Transit van was parked on a piece of waste ground, hidden from the road by tall hedgerows, but open to the motorway across the intervening fields.

Cesar Perales got out of the van and made a circuit of the ground and hedgerows on foot, establishing that no other persons were in the vicinity. He was not worried about being seen from the motorway. Drivers hurtling past at eighty or ninety miles an hour were not likely to spend their time gazing into the darkness outside their headlight beams. He returned to the van and opening its rear door began to lift out and assemble equipment. He also glanced repeatedly at the clear moonlit sky and blessed his good fortune.

Colin Harris slowly paced the high street of Martyrs village. He was extremely unhappy to be relegated to the role of a mere observer. He felt very aggrieved with Sir Thomas Hamilton for excluding him from the scene of action, Ewe Hill, Lambourne Down.

Eastwards in the distance he heard the whup whup whup of a helicopter, but he knew that he could disregard it – It would be the chopper that was carrying the cadets for the abseiling demonstration. He listened hard and heard the muted reports of blank ammunition being fired on the playing fields. He sighed in resignation. At least another two hours would have to pass before he could expect to witness anything to interest him.

Then, from the west he heard the sound of another approaching helicopter. Coming in low and fast.

"It can't be them!" he thought. "It's too early."

Even as the thought flashed through his mind the chopping roar of the prop blades suddenly became deafeningly close, and the helicopter swooped overhead, barely skimming the rooftops.

He broke into a run, heading towards Penfold House and saw the helicopter soaring upwards, circling as it rose, as if its pilot were searching for his objective.

On the waste ground Cesar Perales was presented with a perfect silhouette against the moonlight as the helicopter rose rapidly upwards. He sighted on the black shape, pulled the trigger and with a roaring whooshing of flame the Blowpipe missile streaked towards its target. Within seconds there was a flash which lit up the skies as the helicopter exploded in a ball of fire which instantly disintegrated into a myriad of tumbling flames.

Colin Harris stumbled to a halt. "Jesus Christ!" was all he could jerk out. "Jesus Christ!"

On the playing fields the spectators gasped with wonder at the sheer size of the explosion and applauded the giant firework.

The flash of the explosion momentarily lightened the sky above Spencer as he travelled northwards, and he smiled. Then his fingers began to tap upon the steering wheel in rhythm with the merry tune that was playing in his head.

Bk
156 mor
£10 99